THE QUEEN AND
THE COURTESAN

A Selection of Recent Titles by Freda Lightfoot

The French Historical Series

HOSTAGE QUEEN ★
RELUCTANT QUEEN ★
THE QUEEN AND THE COURTESAN ★

The Lakeland Sagas

THE GIRL FROM POOR HOUSE LANE
THE WOMAN FROM HEARTBREAK HOUSE

The Manchester Sagas

DANCING ON DEANSGATE
WATCH FOR THE TALLEYMAN

The Champion Street Market Sagas

WHO'S SORRY NOW?
LONELY TEARDROPS

Novels

TRAPPED
HOUSE OF ANGELS

★ *available from Severn House*

THE QUEEN AND THE COURTESAN

Freda Lightfoot

This first world edition published 2011
in Great Britain and in the USA by
SEVERN HOUSE PUBLISHERS LTD of
9–15 High Street, Sutton, Surrey, England, SM1 1DF.
Trade paperback edition first published
in Great Britain and the USA 2012 by
SEVERN HOUSE PUBLISHERS LTD.

British Library Cataloguing in Publication Data

Lightfoot, Freda, 1942–
    The Queen and the courtesan.
    1. Henry IV, King of France, 1553–1610 – Relations with
    Women – Fiction. 2. Mistresses – France – Fiction.
    3. France – Kings and rulers – Paramours – Fiction.
    4. France – History – Henry IV, 1589–1610 – Fiction.
    5. Historical fiction.
    I. Title
    823.9'14-dc22

ISBN-13: 978-0-7278-8092-5 (cased)
ISBN-13: 978-1-84751-397-7 (trade paper)

All Severn House titles are printed on acid-free paper.

Severn House Publishers support The Forest Stewardship Council [FSC],
the leading international forest certification organisation. All our titles that
are printed on Greenpeace-approved FSC-certified paper carry the FSC logo.

Typeset by Palimpsest Book Production Ltd.,
Falkirk, Stirlingshire, Scotland.
Printed and bound in Great Britain by
MPG Books Ltd., Bodmin, Cornwall.

'It is a disgrace that a hero who has conquered France inch by inch yet cannot manage two unruly women.'

Ferdinand, Grand Duke of Tuscany

Part One

HENRIETTE

1599

Henriette stamped her small foot, face scarlet with temper. 'How dare they dismiss me from court! Did you not see how the King gazed into my eyes, entranced; how he complimented me on my dancing? The courtiers are calling me "*une femme toute charmante*". He danced with me twice, so how dare anyone send me packing as if I were of no account. It's the fault of that strumpet Gabrielle. She was furious because of the attention Henry was paying me.'

'Hush, my sweet. Take care what you say. Palace walls have ears.' Her mother glanced anxiously around, as if the Swiss guards might appear at any moment to physically evict them. 'The Duchesse de Beaufort is the King's favourite, carrying his child and about to become his queen at last. You must make allowances for her condition. This pregnancy is proving more difficult than the others so she is naturally tense.'

'Bah, more likely she fears she can no longer hold the King's love. They say she's calling me "*une baggage*"!' Henriette stormed, ripping the silver combs from her coiffure and flinging them across the room. She'd been excited to receive the invitation to attend the wedding celebrations of the King's sister, had revelled in the admiration she'd attracted; now it was all spoiled, and she was beside herself with fury.

Pushing Henriette gently down on to a dressing stool Madame d'Entragues began to brush the bright auburn hair, soothing her tempestuous daughter with soft words as well as with strokes of the brush. The former Marie Touchet, one time mistress of Charles IX, had never been one to make a fuss, her gentle manner often providing a calming influence on the excitable young king.

Her daughter was another creature altogether. Quite unlike her younger sister, dear little Marie-Charlotte, who was a fragile, beguiling child, always eager to please. She was even now patiently sorting the ribbons and jewels that her more volatile sister had scattered in her temper. Far too much like me, her mother ruefully admitted.

Sadly, Henriette had inherited her father's scheming, crafty nature. François de Balzac, Baron de Marcoussis and Lord of Entragues and Malesherbes, was utterly tenacious when it came to getting his own way. As governor of the city of Orleans he'd once offered to sell the town to Henry of Navarre, the plan only thwarted when the citizens fiercely objected.

This daughter was equally ruthless.

And if Henriette did not quite possess the beauty of Henry's long-established favourite Gabrielle d'Estrées, the Duchesse de Beaufort, at twenty years of age she had about her that indefinable quality that sent men wild with desire. She was dark and slim with a comely figure and handspan waist. The heavy-lidded, glittering green eyes were shrewd and sensuous, if somewhat provoking; the small, Cupid's bow mouth inclined to curl upwards at each corner in a knowing little smile. Straight nose, finely arched brows and a heart-shaped face with a softly rounded chin, the girl possessed a feline grace. And, like a cat, she could purr with pleasure or just as easily put out her claws and scratch. One moment she would be all sunshine and smiles, the next spitting with fury if something should displease her. While she lacked neither wit nor charm, even her own mother took care not to cross her.

Henriette was expressing that displeasure now. Shrugging off her mother's ministrations, she began to storm about the room, the maids running about in a desperate bid to catch the vases and marble figurines she picked up at random to hurl in the wake of the silver combs. And as she raged, Henriette complained bitterly about the imperfections of the quarters allotted to them and how glad she would be to leave it, while at the same time describing Gabrielle as a bloated fishwife, saying how much more attentive she would be to the King were she allowed to stay.

'Take care what you wish for,' Marie softly warned, gathering up shards of broken china. 'Loving a king can be fraught with danger, child. I was fortunate in that Charles's queen, Elizabeth of Austria, was an undemanding girl who made no protest about his keeping a mistress. She and I became firm friends, each loving the King in our own way, and supporting each other.'

Henriette looked at her mother with scathing contempt, not at all understanding such generosity of spirit. 'That is because you are happy to have people walk all over you, like silly Marie-Charlotte here. I am not so stupid.'

If Marie Touchet felt any urge to defend herself against her daughter's rebellious condemnation of her mild manners, she gave no sign of it, simply returned to folding gowns and laying them in the coffer until Henriette snapped at her again.

'Stop that at once, *Maman*. We keep maids to perform such a task. Do not demean yourself.' Then arching her back and stretching her arms above her head to show off the perfect lines of her lithe body, exactly as a cat might, she softly purred, 'This isn't the end, believe me. Next time I shall capture his heart. The stakes may be high, Mother dear, but I know how to play them. I'm perfectly sure another opportunity will present itself.'

The opportunity came sooner than even Henriette might have expected. Gabrielle d'Estrées died during the early hours of Saturday, 11 April, although whether from complications of a difficult pregnancy or something more malicious, no one dared say. Gossip was rife, suspicions privately held against ministers close to the King as the Duchess had made many enemies. Men with connections in Rome who sought to have an Italian princess on the throne. These included Sancy, who had constantly resisted her rise in favour, and even Rosny, Henry IV's closest advisor, but none dared point the finger. Whatever the cause of Gabrielle's death, the fortune-tellers had been proved right. She had indeed died young, very possibly betrayed by friends as she'd sickened following a supper at Zamet's house. The Italian had personally brought her a glass of lemon juice and Gabrielle had drunk deep.

Henry showed not the slightest suspicion in anyone, possibly because he was too grief-stricken to hear the whispers. But then he was not a man who cared to dwell on unpleasant thoughts and events. His affable, easy-going nature ensured that he person-ally made few enemies, which had been his salvation on numerous occasions in the past. It was a skill he'd learned as a young man, following his marriage to Marguerite de Valois, when the pair of them had been held hostage in the Louvre for some years by Catherine de Medici following the Massacre of St Bartholomew.

Queen Margot was now languishing in the fortress of Usson, first as a prisoner and then taking control of it in her own inimical way. She refused to leave as she claimed to fear for her life. All a nonsense – she was simply holding out for more money – although Henry believed that he'd finally won her agreement to a divorce. Too late. His beloved Gabrielle, his hoped-for bride, was gone, as was their child. There would be no wedding, no crown for his angel.

He'd been so devastated when he'd heard the news that he'd fainted in his carriage, then had closeted himself in the palace of Fontainebleau for days, refusing to see anyone.

Gabrielle lay in state and more than twenty thousand people sprinkled holy water on her bier. She was buried at the Church of St Germain l'Auxerrois under a superb catafalque. Requiems were chanted, prayers read, and all the court was present. No grander funeral could have been provided had she indeed worn a crown.

Henry swore that he would never love again. 'The root of my love is withered,' he cried.

Rosny gently pointed out that her death was by Divine will. 'One day you might thank God for this blow. Think of the impossible position in which you were placed, drawn to her as you were and yet bound by honour and duty to marry a royal princess. Now you can rest easy in the joy and blessing of your people.'

Too overwhelmed by despair, Henry did not trouble to respond. He ordered the entire court to wear black, and Gabrielle's memory was honoured to the extent that Parliament itself offered the King its condolences, normally only given for persons of royal blood. His sister, Catherine, newly married to the Duke of Bar quite against her wishes, sent him her love and deepest sympathies, as did Queen Margot herself. All expressed tender condolences while privately rejoicing in the removal of this inconvenient obstacle.

Like the good father that he was, Henry visited his children to offer them his love, and gave instructions concerning their mother's effects: her furniture and personal jewels, while retrieving those which belonged to the crown.

By the end of the month he'd discarded the black apparel in favour of violet, and was once again writing letters of state.

Studiously avoiding any mention of his loss, he remained swamped in melancholy. He would sit oblivious to the roistering and wit going on all around him from his courtiers, even the charms of the lovely ladies who would readily have offered him comfort. Bellegarde, his closest friend and one-time rival for Gabrielle's affections, did his utmost to cheer him, while the Comte d'Auvergne lost no opportunity of mentioning the charms of his sister, Henriette de Balzac, reminding Henry how he had enjoyed dancing with her.

'She is a woman of great reserve and virtue,' he told the King, raising a collective disbelieving brow among the courtiers at this unlikely description of his sister's charms, a saucy coquette if ever there was one. It was also well known that her father, François d'Entragues, had been one of the most profligate courtiers of the licentious court of Henri III. Auvergne himself, often referred to as the Bastard de Valois as he was the son of Marie Touchet by Charles IX, and therefore the girl's half-brother, was known to be restless and overambitious, and not averse to a little wily conspiracy.

But on this occasion, perhaps weary of lonely days of mourning, and recent trying visits from various ambassadors, Henry responded with a smile. The entire court applauded, so relieved were the noble lords to see their king begin to recover his usual good spirits.

It was this wish to cheer him that his courtiers suggested a hunting trip to Blois. When he agreed, Auvergne quickly dispatched a secret message to his mother, urging her to invite the King to call at the estate of Bois-Malesherbes, the residence of the Entragues family, to rest from the fatigue of the chase. The message was received as the party rode back towards Fontainebleau and Paris.

'Now you can judge for yourself, Sire,' Auvergne told him, 'whether I do not speak true.'

Surrounded by a hundred hectares of parkland, the stately chateau with its tithe barn, chapel and huge *pigeonnier*, overlooked the beautiful valley of the River Essonne, situated in the department of the Loiret. Henry was impressed. Balzac had clearly done well for himself. The fellow had a beautiful wife in Marie Touchet, who had presented him with a son and two daughters, plus he also had a son and daughter from a previous marriage. A fortunate man indeed.

Henry could not help but experience a burst of envy, thinking of his own ill fortune.

Why was he, of all men, denied happiness? Even now his advisers were making plans to marry him off to some dull royal princess, constantly reminding him that Queen Margot would only agree to a divorce if her replacement was considered worthy. He'd battled against this unreasonable stricture, deliberately keeping his wife short of funds in order to force her to bend to his will. But the years were slipping by, he was no longer young, and, if he was to produce the legitimate heir France needed, Henry knew he could hold out no longer.

Not now that he had lost Gabrielle.

He'd had word that Margot had already sent a personal requisition to Rome, in which she'd declared that their marriage had been in opposition to her own free will, and entirely at the instigation of her brother, King Charles IX, and Queen Catherine, her mother. She claimed that she had not even spoken during the ceremony, her agreement invoked when her brother the King had forcibly inclined her head. The letter had concluded, 'And with the King my husband and myself being related in the third degree, I beseech His Holiness to declare the nullity of the said marriage.'

Henry was relieved the battle between them was finally over, that perhaps they might even be friends again, in time. But it would not be long before Rosny would be naming a new royal bride. His heart sank to his boots at the thought.

The bedroom he was given at Malesherbes was most commodious and magnificently appointed, decorated with a series of tapestries depicting biblical scenes. Oh, but it felt so empty, the bed lonely without his angel beside him. At least it was not one they had ever shared. Henry was so determined to avoid the memories of their blissful nights together that he slept in his own bed as little as possible, constantly visiting the homes of friends and courtiers, and refusing to retire until he was dropping with fatigue.

But it was almost the end of May, the trees were fragrant with blossom, the sun warm on his skin, and he was happy to see Marie Touchet again. He remembered her as a sweet girl who, along with Elizabeth of Austria, had done much to calm the madness of Charles IX when he was out for Henry's blood.

Now Marie presented the two daughters of her marriage with François de Balzac, and the moment he set eyes on the elder, he remembered that dance. He recalled the way she had moved with a sensuous grace, scandalously flirting with him even as his would-be Queen had looked on. She was the most bewitching girl he had ever seen. For the first time in weeks he felt that familiar spark of interest that brought him instantly alive again. He was utterly captivated by her youthful exuberance, so like that which had once attracted him to his lovely Gabrielle. That, of course, had been before several pregnancies had plumped her figure. This girl made him feel young again, charming him with her wit and clever conversation, by the way she laughed and teased him as if he were simply an attractive man, and not a king. She did not appear in the least overawed at being in the presence of her monarch, which Henry found exciting.

'Why do you surround yourself with these buffoons?' she chided him, indicating Bellegarde, Montglat, Frontenac and others, including her own brother. 'Do you not realize it is their own vanity they wish to flatter by being in Your Majesty's presence.'

He smiled into her green eyes. 'You wish them to flatter me?'

'You are their king, more worthy of accolades than they. Do not allow them to rule you, or dictate their own wishes as if they were your own.'

Henry sketched a teasing bow. 'I thank you for those kind words of wisdom. But it was their suggestion that I call here at Malesherbes. Was that a mistake, think you?'

Henriette allowed herself to appear slightly flustered as she cast him a sidelong glance from beneath her long dark lashes. She was certainly well versed in the art of flattery, and knew how to fascinate a man, even a king.

'How do you know the invitation came from them? I doubt these so-called nobles are capable of such a very *noble* thought. Do they possess any sensitivity or consideration for others? I very much doubt it. Perhaps the idea for this visit was born of quite a different source, inspired by your good self at some point in the not-too-distant past.' She arched one finely plucked brow and he laughed out loud.

'I think you are cleverer than I gave you credit for, mademoiselle.'

The small pert mouth curved upwards into a bewitching smile. 'I dare say that is something you might discover for yourself, given time.'

'And will you allow me the necessary time to make such fascinating discoveries?'

Henriette sank into a deep curtsey, head bowed for a moment before raising it to look directly into his eyes. 'I would never presume to deny a king, unless he were to ask me to relinquish my good character.'

It was a challenge Henry could not resist. He stayed at the château several days longer than intended, enchanted by the young beauty. He found her to be both vivacious and intelligent, entranced by the secret smile that played about her lips whenever she looked in his direction. Henry was never allowed to be alone with her, as her protective mother assured him she was still a virgin and had no wish for her daughter's virtue to be comprom-ised. Yet unlike his sweet Gabrielle, she did not act like one. There was a promise of passion in those catlike eyes that were as deep and unfathomable as the ocean. Henriette made it very plain that she would not succumb easily, but it came to him with a delicious shock that he wanted her, very badly.

Gabrielle had been dead for just five weeks.

Henriette was jubilant. 'Did I not tell you, *Maman*, that I could charm the King? He could not take his eyes from me.'

Balzac, well pleased with the royal attention to his beautiful daughter, was already weighing up possible advantages for his own future. 'You must not surrender to the royal suit unless it includes the crown matrimonial.'

'Indeed, I will not,' Henriette agreed with a knowing smile.

Marie sighed, wishing to caution both husband and daughter yet knowing they would not listen. She had wanted a respectable life for her girls, but how could she, as a one-time royal mistress herself, deny Henriette such an opportunity? 'Remember that the King is in mourning. Had Gabrielle d'Estrées lived, she would have been our queen by now.'

'But she is dead, and *I* am very much alive. I am young, and

if not quite such a beauty, I am as well born and possess a sparkling wit, or so the King thinks.' Henriette laughed. 'I certainly
know how to play him.'

'Flattering the vanity of a king is not difficult but can easily
lead to disappointment, particularly with this one. Henry has a
fickle nature when it comes to women, so do not set your heart
on having him. You will have many rivals for his affection. I
loved Charles. He loved his beloved Elizabeth, but also adored
me. I was fortunate in that I was his one and only mistress. You
could never be sure of such constancy from Henry of Navarre.'

'Tch, you can be happy without becoming encumbered by
love. Power is far more important.'

'If that is what you seek then you play a dangerous game,
child.'

'Any game with a prize worth capturing involves danger,'
retorted her husband.

'That is true, but does she not also deserve a good husband?
Would love without marriage be enough for you, my sweet?'

'There you go again, *Maman*, judging me by your own standards. You were not ambitious, were content to be a mistress, but
that was *your* choice. It would not be mine.' The green eyes glittered with a new determination. 'Why could I not have both the
King's love *and* marriage? What think you, Papa?'

Balzac smirked with pleasure that this clever daughter's thoughts
so matched his own. 'I see no reason at all, dearest child, why
you should not succeed where the unfortunate Gabrielle d'Estrées
failed. If you can but win the King's heart, you could indeed win
a crown.'

The château of Malesherbes was convenient enough to Paris for
Balzac to take a full part in court life, but as this new plan took
shape he removed his family to their house in the city so that
his daughter would be better placed to pursue her dream. Henriette
preened and prettied herself while she waited in breathless anticipation for the King to come. She was not disappointed. The
moment Henry heard, he abandoned the hunt and hastened to
Paris after her.

To Henriette's complete delight the King was even more attentive, making a point of visiting her daily. One day he brought

her a gift, a rope of pearls, which she cleverly refused to accept, not wishing to appear too grasping, or compromise her reputation.

'My lord, do you think you can buy my favours with such riches?' she chided him, allowing soft tears to form in her beautiful eyes. 'You know how I value your friendship, but you are a king, and I but a humble maiden. Would you dishonour me?'

To her surprise and disappointment Henry did not press her, but put the valuable necklace back in its casket and returned to the Louvre.

'You have played it too cool. You've lost him,' Marie-Charlotte whispered as he strode away.

Henriette slapped her sister across the face. 'Never dare to say such things to me. I *will* have him! He will come again, do not doubt it.'

The next day she was proved entirely right as Henry again presented her with a mysterious box. Fully expecting to find the magnificent pearls still inside, Henriette discovered instead that he had brought her a dish of a hundred apricots. She gazed upon them, stunned and dismayed.

'You know that I seek only to honour you. Where is the harm in a dish of fruit?'

Quickly recovering her composure she laughed out loud. 'You are an incorrigible prince.'

No one had ever called him such a thing before, and, enchanted by her audacity, Henry fell still further beneath her spell.

Casting her sister a triumphant, warning glare, so that Marie-Charlotte quickly scurried from the room, Henriette sank to the floor in a charming puff of skirts, putting her hands to her warm cheeks. 'My head is spinning, my emotions in turmoil. You have touched my heart, Your Majesty, I do not deny it, but how can our destinies ever be joined? I constantly bewail the twist of fate that has placed you upon a throne, and thus beyond the reach of my affection.'

'How can I be beyond your reach when I am your prisoner?' Henry murmured, gently raising her and leading her by the hand to a quiet arbour in the garden where, unobserved, he might succeed in stealing a kiss. 'I am your captive. How can I resist your charms?'

'Or I yours,' she told him, her soft white hands stroking his. 'I am ready to make any sacrifice rather than resign my claim upon your love, save only that which cannot be returned to me intact.'

She referred, of course, to her maidenhead, in fact long since surrendered, although Henriette had no intention of allowing the King to know that.

He grasped her hand and kissed it. 'Some sacrifices are worth making, for the benefits they gain. Say the word and you could enjoy the place and state that my beloved duchess enjoyed. You will be my *maîtresse-en-titre*.'

Henriette rewarded his passionate plea with a furious frown. 'Sire, I am not Gabrielle. I am not your insipid little angel wishing always to please you and do as you say.' Only that morning her sister had brought to her attention some verses called the *Complaint of the Shade of the Duchesse de Beaufort to the King*. She had ripped the paper to shreds. Henriette had no intention of being bound by the ghost of a former mistress less clever than herself. 'I am my own person. I will not be bullied or controlled, even by a king. If I come to you, it will be of my own free will, not because you demand it.'

Excitement pounded in him, the blood roared in his head, the ache in his loins was almost unbearable. So much so that he made no attempt to chide her over the criticism of his former favourite. This one would be very different. Henry could sense the latent passion in her. He could smell it, taste it. It burned like a fever in her eyes, in her teasing little touches on his person. She would be like a tiger in his bed, not the sweet willing participant he'd grown used to in Gabrielle. Henry recognized this aura of sensuality in her and welcomed it. He needed a woman in his bed who knew how to give him pleasure, particularly if the rest of the time that same bed would be occupied by a fat Italian princess. Rosny was constantly impressing upon him the benefits of marrying Marie de Medici, not least for the sake of the treasury. The net was closing in, no doubt about it. He met the girl's furious glare, all jesting gone. 'I would have you come to me for no other reason, but come you must.'

A short, breathless silence, in which a silent acknowledgement passed between them.

'Much as I might long to give in to my desire, how can I?'

she gasped. 'My father would never agree. Nor my mother, who is overly protective of me. She warns me that I would court disappointment, were I to succumb to your pleas. And I dare not go against my father's wishes. His anger would be so terrible he would marry me off in a moment, to the first man willing to take me, however fat or old; a husband I would surely loathe. How dare I take such a risk?'

Mildly irritated by this show of resistance, which he had heard many times before, Henry hastened to offer the usual reassurances. 'I swear you would not be disappointed. I would be true, and I would never leave you at the mercy of a cruel father.'

'You might mean to protect me, but my father has sworn to protect the family's honour.'

Henry longed to explain that he had always generously provided previous mistresses with a rich husband, but thought better of it. In any case, some of those had indeed been fat and old. He'd never enjoyed competition. Girding his patience he decided to try another tack. 'In that case we must employ different skills. I wish for our future destinies to be most certainly entwined, so we must seek some way to pacify your father.'

And on that promise, she allowed him to kiss her.

Following this heartfelt declaration, Henriette grew ever more daring and generous with her favours, cleverly allowing the King increasing liberty with her body, which only encouraged him to press for more. He would blaze a trail of tantalizing kisses along the slender white curve of her throat. She would creep up on to his lap and allow him to dip his fingers beneath the low bodice of her gown. Henry did so love to fondle her breasts; would rub a teasing thumb over her rosy nipple, or flick it with his tongue, surprising her by how quickly it hardened with desire. Henriette discovered to her delight that although the King was quite old, he was a generous and exciting lover. In her turn she would daringly take in hand the King's member and pleasure him too, but she drew firm boundaries. There could be no true intimacy between them, no risks which might damage her reputation, and ruin her chances of a richer prize.

Consequently Henry's frustration grew by the day, his patience stretched to the limit.

In early August, still eager to avoid the loneliness of his own bedchamber, Henry was staying at Zamet's house. Following supper with the Marquis d'Elbeuf, he returned rather late and went straight to bed, only to be roused from his slumber in the early hours by an uproar. Some dispute or other was clearly taking place in the courtyard. Taking up his sword, and clad only in his nightshirt, Henry hurried to investigate. He found his Grand Equerry, the Duke of Bellegarde, and Claude, Prince de Joinville, fourth son of the late Henri de Guise, engaged in a ferocious fight.

'What means this? What goes on here?' Henry asked a goggle-eyed page.

'Sire, the gentlemen fight over a woman.'

Henry snorted. 'I should have guessed. Who is the fortunate, or perhaps I should say *unfortunate* lady this time?'

'Mademoiselle de Balzac.' Enthralled at being in conversation with the King himself, the young page poured the gossip into Henry's ready ear. 'Prince de Joinville has been paying the lady his addresses, but now the Duke de Bellegarde has come forward as a rival.'

'Has he indeed?' Henry growled, remembering how the Equerry had once begged permission to marry Gabrielle, and how he'd been obliged to banish him from court as a consequence. What an unfortunate fellow he was to always fall in love with the wrong woman. Henry called out to them, half-amused by the altercation, which did not appear to endanger life, and yet he was partly irritated that these two should dare to compete with a king. 'Stop behaving like fools, the pair of you. The lady is taken, and by a better man than either of you.'

Certain of being obeyed, Henry had half turned away to return to his bed when he heard the unmistakable sound of a sword being unsheathed from its scabbard. Before anything could be done to stop him, Joinville had rushed at Bellegarde and pierced his rival's thigh with his rapier.

Henry leaped out into the courtyard and was upon him in a second, de Villars and Rambouillet at his side. 'Are you mad?' he roared, knocking Joinville to the ground and snatching the weapon from him. 'You could have killed the Duke.'

'Sire, he has intruded upon my pleasure.'

'And you intrude upon mine.' Turning to Villars, he cried, 'Summon the President of the Parliament. I'll have this young fool arrested and brought to trial. Mayhap that will knock some sense into him.'

But come morning the Duchesse de Nemours called upon the King to beg mercy for her grandson. 'He is as hot-blooded as his father was, and Guise was no enemy of yours, Sire.'

'How can you say that when he was the love of Queen Margot's life.'

The old duchess gave a small smile. 'You never objected at the time. What a pair you were, each outdoing the other with your intrigues and *affaires*. Surely you, of all men, can sympathize with a young blood hot with love for a woman.'

Henry felt obliged to concede the point and contented himself with banishing Joinville from the court. But did not hasten to forgive him. By the time he did allow the fellow back to court, his own liaison with Henriette would surely be settled, and any hope of future rivalry for her favours forever banished. He meant to have her, and although Henry had no wish to share his throne with the daughter of the mistress of Charles IX, there had never been a woman he could not persuade into his bed.

The King took her to meet his children at St Germain. He sent her more gifts including some hangings that were conservatively valued at three thousand *livres*. He flattered and charmed her, freely admitted that he had lost his heart to her. It was not enough. Henriette coolly refused to surrender, and, quite against her father's advice, returned to Bois-Malesherbes.

'Do not push him too far or you risk losing all,' Balzac warned his ambitious daughter.

Henriette smiled. 'Do not worry, Papa, my absence will only serve to show the King what he is missing.'

Her clever game worked as Henry quickly followed her, but yet again she refused him. This time he left in high dudgeon and in retaliation turned his attentions to a maid of honour at Chenonceaux where he was visiting Louise of Lorraine, widow of Henri III.

Later, on his return to Fontainebleau, Henry despatched the Comte de Lude to discuss a certain proposition with Henriette and her father. 'Let her think that my interest is waning, that should bring her to heel.'

The King's emissary did as he was bid and tactfully pointed out to Balzac that His Majesty was now so enamoured of Mademoiselle de la Bourdaisière, a renowned beauty, that he may well cease to pursue Henriette altogether. 'The King's patience grows thin.'

Startled by this news, Balzac instantly changed tactics, adopting a more humble disposition. 'I may well agree, were my family's honour to be properly compensated.'

The Comte hid a smile. 'His Majesty wishes to know what price you would ask for her to concede to his desires.'

Balzac hurried away to discuss the matter with his wife and son. Auvergne had frequently feigned disapproval of the King's pursuit of his sister, even while secretly encouraging it. Marie Touchet cried out in horror when she heard the sum he had in mind.

'You ask too much. You shame us by these demands, husband.'

Lifting her chin with a blaze of defiance in her green eyes, Henriette challenged her mother. 'Are you saying that I am of less value than a pile of old silver? Shall I not need to set myself up in a manner befitting my new status?' In her heart she was secretly growing fearful of losing Henry, of her clever tricks failing to bring off this coup. There was still talk of an Italian marriage, but not for a moment would she admit these fears to her parents.

'On the contrary, we ask too little,' Auvergne protested. 'The King should treat her with better respect. This is not the first time Henry has willingly paid for a woman's favours. But I note he still does not offer a crown.'

Balzac frowned. 'You are right, son. Does he imagine he can buy my daughter's honour with mere money? I shall also request a suitable appointment for you, and for myself. He is hot for her and will pay whatever we ask.'

The pair at once began to devise various military promotions which might be advantageous to them both. After lengthy discussions Balzac returned with a demand for one hundred thousand *livres*, plus suitable positions for himself and his son.

Now it was the Comte's turn to be startled. One hundred thousand was an unheard of sum, even for a maidenhead, and

Henry was surely not fool enough to be convinced the girl was still in possession of it. But who was he to judge what a king would do to satisfy his lust? Skilfully masking his dismay, de Lude bowed deeply and quickly departed to relay these demands to his monarch.

'Are you never satisfied, husband?' Marie protested. 'Think of our daughter's virtue which you so easily barter.'

'Silence, wife! I will not relinquish the family honour for anything less than the sum we demand, plus a crown.'

Henriette burst into a tantrum of fury. 'The King may refuse. How can we force him to agree to what we ask? We have no power.'

'We have more than you might think. Now do not spoil that pretty complexion with tears, and listen carefully, child, for I have a plan.'

Henry heard the demands in silence. How different the bewitching Henriette was from his sweet Gabrielle. He had showered his precious angel with gifts and love but she'd had no desire for a crown, wanting only to marry and be respectable. In the end his persistence had paid off and he'd won her affection away from her previous lover. He'd loved Gabrielle sincerely, and would gladly have made her his queen. There would be no crown for Henriette but he wanted her all the same, and if a hundred thousand *livres* was the price to pay to purchase her favours, then so be it.

The problem was that while he was ready and willing to hand over the sum demanded, Rosny put every possible objection in his path to prevent him from doing so.

'Does Your Majesty not appreciate how difficult it has been for the treasury to raise the required four million for the renewal of the Swiss alliance?'

'Then this is a trifling sum by comparison. I wish her to have status and privacy, away from her meddling father. I demand that you make the payment forthwith.'

Knowing he had no choice but to obey, the wily superintendent of finances made one final effort to change his monarch's mind. The next morning, approaching the King while Henry took breakfast, he slowly and deliberately counted out the coins, in small pieces of silver, spreading the piles across the table in order to demonstrate how large a sum this greedy courtesan had demanded.

The gesture made not the slightest difference. The King's decision was final.

A small château and the estate of Bois-Lancy in the Orléannois was purchased and the deeds sent to Mademoiselle d'Entragues, together with the balance of the money in silver to her father. Henry ordered Henriette to leave Malesherbes and wait upon him there.

Instead, infuriated by the lack of an appointment for himself and his son, Balzac refused to allow his daughter to leave.

As anticipated, Henry quickly followed.

'Led like a fool by the nose, or by the demands of the heat in his breeches,' Balzac scorned, smirking with satisfaction as the King's entourage clattered into the courtyard. 'Order refreshment for His Majesty, wife, and put on your best smile. As for you, daughter, remember the stakes we play for are high.' As if Henriette needed any reminder.

The royal patience might be rapidly failing but Henry could not bear it when a woman wept upon his shoulder, as Henriette was doing now, pressing her warm voluptuous body against his as she proclaimed her distress over her father's obstinacy. Henriette strived not to flinch or recoil at the stink of horse flesh emanating from him, and the sweat he'd worked up on a long hard ride.

Henry's resolve to have her remained strong. 'What more can I do for you, my beloved? You already have my heart, a fine château, and your father a small fortune in silver.'

She stroked a soft hand over his cheek, playfully tweaked his beard and ran a finger over that sensuous lower lip of his, hearing the low groan of desire deep in his throat. 'I would surrender to your will this day, this very moment, but my father will not allow it. He wants more. I confess he is a greedy, cruel man who will beat me if I do not obey his wishes,' Henriette lied.

Fearful of losing her when the promised prize was tantalizingly within his grasp, his hands circled the tiny waist to press her ever closer, hoping to ease the ache in his loins. 'What is it he wants from me this time?'

'I dare not say. It is too shocking.' Pushing the King gently away, Henriette retreated to the window and hid her face in her hands, praying he would follow. 'I swear I do not possess the courage to communicate his demands to Your Majesty.'

'Tell me, my sweet, and I swear I will not blame you, whatever they may be.'

Feeling his arms come about her she closed her eyes in relief and allowed herself to sink back against his broad chest. Then catching a breath in her throat, Henriette spoke quickly, as if in fear. 'My father the Marquis will never consent to my becoming your mistress unless he receives a written promise, signed by Your Majesty's hand, that you will offer me marriage, provided that within a year I successfully give you a son.'

Turning in his arms she gazed lovingly up into his face, and saw a small frown gather upon his brow. Henriette hastened to lay the blame squarely upon her father. 'I did try to point out the futility of such a demand, but my arguments were in vain. My father declares that he seeks only to preserve the honour of his house.'

'Does one hundred thousand *livres* not soften his loss sufficiently that he must demand more?'

Henriette felt the smallest panic start up in her breast as she pressed herself ever closer, showering kisses over his mouth and bearded chin. 'I reminded my father that the word of a king was of equal value to his signature, and that I, a mere subject, could never dare to demand such a promise. But he is adamant, and since he will not relent, can you not indulge this whim? Of what consequence is it? If you love me, and value the love I hold for you, how can you hesitate to comply with his desire? Name what conditions you please, I am ready to accept them, content to obey your slightest wish. In *everything*.'

And leading the King to a couch she gave him most, if not quite all, he desired. The document was duly signed before the day was out.

> *We, Henry fourth, by the grace of God, King of France and Navarre, promise and swear before God on our faith and word as a King, to Messers François de Balzac, Lord of Entragues, a Knight of our Orders, that [he] giving us as companion Demoiselle Henriette Catherine de Balzac, his daughter, in case in six months, beginning*

from the first day of this present one, she should become enceinte, and should give birth to a son, then and instantly we will take her to be our wife and legitimate spouse, whose marriage we will solemnize publicly and in face of our Holy Church according to the rites required and customary in such a case. For greater confirmation of the present promise we promise and swear as herein stated to ratify and renew it under our seals, immediate after we have obtained from our Holy Father the Pope the dissolution of our marriage with Dame Marguerite of France, with the permission to marry again as may seem fit to us. In witness whereof we have written and signed these presents.

At the Wood of Malesherbes, this day the first of October, 1599.

Henry.

Rosny was furious. He picked up the carefully worded document, read it to the end, then ripped it in two.

'Since you wish to know my opinion, that is what I think of such a promise.' Had he not just rejoiced at finally being rid of the obstacle to his plans to provide France with an honourable queen, he most certainly had no wish for another.

'*Ventre Saint Gris!*' cried the King. 'What are you about? Have you gone mad?'

'I fear so, Sire,' Rosny answered. Privately he thought it was his monarch who had lost his wits. 'I am a fool. Would that I were the only one in France. Sire, remember how d'Entragues and his daughters created a scandal in the time of the Duchess de Beaufort. Did you yourself not insist that I give *une baggage* orders to quit Paris?'

Flushed with irritation Henry refuted this. 'It was my dear angel who insisted the girl leave, as she was foolishly beset with jealousy over a simple dance.'

'But the promise of marriage will only serve to bring Your Majesty into derision. In addition, the document would prove a serious obstacle both to the projected divorce from Queen Marguerite and to a suitable matrimonial alliance which might benefit France. I beg you to think carefully on this, Sire. Queen Margot will not surrender her title to any demoiselle, nor will the Pope insist that she does. You could well lose all hope of alliance with the Italian princess, Marie de Medici, who is by all reports a lovely young woman as well as rich, and find yourself once again shackled to Queen Margot with no prospect of escape.'

Furious at being so challenged, yet knowing the argument to be sound, Henry strode from the room. But obstinately refusing to back down he called for his private secretary to write out a fresh promise of marriage to replace the one which Rosny had destroyed. Then he mounted his horse and went hunting, an expedition which conveniently took him to Malesherbes, where he remained for several days.

The matter was far from settled. Balzac decided he would be satisfied with nothing less than the post of Marshal of France, a position for which Henry considered him entirely unsuitable as he did not possess the necessary military qualifications. The Marquis made this further demand as he daringly outfaced the man who lusted after his daughter, even though he was a king. Henry was incensed and refused, point blank, to grant his wish. He'd thought the girl almost in his hands, now it was all going wrong.

'This transaction is turning out to be far more expensive than I bargained for. You have silver in your pocket, your daughter a fine château, and a promise of marriage. Would you have my bleeding heart too?'

Balzac smirked, certain he was winning. The only danger to his plan was that his daughter was like a cat on heat, more than eager to surrender whatever was left of her virtue. In order to separate her from the King while he concluded these arrangements to his complete satisfaction, he dispatched the girl to Marcoussis, then followed himself in order to guard her.

The King fell into a sulk and on 10 October wrote to Henriette.

> Mes chères amours. *You order me to surmount, if I love you, all the difficulties . . . By the proposals I have made I have sufficiently shown the strength of my love for those on your side to raise no further difficulties. What I said before you I will not fail in, but nothing more.*

It seemed the King had reached the end of his tether and Henriette was deeply alarmed. Marcoussis was closer to Fontainebleau than Malesherbes, but it was a stronghold with ramparts, and a keep which was only reached after crossing three drawbridges. The castle had been erected in the fourteenth century, since which time it had more than once withstood a siege, notably by John the Fearless of Burgundy in 1417. It could easily withstand that of a lover, even if he were a brave soldier king.

The protracted argument over her surrender had gone on long enough, so far as Henriette was concerned. She wanted to enjoy some of the benefits of capturing a king's heart. She certainly had no wish to be confined in a prison, as was Queen Margot. 'Why would I wish to be locked behind these stone walls when I could grace the bed of a king?' was her constant cry. 'Advise me, *Maman*, how to keep his interest, as you so successfully retained the love of Charles IX. Am I not as clever and as beautiful as you?'

'You are certainly more ambitious, child.'

'At least I took the precaution of getting this,' she snapped, flourishing the signed document in her mother's face. Soon, I shall be his wife and Queen of France. What say you to that?'

'That Henry of Navarre was never a man for keeping his promises, or for constancy, so do not count your chickens too soon, my love. He could easily grow bored and turn again to Mademoiselle de la Bourdaisière. And I've heard he is also paying court to Mademoiselle de la Chastre,' Marie mildly remarked. 'Did I not warn you of possible disappointment?'

Henriette stamped her foot, her cheeks growing crimson with fury. 'So tell me your secrets. What must I do to win, and *keep*, a king, *and* a crown? He is a man, after all, with a man's weaknesses. What more can I do to fascinate him?'

Marie could have said that Henriette should listen less to her own greed and more to her heart, and not too blindly to her own father, but did not dare. And in truth her younger daughter, Marie, was far less shrewd, having recently eloped with Bassompierre without any promise of marriage. Perhaps this one was cleverer than she gave her credit for. With a sigh, Marie gave Henriette the kind of advice a mother should never give a daughter on how to please a man with pretty and titillating little tricks. However unsavoury and embarrassing, it was the only advice to which she would listen.

When this was done, or Marie could bear to say no more, Henriette merely laughed. 'But I've already tried all of that, save for the falling in love part,' she scorned. 'I've learned a few tricks myself these last few years. Have I not had two lovers fighting over me? Skilled as I am in the art of love, why have I failed to capture the King? Why does he not come to me now?'

'How can he when you are so well guarded?'

Her head jerked up and she grew instantly thoughtful. 'Then how can he get past Papa?'

'Ah, that is a difficulty for you to resolve. I couldn't possibly advise.'

Her mother quietly withdrew, leaving Henriette to restlessly pace her bedchamber, chaffing even more at the restrictions placed upon her. Then an idea came to her. Calling for pen and paper she quickly wrote a note which suggested that the King summon her father to some alleged duty away from the castle, which would leave the way open for her rescue. She quickly dispatched the missive with a loyal page.

The plan worked like a charm. The Marquis innocently obeyed the King's orders, and, once he had left the castle, Henry presented himself and carried off Henriette. No one dared to protest.

She was duly installed at the Hôtel de Larchant in Paris, which had been specially prepared to receive her, decked out with new hangings and flowers in every room. 'A pretty bird should have a pretty cage,' Henry said, gathering her hungrily in his arms.

'I want no cage,' Henriette softly protested. 'Only the freedom to be every moment at your side.' Carefully remembering all her mother's advice, she did indeed shower him with love and fond words of affection, well laced with her own adventurous spirit. That night she gave the King all he had hoped and dreamed of, and beyond. As always, Henry was an eager lover, nor was he disappointed with his prize, and Henriette set no boundaries in her resolve to please him. She let him do with her as he willed, and even showed him one or two tricks of her own. Henry was enslaved.

By the end of the month Henriette d'Entragues was firmly established as the royal favourite. One of her first unselfish acts was to solicit the pardon of the Prince de Joinville. But then he had previously been her lover, so she was determined to help him if she could. Henry generously granted the request, and in early November Joinville came to Saint Germain-en-Laye, accompanied by his uncle, the Duke of Mayenne, to pay obeisance to the King. Henry received him with much kindness. Soon after that, his royal mistress was presented with her new domain and granted a title to go with it. Gabrielle had been the Duchess of Beaufort, Henriette would in future be known as the Marchioness de Verneuil. Not quite so high in rank, but it was a good place to start. Henriette resolved that her next advancement would be the highest in the land, next to the King's.

Part Two
THE ITALIAN MARRIAGE

'The marriage arrangements have been successfully concluded.' Ferdinand I, Grand Duke of Tuscany, beamed exultantly upon his niece. 'In return I have agreed to release France from its indebtedness, the balance to be given in cash to a total sum of six hundred thousand *livres*, which will represent your dowry. The Ambassador has this very day been dispatched to Paris with the signed articles of marriage. What think you of that?'

Marie de Medici gasped. Six hundred thousand *livres*! How could she be worth such a sum? It terrified her. So many projects of marriage had been mooted and failed. She had once hoped to marry her cousin, Don Virginio Orsini, Duke of Bracciano, a handsome and chivalrous *chevalier*, but it had come to nothing, as had this one with Henry IV, which had rumbled on for years. By now the King of France must be approaching fifty, and with a reputation for philandering, so she'd rather hoped that too might similarly flounder. No doubt he was pressed for cash, and she, as a rich royal bride, was seen as a solution to his troubles. Marie sighed. She should not complain. Was that not always the lot of princesses?

'Will I suit him, do you think?' she asked in tremulous tones.

She was twenty-seven years old and eager for a husband and children of her own. If she loved him well, mayhap he would no longer feel the need for a mistress.

As if reading his niece's mind, and being of a kindly nature – if a little hectoring at times – the Grand Duke came to put his arms about her. 'Any man would be a fool not to appreciate your youthful loveliness. You are a handsome young woman, never forget it.'

Marie gave a wry smile. 'Handsome? I'd sooner be a beauty.' She did not see herself as beautiful. Her oval face she thought pale and unremarkable, the nose rather too long, the chin too pointed. But she was of reasonable height and slender, with a shapely figure. 'How can I compete with the late Duchess of Beaufort for whom the King must still secretly mourn? And his new mistress, the Marchioness de Verneuil.'

'Remember that whatever affections have gone before in Henry's life, you must ignore them. You are a Medici, and the daughter of the Archduchess Joan of Austria. Be proud of that.'

She looked up at her uncle, all the pride she felt in her heritage and her Italian blood gleaming in her dark, shining eyes. Besides, she longed to please him as he had improved her life exponentially since his accession. 'Oh, I *am* proud, I am.' Even as a small child her beloved mother had taught her to lift her chin high and walk with assurance in every step.

'You will be queen, and therefore have no need to compete with anyone. You possess the proper dignity and presence, have inherited your dear mother's pretty Hapsburg mouth, as well as her soft brown hair and porcelain complexion. And from your father, my wayward brother Francesco, his intelligence and confidence, though not his cold, unfeeling nature, praise God. Were your parents still with us, I believe they would be proud of you this day.'

Marie smiled with warm affection, grateful for the care her uncle gave her, while privately acknowledging that her neglectful father had never shown the least pride in her. Following the death of her mother he'd dispatched her to the Pitti Palace in Florence, just days from her fifth birthday, where she'd spent a sad and lonely childhood. But it was surely true that her intellect was quick and cultivated, thanks to the excellent education she and her half-brother, Antonio, had been given by the formidable Donna Francesca. Marie had particularly loved the arts and poetry, and developed a gift for languages. She'd loved to walk in the Boboli Gardens, created by her grandfather, Cosimo. But if she did not suffer fools gladly, wasn't that only right and proper in a royal princess?

She became aware that the Grand Duke was still speaking, offering her his valuable counsel, as he so loved to do.

'You must remember to exercise restraint and learn to submit to the King's will. Keep your thoughts private and your temper cool.'

'You know that I am not hot-tempered, Uncle, but I shall expect to be treated with respect, my opinions listened to.'

Ferdinand gave her hand a reassuring squeeze. 'I'm sure that will be the case, so far as state affairs allow. I know that you are ambitious, my dear, which is a natural family trait and necessary in any would-be queen, but do not be impatient, or too impulsive, which can result in poor judgement.'

Marie frowned. 'I will not be his cipher by saying and doing nothing to displease him. I am as royal as Henry, and a true marriage should be a partnership.'

'Indeed, in an ideal world that would most certainly be the case. Sometimes life is not quite as perfect as we would like it to be. Henry is a good man with an easy nature, one who loves women but is also desirous of a pleasant domestic life. If you can but be tolerant of his flaws, you will do well together.'

She troubled him somewhat, this beloved niece of his, as there was a paradox in her. Marie longed for marriage and was needy for love, yet she bore some of Joanna's hauteur, and was instinctively distrustful of men. A natural reaction, perhaps, to losing a mother so young, and considering the mysterious circumstances of her death. Outwardly proud, but emotionally vulnerable. 'You are strong and healthy. Once you have given Henry a dauphin for France, he will look at no other woman.'

Marie hoped and prayed that would be true. She did not think she would be very good at sharing. She remembered the suffering her own mother had endured at the hands of the scandalous Bianca, her father's young mistress. And her own, after the unexpected and convenient death of Bianca's husband had allowed the two lovers to marry.

As if a neglectful father had not been bad enough, her young life thereafter had been ruled by the tyrannical regime of an overambitious stepmother. Marie knew that it was expected for a king to keep a mistress, but she made a private vow that she would never allow herself to be so ill-used.

Henry was well aware of Rosny's machinations on his behalf but had chosen to ignore them. He never questioned his advisor as the minister had been with him a long time. Born at the Château de Rosny near Mantes-la-Jolie of a noble Flemish family, Rosny had been brought up in the Reformed faith. As a young man he'd been presented to Henry of Navarre in 1571 and remained loyal ever since. Now he worked quietly and speedily, using every means at his disposal to bring about the marriage of his sovereign to a European princess worthy of sharing his throne. No obstacles had been put in the way of a successful outcome as the King was too taken up with the delectable Henriette to pay proper attention. So on Rosny's return from signing the articles with the Italian Ambassador, who had recently arrived in Paris, the King asked, with careless curiosity, where he had been these last few days.

'We come, Sire, from marrying you.'

Henry stared at him, too shocked to speak. It was some moments before he could find the words to demand an explanation.

The superintendent of finance answered in bland formal tones, as was his way. 'I mean that I have come from meeting with Baccio Giovannini, an envoy from the Grand Duke of Tuscany. It took a few days of negotiation but, as a consequence, the articles of marriage are signed for Your Majesty to marry with his niece, Marie de Medici, and a dowry agreed.'

Henry sank into a chair as if his knees had given way, only to at once leap up and start pacing about the chamber, nibbling on his nails, lost in thought. He paused before Rosny. 'There is no way out of this?'

The minister raised a brow in polite enquiry. 'Why would you seek one, Sire? Your Majesty had agreed that you must marry, for the sake of the nation. The treasury has been saved.'

'There is no escape?'

'None that will not greatly offend or create possible conflict with the Grand Duke, as well as leave us in a poor bargaining position against the Duke of Savoy. A contract will be drawn up and signed, and a proxy marriage held in due course, in Florence, before the princess sets sail for France.'

'Can it not be delayed a while longer?' He was thinking of Henriette, and how she had hopes of fulfilling her part of the bargain by giving him a son in just a few months' time.

'No longer than it takes for these matters to be arranged: a few weeks, a month or two at most.'

Henry continued his pacing, scratching his head and muttering to himself. Finally reaching an acceptance of his fate, he heaved a great sigh and slapped his hands together. 'Very well then, so be it. There is no alternative, since for the good of my kingdom you say that I must marry.'

'I am glad to see Your Majesty so amenable,' Rosny drily remarked. 'We will proceed with the arrangements,' and after bowing low, quickly departed before the King could change his mind.

Henriette was sitting up in bed enjoying a late breakfast when the King came to her. She instantly reached out her arms to him, her mood warm with affection for she had recently discovered she was *enceinte*. The King's marriage with Marguerite de Valois had been dissolved to allow him to marry his darling Gabrielle. But with that plan dying with his former mistress, Henriette was quite certain it would now be herself who would soon be Queen of France. Did she not have his signed promise of marriage tucked safely away?

Henry came to sit beside her on the bed, declining the sliver of peach she offered him. 'I have already breakfasted, thank you, dearest, some hours ago before my ride.'

'I insist. It is but a small morsel of my love,' she said. Henry let her feed him the piece of fruit, her mouth coming to his to nibble it with him, her tongue sliding between his lips in a most erotic fashion. She smelled of musk and the sex they'd enjoyed only an hour ago. How could he refuse her anything?

With steadfast resolve he brought himself back under control and tried again. 'My love, you are aware that attempts have been made to negotiate a marriage with the Grand Duke of Tuscany's niece, Marie de Medici?'

Henriette sighed. 'Who could not be? Your ministers have been attempting to bring about that union for years, even in the time of your little Gabrielle. And consistently failed.' She sucked on another sliver of peach, uncaring. Rosny's politicizing did not trouble her in the slightest. The sour-faced minister may well make his dislike of her very apparent, but she had almost achieved her object. A few months of careful rest and her future would be assured. She took the King's hand and smoothed it over her belly. 'Feel how your son grows in strength daily. He will be a fine boy, like his father.'

Henry felt only a flat stomach. It was far too early for her to be showing, or to be certain a child would even be born. He withdrew his hand. 'My dear, do you still have the promise of marriage I gave you?'

'Of course.'

'May I see it?'

'Why would you wish to?' She laughed, offering him another slice of fruit, which this time he wisely declined. 'You are familiar enough with its contents. You are my affianced husband.'

'Dear heart,' and here he paused to clear his throat, or gather his courage. 'The fact of the matter is, I fear I must insist that you return it to me as I am now unable to comply with that promise.'

'Not comply . . .' She stopped, her green eyes narrowing with suspicion. 'Why would you not?'

'Because, my love, quite without my realizing it, a marriage agreement has been signed with the Italian princess. The contract is even now being drawn up, and the proxy wedding will take place within weeks, a few months at most.'

For several long seconds Henriette did not respond, only stared at him in stunned silence. Then she let out a horrendous scream. It echoed around the cavernous bedchamber, carrying all her fury and torment with it. The King almost fell off the bed in alarm but when he rushed to calm her, he managed only to catch the dish of peaches that she flung at him.

'How could you do this to me?' she yelled. 'You liar! You cheat! You promised me most faithfully! This is Rosny's doing. I insist you dismiss him forthwith, and that cringing Villeroy who does his every bidding.'

'Villeroy is still with the Tuscan envoy.'

'Then dispatch the greedy fool back to Italy.'

'You must be calm, my love. Think of the child.'

'Why did not *you* think of this child?' she cried, in a frenzy of temper. 'Your *son*! *I will not be ignored!*' And falling into his arms she began to sob. Her distress was such that Henry had not the first idea how to deal with it. Fortunately, on hearing the disturbance, her maid came running and he made good his escape.

Henriette was not a woman to give up easily. She thought perhaps her tantrum had been unwise on this occasion, and as her sobs had failed to move him she sent for her father and brother, certain they would be on her side. They listened in horror to the awful news.

Auvergne was outraged. 'He cannot be allowed to get away with this. Do you still have the King's signed promise of marriage?'

'I have it safe. He demanded I return it but I refused.'

'Very wise. We must guard it well. Surely such a promise is equally binding in law as any contract that Rosny could produce?' He looked to his father for an answer.

Balzac, equally alarmed by this threat to his carefully devised plan, promised to secret it away where it could not easily be found, and hurried off to discuss the matter with lawyers forthwith.

'If the document has indeed been drawn up in proper form, it might well invalidate any marriage agreement between the King and Marie de Medici, certainly in the eyes of the Church,' he assured them on his return some time later. 'So if the proxy wedding could be delayed on the grounds of your needing to comply with what is stipulated in that document, and you do successfully present the King with a son, then he could do naught but comply with it and make you his queen.'

'Then all we have to do,' Auvergne agreed, 'is to devise some way to delay the proceedings until Henriette has given birth. In the meantime, sister, you must keep the King content. Make yourself indispensable to his happiness.'

Henriette had sat avidly listening through all of this, growing increasingly certain of success. How could she fail? Did she not have the King eating out of her hand? She would not allow her resolve to weaken. But her brother was right, she must make more effort to behave with proper decorum, and to please him.

Going at once to Henry she sank in a deep curtsey before him. 'Sire, I have come to prostrate myself before you. I fear I may have offended you by my reaction to your glorious news. In my own defence I can only say that the shock I displayed was born out of my great love for you. I cannot think what I would do were I to lose your love.' She allowed tender tears to slip down her pale cheeks and Henry's heart softened, as always at sight of a woman in distress.

'My love, the fault is mine, I should not have told you so

bluntly.' He'd been miserable these last days without her. She so livened his life with her risqué jokes, her indiscreet gossip, love of dancing and derring-do attitude to life. 'There will always be a place for you in my life, and in my heart. Come, let us not consider the matter again. It is forgotten.'

But not by me, Henriette thought, as he raised her up to kiss her and led her to his bed. Even as she let him peel off her silk stockings and pleasure her beneath her skirts, her mind was busily devising how to dispose of the Italian threat.

Assistance came in the shape of Charles Emmanuel, Duke of Savoy, a son-in-law and ally of Philip II of Spain. He arrived at Fontainebleau on the fourteenth of December with an entourage of his most important ministers and nobles, and twelve hundred horse. Henriette took a dislike to him on sight.

'What a strange little man he is,' she whispered to her brother as the court gathered in the cold courtyard to receive him. 'Like an ugly dwarf with that humpback, and overlarge head with its abnormally broad brow.'

'Hold your waspish tongue, sister. He is a powerful man, and whatever his deficiencies, rumour has it that he has enjoyed as many mistresses in his time as Henry of Navarre, and consequently acquired as many children.'

'Poor souls,' Henriette giggled. 'I trust they do not resemble their father. His head looks like a brush with that great tuft of bristled hair atop it.'

'Be nice to him,' Auvergne warned. 'He could be important to us. He bears many grudges against both France and the King. Apart from ongoing disputes about land, he had hoped to marry one of his daughters to Gabrielle's son, little César, whom, had she lived, would have become the next Dauphin. Now that alliance has been lost, which he sorely regrets.'

Henriette considered this titbit of gossip with eager interest. 'You think he might help us then?'

'It would not be in his interests for the Italian alliance to go ahead as the huge dowry offered might well be deployed by France to start a war against himself. Much of the territory he once captured from the French in the religious wars has now been restored, save for the Marquisate of Saluzzo. We, of course, regard that piece as of great strategic importance to our nation, being situated as it is on the Italian side of the Alps, but he resolutely refuses to surrender it. So guard that virulent wit of yours, sister, and practise more charm.'

The Duke was given a warm welcome by the King, and made much of with endless balls, jousts, masques and hunting-parties. After a week of this the court moved to Paris where the festivities, many devised by Madame la Marquise herself, continued over Christmas and into the New Year of 1600. Henriette was striving to be agreeable, and to please Henry, which was in her own best interests, after all. She even allowed the Duke to lead her out in a dance, although she returned to her brother's side with a sardonic curl to her lip.

'I do not care for that odious little man. Small of stature, large in ego.'

'Remember what I told you. Ah, he is coming for you again, now put on your best smile and be gracious.'

Henriette danced and pirouetted, smiled and charmed him as best she may. The Duke was ever courteous and deferential towards her, and to the King and his ministers, yet whenever Rosny brought up the subject of Saluzzo, he remained intransigent in his determination to retain it.

Savoy was no fool, and in preparation for possible conflict had mustered what support he could. He made a point of seeking out malcontents and had chanced upon Marshal Biron as he passed through Burgundy on his way to France. That one-time loyal subject likewise bore a grudge against the current regime as the Duchess of Beaufort had promised him Perigord and Bigorre, as well as the post of Constable of France on Montmorency's death. All now lost with her unexpected death. The Duke of Savoy had offered Biron a bribe in the form of the sovereignty of the Duchy of Burgundy. In addition, he would be granted the hand of one of his daughters in marriage, together with a splendid dowry.

Now Savoy responded with equal cunning to the charms of Henry's new mistress. 'I thank you for your company,' he told her with a bow as he returned her to her seat. 'Mayhap we could talk more tomorrow. A walk in the garden in the forenoon would be most pleasant.'

'I shall look forward to it,' Henriette graciously accepted, striving not to reveal how the touch of his hand made her skin crawl.

The walk took place, as agreed, in the Tuileries gardens, and as they strolled together along the avenues of poplar, lime and white mulberry that Catherine de Medici herself had planted, the Duke readily offered his services without even being asked.

'I am aware of the delicacy of your situation, and wish you to know that I would be most happy to put any obstacle in the way of this Medici marriage. France is powerful enough, without the might of Rome and Florence behind it.'

'I thank you, Sire.' Henriette politely inclined her head, heart thumping with hope. Her brother would be pleased if she could land this big fish. 'And would you agree to offer your support for a certain document in my possession, written and signed by the King's own hand at Bois-Malesherbes, which makes me a promise of marriage provided I give him a son? As you see, I truly hope soon to do so.'

'I see that delay of the Italian marriage is essential, but I'm sure we can reach an agreement, you and I, how best you could show your gratitude if I helped you.' He smiled at her, ever the lecher, and Henriette stifled a shudder as she smiled sweetly back. 'Once my own position has been clarified, I'm sure we can come to mutually beneficial terms.'

'I'm sure we could, in the fullness of time,' she hedged, patting her stomach as a gentle reminder of her condition. There seemed little point in pretending she did not understand his meaning, but so long as she could keep him dangling, there was really no necessity for her to actually deliver. She licked her lips with her small pink tongue and saw how his face suffused with flushed desire.

Henry had drawn up a long list of territories, including Bresse, and the Alpine valley of Barcelonnette, among others, which he would accept in return for allowing the Duke to retain ownership of the Marquisate of Saluzzo. But Savoy had no greater desire to part with any of those either. He refused, however, to engage in argument over the matter. Instead, he showered gifts on the King and his courtiers on New Year's Day, when the French Court traditionally exchanged gifts: crystal vases for Henry, valuable diamonds for Madame la Marquise. There were many more presents, and huge sums of money, in a bid to win support from some of the most influential nobles in the land, even at the cost of civil war in France. All were accepted with gracious courtesy, save for Rosny, who, when offered a snuffbox enriched with diamonds estimated to be worth fifteen thousand *livres*, he politely declined it.

'I made a vow never to accept any present of value except from my own sovereign.'

The wily minister clearly construed the gift as a bribe. 'Let him judge me as he wishes,' Savoy told his men. 'My generous gesture has cost several hundred thousand *livres*, money well spent if it impresses the French with our wealth and resources. Mayhap they will think twice about challenging us.'

He amazed the nobles still further by appearing at a ball in an outfit richly embroidered with precious stones. But eventually, the Duke declared his readiness to return home, with a promise to consider the alternatives Henry had offered.

'You must come again soon, Monsieur le duc. We always enjoy your company, so long as you appreciate our determination to enforce our right to the Marquisate which you stole from us,' Henry told him, in his usual friendly but forthright fashion, showing no fear whatever of any possible conflict.

Savoy frowned, not caring for the thought that his huge invest-ment had been wasted. 'Perhaps a commission might be appointed to examine our conflicting claims,' he suggested.

'Perhaps so,' Henry pleasantly agreed.

One was set up forthwith and Savoy postponed his departure while arguments for each side were considered. But while some agreements were forged, other issues were left in abeyance. It was March before finally the Duke left Paris, and only then with a three month grace to consider his options.

The delay had done nothing to help Henriette in her own dilemma. The Duke of Savoy's promises to help had become almost meaningless, her cause more precarious than ever. Henriette's smile became daily more fixed, her efforts to tanta-lize and ingratiate herself with the King lacking her usual enthusiasm and energy. And as her pregnancy advanced

Henriette was compelled to take life quietly, and to rest more. Producing a child, and thereby gaining a crown, wasn't proving to be quite as easy as she had imagined. Each night she prayed that the babe would be kept safe.

'The life of Marie de Medici should be one long period of repentance for her shameless usurpation of *my* conjugal relations with His Majesty,' she told her brother.

'We still have hopes the Italian marriage can be stopped. You have only to produce a healthy son.'

'But it could be too late!' she screamed.

'I beg you to remain calm, sister. All is not yet lost.'

But she was fast losing patience as well as her temper, and frequently forgot the promises she'd made to her brother to be more discreet. 'Have you thought yet how to stop that woman from coming?' she would snap at the King. Henry would give her a mournful smile, or scowl and insist the matter was out of his hands.

'But you promised to marry *me*! You should dismiss Rosny for getting you into this muddle.'

Henriette might stamp her foot, or fling her hair brush across the room as often as may be, but to no effect. Henry remained obdurate, and her resentment grew as he persisted in his pursuit of the Medici. Fear snapped at her heels and she daily became more irritable and unhappy.

Henry was by now over the first flush of passion and beginning to see the quagmire into which he'd landed himself. He'd seen a portrait of Marie de Medici, and rather liked the look of her. She was handsome enough and he thought she had the makings of a good wife and queen. He felt excited at the prospect of meeting her and saw no reason why she should object to his keeping a mistress, for were not all kings entitled to at least one? Yet he could not stop himself from considering how things might change if Henriette did indeed present him with a son in a few months' time. How would he feel then about the Italian marriage?

The wedding arrangements continued inexorably and Henry became increasingly desperate to retrieve the promise of marriage he had made to Henriette. It would surely be seen as an insult to the princess were it not destroyed. It might even create problems in the future.

Once again he asked for its return.

> *MADEMOISELLE, The love, honour and benefits you have received from me would have checked the most frivolous of souls had it not been accompanied by such a bad nature as yours. I will not scold you further although I could and ought to do so, as you know. I beg you to send me back the promise you know of, and not to give me the trouble of recovering it by other means. Send me back also the ring which I returned you the other day. Such is the subject of this letter, to which I require an answer by tonight.*
>   *Friday morning, 21 April 1600, at Fontainebleau. Henry*

Henriette did not comply. Four days after receiving a second letter from the King, on the fifth of May, news arrived that the contract of marriage between the French monarch and the Princess Marie de Medici had been signed at the Palazzo Pitti, in the presence of the Archbishop of Pisa. The Savoy issue had indeed delayed matters, but the inevitable had happened nonetheless.

Henriette was distraught, and now banked all her hopes on the successful delivery of a son.

Henry made it clear to his courtiers that the subject of the Italian alliance must not be mentioned in the presence of Madame la Marquise. 'She must be kept calm at all times, for the sake of the child.' He was irritated that she had not responded and returned the promise, as instructed, but pragmatic enough to realize that were she to deliver a healthy son, he may well carry out his promise to marry her, and risk Rosny's displeasure.

But for now he was more troubled by the fact that no decision had yet reached him regarding Saluzzo. Henry understood perfectly that the Duke of Savoy had sought a delay of three months only as a means to avoid surrendering any territory at all. Thus, as the month of June progressed preparations were made for hostilities to begin.

'I am reluctant to leave you, dear heart, when you are so close to your time, but I am being urged to make plans to advance to Lyons, whither Rosny has already despatched troops and artillery.

Will you accompany me? Gabrielle often came with me on campaigns. Do you feel able to do likewise?'

Henriette would love to have been able to do so, if only to prove how necessary her presence was for his happiness. But her state of health was too delicate, and the outcome so important, that she dare not take the risk. 'I fear it would be too fatiguing for me, Sire. I must guard the health of our son.' She lived in hope that once she was safely delivered, all talk of the Italian woman would be over. 'Can you not delay the campaign for a little while?'

Henry did just that. He put off his departure until Rosny wrote demanding to know what had happened to the vital support he needed. 'I can delay no longer, my sweet. Know that I love you, that if you are successful in delivering on your promise, then I will keep mine. I have demanded daily reports of your state of health. Farewell, my own. I kiss your hands a million times.' And with great reluctance, Henry left.

A bare two weeks later, on a summer's day sultry with heat, a terrible thunderstorm erupted, and lightning struck the Palace of the Louvre. Pictures tumbled from the walls in the Great Gallery, and the entire building seemed to shake and tremble. The shock was so great that it caused Henriette to go into premature labour. She did indeed produce a boy child, but he was stillborn.

Henriette was distraught. Her health was at its lowest ebb and her dream of being Queen of France had crumbled to dust. Worse, Henry was unable to come to her immediately as he was too occupied preparing to invade Savoy. She wrote to him in her sadness and bitter disappointment.

> . . . *my happiness depended more on you than on the power of destiny, to which I will not ascribe the cause of my grief . . . a grief which I am constrained to confess, not because you have to fulfil the desire of your subjects, but because your nuptials will be the funeral of my life, and subject me to the power of a cruel discretion which will banish me from your royal presence, even as from your heart . . . O my King, my lover, my all!*

She wrote at some length, pouring out her heart, flattering the King and humbling herself with almost maudlin self-pity, signing the letter:

> *From your humble servant, subject creature, and (shall I say?) forgotten lover, Henriette de Balzac.*

Since she had no hope now of being a queen, far better to be a king's mistress than to return home in disgrace with nothing at all.

On 6 August, negotiations having broken down over Saluzzo, Henry invaded Savoy. He wrote to Henriette from Chambéry expressing his sorrow for her loss, and his love. He then instructed Varenne, his loyal attendant, to accompany the Marquise south as soon as she was fit enough to travel.

On reaching Lyons, Henriette made a triumphal entry into the city as if she were indeed a crowned queen and not a fallen woman. The people honoured her with the same enthusiastic welcome they had once given Diane de Poitiers, the famous royal mistress of Henri II, when she had visited their city many years before. Henriette was presented with a number of standards taken by the King's forces and sent to her by Henry with pride, as he had done long since for Corisande. Very cleverly she presented these to the ancient church of St Just de Lyons on the King's behalf.

Her sister Marie-Charlotte was with her, as companion and attendant. As her lover, François Bassompierre, attended on Henry, it seemed sensible that the two sisters should support each other. She loved to stir gossip and would often bring many a naughty titbit, even those Henriette would much rather not hear. 'They are saying that Mademoiselle de la Bourdaisière and Mademoiselle de la Chastre have accompanied the King on his latest campaign,' she told her now, eyes agog.

Henriette was not amused. 'I do not believe you.'

'I swear it is true.'

Henriette slapped her. 'Don't bring me any more lies.'

The two lovers met on the road to Grenoble and immediately began to quarrel. 'Is it true,' Henriette demanded, 'that you have Bourdaisière and de la Chastre with you?'

Henry was taken aback, expecting to be harangued on the

approaching royal marriage, not on his choice of companions on the campaign. 'My love, why would I have eyes for anyone but yourself?'

'I appreciate that your high rank has placed an inseparable barrier between us, and that my own insignificance precluded the possibility of my ever becoming your wife. But I implore you to leave me the happiness of at least remaining your mistress, so that I might continue to bask in the same tenderness which you have hitherto accorded me. Do not, I beg you, banish me from your heart completely.'

He attempted to pacify her. 'My sweet, why would I do such a cruel thing?'

'Rumour is rife. They are saying that you are done with me,' Henriette challenged him through floods of tears. 'Would you betray me when I'm at my lowest? Why not stab me through the heart in very truth. I am already mortally wounded.'

Henry was filled with guilt, mortified that she had discovered what he considered a very small transgression. 'Dear heart,' he wheedled, 'it was of no account. I would not hurt you for the world, and I apologize profoundly. It will not happen again.'

She looked up into his dark Gascon eyes and knew that it would. He loved her, it was true, but then he loved all women, and simply could not resist them. But she dare say no more. Henriette was far too unsure of herself now, a feeling she hated, to risk criticizing the King too fiercely. Nor dare she allow herself to reflect on how different it all could have been, were it not for that terrible storm. Yet as she gazed, she saw again that flare of need, and knew that he wanted her as much as ever. Flinging herself into his arms she began to smother his face with kisses. Whenever she was at a loss for words, Henriette always resorted to passion.

As usual after one of their quarrels, they made love passionately and without restraint. Afterwards, Henry was full of fresh promises.

'I shall procure you a rich husband.'

'You would fob me off with some old toad who is no good in bed?' she sighed. 'I swear that you have naught to fear from any husband. He could never compete with you, my King.'

He was pleased by these soft words of flattery. 'What about the Duke of Nevers? A Prince of the Blood no less.'

'I care not for a husband. You know that I want only you,'

she murmured, kissing him with renewed passion, even as her mind turned over this new idea. A rich husband would be no bad thing, and surely could be largely ignored. Mayhap she would give the matter some thought.

On hearing what was being arranged on his behalf, the gentleman in question hastily married Catherine de Lorraine, daughter of the Duke of Mayenne. But it mattered not, for there was no more talk of husbands, rich or otherwise. Henry and his favourite were reconciled, and all was well so far as Henriette was concerned. She may not have won a crown, but she still had the love of a King.

Marie de Medici, meanwhile, was reading one of her new husband's frequent letters.

> *Frontenac has pictured you to me in such a manner that I don't merely love you as a husband ought to love his wife, but as a passionate* serviteur *should love his mistress. That is the title I shall give you until you reach Marseilles, where you will change it for a more honourable one. I shall not allow any opportunity to pass without writing to you, and assuring you that my keenest desire is to see you and have you near me. Believe it, mistress mine, and believe that every month will seem to me a century. I received a letter in French from you this morning; if you wrote it without help, you are already a great mistress of the language.*

Marie had spent the last few months refreshing her language skills and quickly regained command of French, determined to be able to converse properly with her husband and be a useful wife to him. She felt excited at the prospect of meeting Henry, and yet nervous. Would he like her? It was one thing to approve of a miniature portrait, but quite another matter to like the living, breathing person. And could he ever come to love her? she wondered.

The King had already shown himself to be kind, sending her dolls dressed in the fashion of the French ladies, and offering the services of good needlewomen, perhaps in order to ease her reception into his country. He begged a favour of hers to wear in his campaigns in Savoy, and replied the day he received it.

I thank you, my beautiful mistress, for the present you have sent me.
I shall fix it to my headgear if we have a fight, and give a few sword
thrusts for love of you.

Unbeknown to Marie, he wrote also to Henriette, who was
in Lyons. On 11 October he sent his mistress two letters, apologizing for the fact that he would not see her before Sunday, and
that the wait would seem longer to him than it would to her.

My Dear Heart, Since I could not kiss you, I have kissed your letter
a thousand times. You may be sure I shall have much to say to you.
It could not be otherwise, as we are so well together . . . But this is
too much talk . . . Goodnight, heart of mine; I kiss and kiss thee
again a million times.

Henry was engaged in further campaigns against Savoy during
September and October and his next letter to his wife urged her
to hurry to him as soon as the ceremony was completed, reassuring her of his love. He finished by saying she must take every
care of her health, as was he by drinking the mineral waters. This
brought a smile to Marie's face as she imagined a strong king
fighting in a brutal war, yet worrying about his health, or more
likely perhaps, their age difference. She knew Henry of Navarre
to be a fine figure of a man and did not see this as a problem.

Lastly, he promised to send his closest friend, Bellegarde, to be
with her at the proxy wedding.

But I shall be with you in spirit, if not in person.

The Duc de Bellegarde, Grand Equerry of France, together with
an entourage of forty nobles, reached Livorno on the twentieth of
September. Seven days later he entered Florence, and on 6 October
1600, the proxy wedding took place, the Grand Duke Ferdinand
himself standing in for the absent husband. His Eminence made
his entry on horseback beneath a canopy held high by eight young
Florentine nobles, preceded by all the ecclesiastical and secular
bodies, sixteen prelates, and fifty gentlemen bearing halberds.

Marie wore a gown of gold filigree on white satin with draped
sleeves and a lace ruff about her neck, and at her wrists. Her

glorious shining brown hair, tastefully ornamented with pearls, was caught up away from a face even more pale than usual; a matching string hanging low over the neatly fitted bodice. The Pontiff himself pronounced the blessing, to which the bride replied with grace and dignity, and the sweetest of smiles.

There was the usual celebration of High Mass, then the Duke of Bellegarde led the Princess to the right hand of the legate. The Grand Duke, placing himself upon his left, presented his Eminence with the procuration by which he was authorized to espouse his niece in the name of the King. The document was read aloud by a prelate, the authority given by the Pope for the solemnization of the marriage, and the remainder of the nuptial service carried out with all due majesty, followed by several rounds of gunshot

Marie felt a mix of fear and excitement churn in her stomach. The deed was done.

The ceremony was celebrated with a ball and banquet, the days following filled with hunting-parties, jousts, races, tilting at the ring and other manly sports, while the nights were devoted to more dancing, plays, masques and ballets. There was much rivalry between the local Florentines and the noble lords from France, not all of it friendly. No expense was spared in the joyous festivities, and when it all finally came to an end, preparations were quickly concluded for her departure.

Marie was delighted to learn that the daughter of her old nurse, one Leonora Dori, was to attend her. She was a skinny little woman with no marked good looks, her dark eyes seeming too large for her elfin face, and most prominent. But she possessed great skill in dressing hair. And there was a stillness about her gracious movements, quiet voice and humble demeanour, of which Marie rather approved.

'I am grateful that you should agree to my appointment, Your Majesty. I will do my utmost to give satisfaction,' the woman humbly assured Marie.

'The *King* has granted permission for your appointment. I'm sure we'll do very well together as I was always fond of your mother. What of your father? Is he not a carpenter?'

'He was, Your Majesty, but he passed away some time ago. I have nothing to hold me to Italy. I am yours, body and soul.'

Leonora was outwardly timid and unobtrusive, the kind of woman most people would not even notice when present in a room. But she was nothing if not ambitious, and recognized a good opportunity when it was offered. Being of lowly stock she was concerned about how she might be received in the French Court. Having Carlo Dori, a carpenter, for a father would not impress the aristocratic nobles of France. As a consequence she had done some research and discovered that at some distant time in the past the Dori family had been loosely connected with the noble Galigai, and for a sum of money the Florentine family's only survivor, a childless old man, was willing to acknowledge the kinship. Leonora showed this proof to the Queen.

Feeling rather sorry for her, Marie did not examine the document too closely, but accepted it as true. 'Then from now on you shall be Donna Leonora Galigai, and my *dame d'atours*, albeit in an unofficial capacity until we have the King's blessing.'

Leonora was delighted. The role of the *dame d'atours*, or mistress of the robes, was the most senior rank in the Queen's household at the French Court. As well as taking care of the royal garments she would attend the sovereign at her *levée* to hand her a petticoat or gown. The *dame d'honneur* assisted, as did the *première femme de chambre* and perhaps as many as twelve *femmes* and *lavandières*. But her position would be the most important and much coveted.

Donna Leonora was well satisfied, and particularly pleased with herself today. Among the cavaliers who were to be a part of the Queen's entourage was one Concino Concini, a handsome young man who had quite caught her eye. He was to be included because he was the son of Giovanni, once a loyal and wise minister to Cosimo I. Admittedly, the younger Concini had not inherited his father's eminence or good fortune, Duke Ferdinand accusing him of leading a somewhat dissolute life. But then he was young and hot-headed. He was tactful and courteous, and had certainly managed to charm the Queen. Leonora had caught him casting interested looks in her direction, which thrilled and excited her. It seemed that her dull, quiet life had suddenly taken a turn for the better, and with everything to play for to make it even brighter in the future.

On the thirteenth of the month Marie de Medici set forth upon her long journey, accompanied by her new *dame d'atours*, her aunt the Grand-Duchess, her sister the Duchess of Mantua, half-brother Don Antonio, and her handsome cousin the Duke of Bracciano, whom she'd once hoped to marry. There were numerous other ladies and gentlemen of the Italian Court, as well as the French Ambassador, and she felt excited at the prospect of leaving Italy to at last meet her husband.

Part Three

FOR THE LOVE OF A KING

They were quarrelling again. In December Henry and his men, having effectively starved the armies of the Duke of Savoy by trapping them in the mountains, withdrew into Piedmont where word reached him of the arrival of his young bride at Marseilles. Now the Marchioness de Verneuil was refusing to attend Her Majesty's reception.

'It would be an insult to myself,' Henriette stormed, tossing her fiery locks. She was sitting beside him in bed, completely naked and all too sensually aware of the effect she was having upon her royal lover.

Henry fingered an auburn curl that fell on her bare shoulder. 'How so? You know that I love you. Have I not given you sufficient proof of my affection this night?' He gave a low chuckle. 'Every night, in fact.'

'If you insist on attending your *wife*, I shall make haste to Paris.'

'Whether in Paris or Marseilles you must be presented, dear heart. She is the Queen.'

'*I* shall do as I please.' Henriette turned the full fury of those glittering green eyes upon him. 'Did you not deliberately set out to humiliate me by selecting the Duc de Bellegarde to carry the marriage papers to Florence? Of all the high nobles you could have chosen, Your Majesty saw fit to select the one you had previously accused of paying court to me. A cheap revenge, was it not, used as a deliberate affront against myself?'

Henry looked faintly surprised by this outburst and then laughed out loud. 'Is that what is troubling you? Then I swear the thought never entered my head. I forgave Bellegarde for that petty fight he picked with Joinville a long time ago, as I have forgiven him many times in the past for his indiscretions. We have had our differences, he and I, but he is my most loyal friend. As are you, my love, I trust,' he murmured, teasing a pert nipple with the heel of his thumb. 'So have done with your sulks, put on your most glamorous gown and be presented to your new queen.'

'Never!' In one swift movement Henriette leaped from the bed, reaching for her *robe de chambre*. But Henry was too quick for her, and catching her by the wrist pulled her back into his arms. The heat between them instantly ignited and he was astride her in a second, pinning her down and taking her with all the force of his passion. Henriette yielded willingly, giving of herself with generous abandon, the harsh words between them forgotten.

Nevertheless, she departed for Paris the very next morning.

Marie was weary of travelling. Being November, the normally calm blue waters of the Mediterranean had been choppy, the rough crossing demanding they frequently put ashore to shelter. Her uncle the Grand Duke had again counselled her before she'd embarked, warning Marie that it might have been unwise of her to make such promises to Leonora. 'Make no demands upon your new husband the King until you have spent some time in his company.'

'It was a very small promise,' Marie excused herself, beginning to grow weary of her uncle's constant admonishments. 'Merely an appointment in my own household.'

'No promise is ever small, not to a king. There are always . . . implications.'

To Donna Leonora herself, Ferdinand advised that she not interfere between their Majesties. 'Nor usurp the prerogatives and offices of the great ladies of the court.'

'You have my word, Sire. I wish only for a quiet life, and covet no honours for myself. Only the permission to devote myself to my royal mistress.' Keeping her eyes suitably downcast, Donna Leonora offered this assurance as she kissed the Grand Duke's fingers, even as she inwardly calculated how she could not only hang on to her new role, but better it.

The grand-ducal fleet had set sail on the eighteenth of the month, comprising seven galleys, one French ship, five papal frigates and five galleys of Malta; persons on board numbering upwards of a thousand. The royal standard of France flew above the main galley, a most magnificent vessel belonging to the Grand Duke. Seventy feet in length, it was richly gilded from stem to stern, inlaid with a profusion of lapis-lazuli, mother-of-pearl, ivory and ebony. The ship needed fifty-four oarsmen to propel her. Marie's own cabin had been decorated in regal splendour, hung with cloth of gold; the *fleur-de-lis* of France, profusely decorated with sapphires and pearls, and the shield of the house of Medici, suspended side by side opposite the state chair. But it was with great relief that the young Queen finally arrived at Marseilles.

When she stepped ashore, gasps of admiration came from the watching crowds. Marie was magnificently gowned in dove brocade threaded with gold, fashioned in the Italian manner, a carcanet of pearls about her throat and her light-brown hair left loose and without powder. She was welcomed by the Chancellor, the consuls and citizens going down on their knees, the former carrying out the traditional ceremony of presenting her with the golden keys of the city.

Marie felt oddly nervous, and disappointed that Henry was not here to welcome her. When would she ever meet her husband? And there were still many more miles to go before she reached Lyons. But bells were ringing, flags were fluttering in the breeze, and salvoes of artillery from the guard of honour on the quay told of a rousing welcome from the people. Marie de Medici, royal princess that she was, drew breath and smiled upon them all.

And all the while the French eyed her carefully and gossiped among themselves. 'The figure of Her Majesty is magnificent,' the Duchesse de Nemours whispered to Mademoiselle de Guise. 'See how her eyes sparkle with health and vigour.'

'And her complexion is superb, with neither rouge, paint nor powder needed to enhance it.'

The Duchesse advanced to make obeisance, and to introduce the ladies of the French retinue. 'The King sends his apologies as he is in Savoy fighting a campaign, and asked me to welcome Your Majesty to France in his place.'

'I thank you, Duchess,' Marie warmly responded.

Then the cardinals and prelates, preceded by the Constable, conducted the new queen to the palace beneath a rich canopy. The ladies of the court followed on behind, led by the wife of the Chancellor. There was some slight altercation over precedence between the French and Italian courtiers, but Marie was too fatigued to pay them any heed.

It delighted her hosts when she thanked them for the courtesy of her reception in fluent French. They were deeply flattered that she should take the trouble to learn their language so well. Her dignity and demeanour, the magnificence of her apparel, and the flush of health and happiness which glowed about her, filled the people with joy and hope. Here was a fine young queen indeed, one to be proud of.

Festivities and celebrations went on for some days, and Marie ached for it all to end. She felt weary of travel, and of civic celebrations. She had endured several as she'd progressed through Italy, now she must suffer them all over again in France.

The King had sent a royal coach to transport her to Lyons, and ultimately to Paris. Outwardly adorned in brown velvet trimmed with silver tinsel, inside it was lined with carnation velvet embroidered with gold and silver. Henry had certainly done her proud. Yet despite being drawn by four fine greys, the vehicle was cumbersome and uncomfortable to ride in, being crudely sprung. More decorative than fast.

But as she was driven around, Marie would draw back the heavy curtains to show herself to the crowds who threw flowers and fronds of evergreen upon her path. Every street was richly decorated, hangings suspended from windows, and draped over balconies. There were triumphal arches splendidly decorated with emblems and devices, and everywhere people waving, or running alongside the coach to shout and cheer.

'How excited they are,' she said to Leonora, feeling a flush of exhilaration herself. 'I do hope I can be a good queen for them.'

'You will make them proud,' her companion assured her. 'But you should decline the services of these French ladies until after you have been joined by the King. They create only dissension.' Donna Leonora did not care to have her nose pushed out of joint by what she viewed as the foreign contingent.

'How can I refuse? Henry has made it clear that they must attend me the moment I have disembarked. I cannot go against the word of a king.'

Though outwardly serene and gracious, deep down Marie felt a little uneasy, a stranger in this new land, and largely ignored by her new husband thus far. She was uncertain of when Henry intended to join her, and what she was supposed to do with herself in the meantime. Could he, she wondered, be with Madame de Verneuil and not in Savoy at all? If only she knew for certain then her situation might be less embarrassing. She'd had word that La Marquise was at Lyons. If that were the case then she determined to protect herself as best she could. She made one demand of Bellegarde.

'I would be escorted to Lyons by my brother Don Antonio de Medici, and by the Duke of Bracciano, my cousin.'

'That will not be necessary, Your Majesty. The King expects these gentlemen to return to Italy with your ladies.'

Marie panicked at the thought of being left alone. 'No, no, I insist upon their presence as representatives of my uncle, the Grand Duke. Otherwise I will remain here in Marseilles until the King has concluded his campaign.'

Faced with such an alternative, and seeing the fear in her eyes, Bellegarde took pity on her and conceded to her request.

Marie's lowest moment came on a day late in November when the Grand Duchess her aunt, and her sister the Duchess of Mantua, took their leave to return to Florence in the galleys, which stood ready to embark at the quay.

'How will I survive without you?' she mourned, keenly feeling the pain of their parting, an ache of loneliness already starting up in her breast.

'You will survive because you are a queen,' her aunt assured her, kissing her on each pale, cold cheek. 'You have only to give the King a Dauphin, and you will have fulfilled your destiny.'

'I will pray to God to grant me that grace!'

'You are not alone, Majesty, you still have me,' Donna Leonora reminded her mistress as the Italian retainers started to board the ships.

Marie hugged her companion warmly. 'So I do, dear friend.'

But she waved farewell to her relatives and friends with a heavy heart, even as she strove to be brave and strong.

Marie set forth the very next day to Avignon, escorted by her brother and cousin, the French contingent, and 2,000 horse. As she continued on her journey, a letter reached her from Henry announcing the success of his campaign, and assuring her he would be with her soon.

I am delighted at the account of your reception in Marseilles. It is only a foretaste, however, of the enthusiasm which will everywhere greet you . . .

Her heart leapt at the thought of finally meeting him, feeling a surge of hope at this good news. How thankful she would be when she was finally settled in Paris with her husband. Marie still did not feel entirely comfortable with the French ladies, although she favoured Mademoiselle de Guise above any other. Now that her sister and aunt had left, she relied more and more upon the friendship of Donna Leonora, who had become such a favourite that Marie insisted she sleep at the foot of her bed. The woman was faithful and unassuming, they could speak in Italian together, of people they knew and now missed, and share memories of the country they both loved. What would she do without her?

So when her *dame d'atours* came to her in a fervour of excitement one day, asking if she may beg a favour, Marie was surprised, as the woman was usually so self-effacing and unruffled. But she was prepared to listen most sympathetically to her favourite's request. 'You know that you can say anything to me, Leonora.'

'Concino Concini has asked for my hand in marriage. May I have Your Majesty's permission to accept?'

Marie was not simply surprised, she was shocked. No one could call her loyal attendant beautiful, in fact many would dismiss the poor creature as downright ugly. Nor was she a flirt. She shrank away whenever the French *chevaliers* approached, and not for a moment had Marie thought to lose her to marriage. Yet this man was an Italian. She managed a smile. 'Are you in love with him, Leonora?'

The woman blushed, betraying her emotion. 'I am, Your Majesty.'

'And what of his feelings towards you?'

Donna Leonora paused before answering. She had no illusions about herself, and if Concini recognized that allying himself to the Queen's favourite might possibly assist his advancement, Leonora had no quarrel with that either. She thought they might well help each other in that respect. For a woman such as herself with no claim to beauty, the attention of a handsome cavalier was deeply flattering. She had never thought to have a lover let alone a husband, and had already succumbed to his charms and embarked upon a love affair with him. 'I am satisfied that his suit is honourable.'

'Then I give my consent, and will do what I can to gain the King's permission, and see that you both receive offices of distinction in my household.'

'Your Majesty, I am most grateful.' It was no more than she had hoped for, and Leonora reported back to her lover, well pleased.

It was early December by the time Marie reached the city of Lyons, where she found preparations for the royal marriage were well in hand. She was informed that the King was already on his way; letters awaited her from Henry, who had also sent her a magnificent pearl necklace.

> *The bearer of this will recount to you my disappointment at not being able to surprise you on your road to Lyons . . . Certes, my trial is hard to bear for it will be eight days before I shall be able to see you . . . I embrace you a million times. This 29th day of November, from Chambéry.*

'I shall be glad to rest a while,' Marie admitted to Donna Leonora. 'And I trust the feuds between the Italian and French will now cease and give me peace.'

It was not to be, as the dissension between the rival retinues continued unabated. Marie did her utmost to ignore the silly squabbles over rank and status, but they were nonetheless distressing. She was further upset when she heard how Madame de Verneuil had departed from Lyons only the day before her own arrival, and publicly boasted that the King's visit to his new bride would be brief.

Each day she waited, hoping for him to come. But the hours would drag by, dusk would fall, the curfew sound, and still there would be no sign of her husband.

One evening following a day of inclement weather, the rain continuing well into the evening, Marie announced that she would take supper and retire early. 'I am told the King may well be with us on the morrow, and I wish to be fresh for when we meet.'

Nerves had again beset her at the prospect of his imminent arrival, yet her heart was racing with anticipation. Marie felt she had already come to secretly love Henry – a love born in her from his endearing letters, his portrait which she kept by her side always, and the mere image of him in her mind. What if he had enjoyed a dalliance or two in the past, and a previous queen? Marguerite de Valois' failure to produce an heir had proved to be her own good fortune. Marie was hopeful that she would succeed. This was a new beginning for herself, and for the King. One to be rejoiced.

Hot water was brought for her to bathe, fragrant with bergamot, then she took a short rest before proceeding to the dining room. As they descended the great staircase Marie paid little attention to a group of gentlemen gathering in the hall. But then some slight movement of the Chancellor alerted her, and casting a swift glance in his direction she guessed beyond doubt that one of the assembled group was the King himself. Giving no indication that she was conscious of her monarch's presence she walked serenely into supper.

Throughout the meal Marie was only too aware that her new husband, Henry of Navarre and France, must indeed be in the room, even now watching her as she ate. Yet she gave no sign. She smiled and chatted to her ladies, and helped herself to the meat that was offered.

'Do you see him?' she whispered to Donna Leonora.

'I believe he may be one of that group of soldiers by the door.'

Marie at once lost her appetite and began to decline the next dishes that were brought to her, anxious to be done with the meal. The moment the chaplain had said grace, she quickly retired to her chamber.

'If he should come, you must let him in at once,' Marie instructed her attendant, almost shaking with nerves.

'But what if you should be asleep?' Leonora sounded disapproving, and Marie almost laughed, although as her companion's small ugly face looked so stern, she managed to restrain herself.

'We cannot refuse him entry, he is my husband.'

Moments later there came a loud knocking on the door. Leonora had only just begun to unlace her mistress's bodice and quickly struggled to fasten it again, all fingers and thumbs. 'Oh, my goodness, why would he come just now?'

Marie was feeling equally shaky, but putting a gentle hand on her companion to calm her, urged her to stop. 'You go and let in the King. I shall finish adjusting my dress.'

But it was too late. Henry had pushed open the door and was already striding into the room. Ignoring Leonora completely, he beamed down upon his new bride. 'Madame, how delighted I am to see you at last.'

Marie was about to sink into a curtsey but instead found herself enveloped in a warm embrace. 'And I you, Sire,' she gasped, rather breathlessly.

'I regret that affairs of war kept me from meeting you at Marseilles, but I believe you were well received. Our meeting has been too long in coming, but here we are now, and I welcome you with all my heart.'

Marie looked up into the merriest dark eyes she'd ever seen, set beneath a high forehead, which must surely be indicative of a sharp and inquisitive mind. His hair was a tangle of thick black curls, the nose long and straight, the chin pointed. She had heard that Henry was an affable, good-natured fellow with a droll wit. Even-tempered and easy-going, yet a fine brave soldier who was fearless in battle. Yet he could take criticism and was said to be willing to listen patiently to advice, even if he did not necessarily take it. Marie speculated on how well he might welcome advice from a new wife. Not that she had any intention of offering any right now as he bowed over her hand, cradling and kissing it with great affection.

He was known as a gambler and a sportsman, an adventurer who laughed at life and went about his duties with a Gascon song upon his lips. But what none of her advisers had found the words to express was that indescribable something which made him irresistible to women. As Marie felt her heartbeat quicken she knew that she was no more immune to his charm than any other. But she also recognized in that shrewd gaze a sparkle of interest in herself, which was most flattering.

'Madame,' he said. 'I find myself embarrassed.'

'How so?' He was still holding her hand, smoothing the back of it with his thumb, a sensation that was having a most disturbing effect upon her.

'The fact of the matter is that so eager was I to come to you that I arrived earlier than expected, and no room has been prepared for me. I fear I am without a bed for the night.' He glanced meaningfully over her shoulder to the commodious bed where she had slept alone until now, waiting for him.

Marie's heart almost stopped beating. She understood well enough his meaning, and the kick of excitement that beat in her chest told its own tale. 'I have room enough in mine for two,' she told him with a smile.

He returned the invitation with a kiss. 'I rather hoped that may be the case.'

It was a night that Marie would never forget. She took him to her bed gladly, this stranger who was her husband. And virgin though she undoubtedly was, she knew instinctively there was nothing to fear from this man. With languid courtesy he made her ripe for love, kissing her mouth till it was rosy from his kisses. Her tongue moved shyly against his, uncertain how to please him, how to respond. Her mind was a torrent of emotion, cheeks flushing with hot desire when he touched places never before explored, which only made her want him all the more.

This was not just a man, this was a *king*, and her *husband*. And for all she might be an Italian princess of royal blood, she was but an untried girl of little beauty, with no experience of men. Why would he find anything the least attractive about her? Yet for some reason he did.

'You have known no man before?' he softly enquired.

'None,' she replied in a breathy whisper. 'I am ignorant of what I . . .'

'Hush,' he murmured against her soft lips. 'I shall be your teacher.'

And he was. Taking his time he taught her the exquisite ecstasy of loving. He gentled and caressed her till she purred with pleasure. Marie had no recollection afterwards of how he had gone about removing her clothing, but somehow he had managed that seemingly impossible task with commendable skill in no time at all.

And lying naked beneath him she felt no shyness, only a delicious vulnerability.

He poised himself over her, holding back while he nibbled her ear, trailing yet more kisses along the sensitive skin of her throat. Then curling his hands beneath her buttocks he lifted her to him and took her, at first gently and then with more force as he sank deeper. Marie cried out, although not with pain. Never had she known such joy, such delight. Was this then how love felt? She saw now that all her life she had ached with loneliness, a hollow emptiness deep inside that only this one man could fill.

A thrilling warmth spread through her, and as his mouth grazed her breasts she arched her back, wanting more, needing to be a part of him.

He had not come to her powdered and scented, as the fops and dandies seen about court. He had come to her as an ordinary man, a soldier, one seemingly impatient to bed her.

He had wanted to stay with her this night, therefore he must like what he saw.

He desired her.

He might even love her, as she already loved him.

They were married the next day in a ceremony officiated by the Cardinal Legate who had conducted the proxy wedding in Florence, although the royal couple had arrived two hours late for the High Mass beforehand. Henry had insisted on making love to her all over again at first light, as if he couldn't get enough of her.

'I much prefer to make love than war,' he told her with a teasing smile.

Now, as Marie knelt beside her new husband, she felt deeply content. Dressed in a gown of crimson, blue and gold, fashioned in the Italian style and glittering with jewels that represented a goodly portion of her dowry, she looked a queen in every respect, even one not yet crowned. About her neck she wore the valuable pearl necklace, given to her by the King, but the most magnificent ornament consisted of an octagonal diamond brooch. Worn on her stomacher it was framed by several smaller stones, each enclosing a portrait in enamel of one of the princes of her house, beneath which hung three large teardrop pearls. It became known as the Queen's Brilliant.

Henry, too, looked magnificent in *haut-de-chausses* of white satin, elaborately embroidered with silk and gold, a black velvet cape draped from one shoulder. Upon his head he wore a velvet toque, rather in the fashion of that once worn at the French Court by Henri III. It bore a string of costly pearls and a regal star of diamonds. Throughout the ceremony he would constantly smile at her, or secretly give her hand a reassuring squeeze.

Had a royal bride ever been more fortunate, she wondered.

The ladies and gentlemen of the court attempted to outdo each other by their own grandeur, looking very like strutting peacocks with their feathers, satins and silks in brilliant colours, their ermine and lace, powder and paint. Even the high altar likewise blazed with gold and precious stones, the scarlet robes of the prelates and priests no less glorious.

At the end of the ceremony, gold and silver coins were thrown to the crowd, and the court processed in stately fashion to the palace, to begin the celebrations.

The son of Gabrielle d'Estrées, the little Duke of Vendôme, was also allowed to join in the festivities and Marie took quite a delight in him. 'He is a charming child, Henry, and must feel free to visit me at any time.'

The King, who was deeply fond of all his children, even though none of them were legitimate, smiled his approval. 'I am glad to see you so happy.'

How could she not be happy with a bridegroom so attentive? Marie was caught up in a whirl of enchantment. She fell more in love with her husband with each passing day.

The honeymoon lasted for more than a month, and despite being obliged to deal with some matters of State, not least the dispute over Saluzzo, Henry was most diligent in pleasing his new wife. He was indeed well satisfied with her. 'Is she not an elegant, charming and handsome woman? She has quite captivated me,' he would say to his friends and courtiers.

They would nod and smile then whisper behind their hands, knowing that the King wrote every day to the Marquise, and that all too soon the honeymoon would be over.

The disputes between the French and Italian nobles did not ease and one morning Rosny, convinced he was losing influence, came to see the King. 'May I recommend, Sire, that you arrange an early departure for the Queen's half-brother, Don Antonio, and her cousin, the Duke of Bracciano. They have served their purpose, and the presence of so many Italians in the Queen's household is creating discord.'

Henry frowned, giving serious consideration to the suggestion. 'I confess I have been irritated by their condescending manner, but I have no wish to offend the Queen. Of course, she would still have her favourite, Donna Leonora, with her.'

Rosny cleared his throat. 'I beg you, Sire, to dismiss La Galigai also, together with her lover, Concini. He is profligate and self-seeking. The woman may appear quiet and timid, but she is neither ineffectual nor lacking in ambition, although I suspect she's gullible to the fellow's charms.'

Henry laughed. 'She is a mouse, and the Queen loves her.'

'I fear the pair intend to establish themselves at any cost in order to make their fortunes in our land, not necessarily in the Queen's, or Your Majesty's, interest.'

'And I think you make too much of this, although I agree that I too am weary of the petty squabbling between these two factions. But surely we can find a less radical solution.'

Rosny was disappointed, but did his best not to show it. 'Perhaps, if Your Majesty were to draw up a list of appointments for the Queen's household, the woman could at least be deprived of some of her power.'

Henry agreed, and granted the post of household superin-tendent to the Duchesse de Nemours. Madame de Guercheville was made *première femme de chambre*. But the coveted title of *dame d'atours* that Donna Leonora had expected for herself was given to Madame de Richelieu.

When the King presented her with the list, Marie was disturbed to find there wasn't a single Italian name on it. Wisely she chose not to comment on this fact, as she was equally tired of the quarrels and silly arguments. But she did make a stand on behalf of her favourite. 'I cannot agree to this last appointment,' she protested. 'I wish for Donna Leonora to remain in the position of mistress of the robes that she has been so ably fulfilling these last months, albeit in an unofficial capacity.'

Surely, even her uncle would consider she'd waited long enough before making this request? But, motivated by fondness for her old friend, and a generous heart, she did not stop there. 'I would also ask Your Majesty's consent for Donna Leonora's immediate marriage with Concini, whom I intend to make my chief equerry.'

Henry was instantly irritated, and bluntly refused. 'I believe I have made my wishes quite clear, Madame.'

'And do I have no say in my own household?' Marie was distraught, her dark brown eyes instantly filling with unshed tears. 'I see no reason why Donna Leonora cannot be allowed this small happiness.'

The King was at once discomforted by the sight of his wife's distress, and attempted to mollify his decision with a compromise. 'If the pair are determined to marry, then they must return forthwith to Florence.'

The prospect of losing Leonora was too much for her to bear and Marie burst into tears. 'How can you be so cruel as to deny me my only friend and companion?' She felt deeply hurt and angry by the King's lack of sensitivity for her feelings.

Henry, however, alert to Rosny's warning, stood firm, which only brought out the worst of Marie's own stubbornness. She did her utmost to persuade him, hoping he would soften, or grow weary of the argument, but to no avail. In the furore, Madame de Richelieu resigned, but the office of *dame d'atours* was given to the widow of a brave soldier and not to her beloved Leonora. It appeared to be a stand-off between the royal couple.

News of this argument somehow reached the ears of the Grand Duke and Marie's uncle wrote of his disappointment that she should so soon fall into a quarrel with her husband.

'I could have disposed of your hand to the Duke of Braganza, or the Duke of Parma, and thus doomed you to a career of comparative obscurity.' He wrote at length, upbraiding her for her folly. 'You have alienated your royal husband by paying heed to these audacious intriguers.'

Feeling herself even more neglected and ignored, Marie miserably replied, 'I am without influence. The King is governed by La Marquise, therefore I intend to retain the friends of my youth.'

Perhaps moved to pity by her distress, Henry relented his stance a little. He would not sanction an appointment in the Queen's household for La Galigai, but she could remain in France.

'So long as she seeks neither office nor precedence.'

It had been an unfortunate incident, and although Marie felt her stubbornness had won her some sort of victory, she hated the fact that this had been their first matrimonial dispute. And the first seeds of discontent had been sown.

The day came when the court set out on its regal progress towards Paris. But after only a few miles, anxious to escape the petty bickering of courtiers and find some release in the arms of his mistress, the King came to the Queen with an apology. 'My love, though it breaks my heart to leave you, I must make haste to the capital. I need to conclude the treaty with Savoy as I have neglected state affairs too long.'

'Oh, but can I not ride with you?' The thought of yet more official functions, without her husband at her side, filled Marie with dread.

'There is no need of that. Our parting is but temporary. You shall take your time and enjoy the sights of your new kingdom.'

Marie was disappointed, but dutifully expressed her understanding. 'If I have offended you then you must tell me, so that I can put the matter right.'

'My dear,' he said, bringing both her hands to his lips to kiss her fingers. 'Do not doubt that I love you dearly, for now you obey my will. Believe that this is the true way to govern me – in short – the only way.'

It was a warning, a gentle one, but a warning nonetheless. But even as Marie strove to think of a response, he was already doffing his cap and making ready to mount his horse. She blew him a kiss and watched him ride away with tears in her eyes.

It was Leonora who brought her the unwelcome news. 'Your Majesty, they are saying that instead of riding straight to the capital, where his presence was allegedly needed so urgently, the King has in fact called at the Château de Verneuil to meet with his mistress and urge her to return with him to Paris.'

Marie stared at her loyal servant in stunned dismay. She'd been distressed by Henry's apparent abandonment of her, her female pride hurt by his ability to leave her so abruptly, and so soon after their wedding. Now she felt a burning indignation, and the first stirrings of jealousy. Marie had been but a small child when she'd witnessed her mother's tears when her husband of just a few years had brought a sixteen-year-old girl to live close by in a fine palazzo in Florence, so that he could visit her daily. Now she understood fully how Joanna must have felt.

'His Majesty was seen to arrive at the château where he flung himself into her waiting arms.'

'Are you saying that urging me to take my time to explore my new kingdom was a deliberate ploy on his part?'

Leonora lowered her gaze, unable to witness the pain this knowledge brought to her mistress, yet feeling a need to take her revenge against the King for his slight against her. 'I cannot say.'

'Then you are kinder than the thoughts rattling in my own head,' Marie tartly replied. 'To go to his mistress now, so soon after our wedding, is a gross and stinging insult.' If at the outset of her marriage she'd ridden on a tide of happiness and joy, now Marie was plunged into the depths of despair. Perhaps he had not cared for her at all. He had simply been performing a duty, admittedly with great skill and artifice, and undoubted charm, laced with a natural earthy desire. Yet all the while Henry had been longing to return to his mistress, who was clearly far more beautiful and desirable than herself.

Marie was mortified, deeply insulted, and somewhat alarmed, feeling suddenly insecure and unwanted in this new land. 'He does not love me.' The words were out before she could stop them.

'The King shows every sign of indifference, that is true,' Leonora agreed, revelling in her power to insult him. 'But you must guard your pride well. Do not let him see how he has hurt you, how you feel spurned by this callous neglect.'

Neglect! It was the one word Marie feared more than any other. Had not her own father neglected her to such an extent that he had not even troubled to visit his own child in years. How would she tolerate such treatment from a husband? And after believing that he cared.

Wringing her hands together she began to pace about the room. They were staying in yet another anonymous hostel on the road somewhere between Bourges and Orleans. It was a bitter winter's night, rain beating on the windows and a draught swirling beneath the door. Marie had been fondly imagining how much warmer and more comforting her cold bed would be were her husband beside her; how in just a few more miles she would reach Paris and could nestle again in his arms. Now she was stricken to the core.

'It is an insult to your royal person,' Leonora was muttering. 'Oh, Your Majesty, you are growing agitated, let me calm you.' Snatching up a brush she attempted to smooth the long brown tresses, but Marie did not have the patience to sit still and again began to walk up and down in a lather of distress.

'Mayhap it was not deliberate on Henry's part,' she said at last, pausing in her fretful pacing. 'The meeting might well have been arranged by *that woman*, by the Marquise herself. I am not so blind that I cannot see it would be to her advantage to delay my arrival for as long as possible. Perhaps things will be different when I am in Paris.'

With this somewhat forlorn hope, she curled up alone in her bed and dreamed of a contented life together.

Because of the constant stops on the road, the dreary ceremonies, civic functions, and endless speeches, Marie did not reach the capital until early February. She was met by the King at Nemours, and he personally conducted her to Fontainebleau. To her relief she saw no sign of the royal favourite, and Henry was as friendly and warm as ever.

'How can you be so susceptible to his charms?' Leonora scorned, her monkey-like face tight with disapproval as she helped her mistress prepare for their first night together. 'Why do you not challenge him?'

'Because he is the King, and I am his queen.'

Oh, but it was hard not to start a quarrel with him. Marie was burning to ask the million questions that swarmed in her head. Except that when he came to her with his smiles and took her in his arms, she could ask none of them. His tantalizing touch made her shiver with desire, and when he bent to kiss her she eagerly yielded herself to the ecstasy of her own ardour. Intoxicated by his lovemaking, which was as passionate and skilful as ever, she banished all such miserable doubts from her mind.

For the few days of their stay at Fontainebleau, Marie held her complaints in check, savouring some of the early joy she'd found in her marriage, albeit tinged with a private sadness. Henry

regularly took her riding in the magnificent forest, showed her
his favourite haunts, but then one morning received word that
his sister, Madame Catherine, was ill, and begged leave to depart
for Paris.

'I must see that my physician is dispatched to her.'

Marie longed to say he could surely order that to be done
from here, but held her tongue.

At last the new queen entered Paris, and found that the delays
to her arrival had been so prolonged that it seemed the people
had forgotten she was even coming. The streets were quiet as
her coach rode through. No decorations or cheering crowds here.
There was none of the pomp she'd become accustomed to on
her progress through the provinces. When she asked the Constable
the reason, she was informed that although the civic authorities
had been eager to afford her a magnificent state reception,
the King himself had commanded that the ceremony should be
deferred, for the sake of cost.

'His Majesty is rigorous at controlling the treasury,' the official
explained with a smile. 'He often insists that his garments be
mended, in order to save the expense of buying new.'

'Is that all I am to him now?' she complained to Leonora as
they jostled along, hiding from the empty darkness behind
the heavy carnation curtains. 'An expense! And that despite the
fortune I have brought to him in the form of a dowry.'

'I suspect it was Madame de Verneuil who has instituted an evil
influence upon His Majesty in the matter. The last thing she would
want would be for you to receive the kind of welcome you have
received thus far in every town you have passed through. Not here
in Paris, the city in which she imagined herself being queen.'

'You may well be right. I must give Henry the benefit of the
doubt.' If only because of the stirring nights she spent in his arms.

Marie shivered, her feet frozen on a foot-warmer that had long
since lost its heat, consoling herself that she would be the one to
wear the crown, after all. Little César was with her and the poor
child was falling asleep in her arms. She drew him close to keep
him warm, telling herself to stop fretting about one mistress. Did
not every monarch consider it his right? She must learn to accept
that, and what did it matter, so long as Henry was discreet?

'I doubt he is even faithful to her,' Leonora inexorably

continued, as the older woman did so love to gossip. 'I have heard rumours that he constantly entertains other ladies of the court at supper.'

Marie was startled by this news, not sure whether to be relieved by this lack of constancy on her husband's part towards his mistress, or further insulted by it. She let out a heavy sigh. 'No doubt things will not look half so bleak when we can actually step down from this tiresome coach for the last time.'

But there was little consolation to be found when they did. The Louvre appeared dingy, the furnishings outdated, certainly to Marie, an Italian princess accustomed to Florentine elegance. She was shocked by the evident lack of preparation for her arrival. There were no fires lit, no clean sheets on the beds. 'We cannot possibly stay here. I doubt it has even been cleaned. Please find us a more comfortable abode while something is done to improve this place.'

Marie installed herself and her entourage in the finest private mansion in Paris, the home of Cardinal de Condé. Here she waited for the nobles, the Princes of the Blood and other high personages, to call and pay their respects, as was only right and proper to a new queen.

The squabbles between the Italian and French retinues had left a sour taste in everyone's mouth, and Marie was doing her utmost to keep her spirits high, despite the poor reception in the capital. But she was also suffering from that dreaded sense of neglect by an easy-going, but careless, husband. Holding fast to her dignity she smiled as she entered the ballroom the following evening, having spent a long afternoon receiving the principal ladies of the court, and derived some small pleasure from hearing murmurs of admiration as she passed by.

Her gown was of gold cloth trimmed with ermine, her fine bosom framed by a ruff of rich lace stiffened by wire that rose high behind the neck. The fashion was instantly christened by the admiring courtiers as a 'Medici'. And wishing to be in keeping with the French Court the Queen's hair was arranged in stiff rows of thickly-powdered curls. As always she looked magnificent, but her confidence, already at a low ebb, dipped lower within moments of reaching the dais.

Henriette stood framed in the open doorway, her pretty head
held high as she glanced disdainfully about her with a dignity
befitting a queen and not a mere courtesan.

Some instinct told Marie who the woman was, confirmed by
the rush of whispers that flew about the room, followed by a
stunned silence. Marie de Medici, that most royal of princesses,
watched in open disbelief as her husband's mistress moved gracefully towards her. She could hardly believe her own eyes. Or her
ears either when, curtseying low, the Duchesse de Nemours – the
famous Anne d'Este, mother of the Duke of Mayenne, Cardinal
de Lorraine, and Henri de Guise who had inherited his father's
sobriquet *le Balafré* and been loved by Queen Margot – introduced
her.

'May I have the honour of presenting to Your Majesty
Madame Catherine Henriette de Balzac d'Entragues, the Marchioness
de Verneuil.' The elderly duchess made a small obeisance.

But if her *grande-maîtresse* looked uncomfortable over having
been placed in this invidious position, Marie did not notice. She
was far too concerned with examining the insolent expression
and startling good looks of her rival. Dark and slim with a tiny
waist that made Marie almost weep with envy, the girl blazed
with jewels, her triumph radiating from her almost as brightly.
Marie instantly decided that her brow bulged somewhat, that her
mouth was sulky, and the chin somewhat fleshy. The heavy-lidded
eyes were too large for real beauty, and the mouth too small.

Henry leaned close to whisper in the Queen's ear. 'Behold
Madame la Marquise, a lady, as you know, well affected towards
myself, but who desires also to become your very humble servant.'

Fully aware though she indeed was that her husband kept a
mistress, Marie had not expected the Marquise to be presented to
her at court. She was outraged that this wicked jade should even
be here, let alone under the wing of one so high as the Duchess
of Nemours, or for the King himself to push her forward. She
sensed, rather than heard, the indrawn breath of the gathered assembly
as they awaited her reaction to this apparent insult. Only her own
strict upbringing and pride in her Italian blood helped her to hold
on to her dignity. Marie's upper lip trembled slightly but she quickly
stiffened it. Not by the smallest degree would she give this slattern
the pleasure of seeing how her very presence wounded her.

Giving no indication by her expression of the turmoil of her thoughts within, Marie carefully studied her rival. Henriette gave a mocking little curtsey, a satisfied little smile playing about her pretty mouth. Apparently dissatisfied with this supposed show of obeisance, the King stepped quickly forward, placed his hand upon his mistress's head and pushed her down further, compelling her to kneel and touch her lips to the hem of the Queen's robe. Marie stood rigid, making no attempt to offer her hand to be kissed, but as the girl scrambled to her feet again nor did she miss the flash of resentment that darted from those catlike eyes.

The King was casting a fierce glare in the Duchess's direction. 'Most ungracious,' he muttered, as if the blame for this effrontery were entirely hers, and that he had not insisted she do this difficult and embarrassing task for him so that Henriette could remain at court, within his reach. Then he strolled away, suddenly finding urgent business requiring his attention in the anteroom, closely followed by the officers of his household.

Madame la Marquise remained where she was.

Assiduously ignoring her, Marie felt the insult like a lash, the colour draining from her face, and she quickly turned aside to converse with her ladies. She was eager to give the impression that the woman was of no consequence, that she'd interrupted a most important and pressing discussion.

Taking a quick step forward the Duchesse de Nemours attempted to salvage the situation by catching the eye of the Queen, but Marie turned away from her too. She made it very evident that the elderly Duchess, once referred to as the Fury of the League, had also incurred her royal displeasure. The unfortunate lady almost shrank from the fierce glare those soft brown eyes now fixed upon her. She'd made every effort to befriend the new Queen, yet had felt obliged to obey the King in this request, because Henry had so graciously pardoned her grandson, the Prince de Joinville, for his murderous attack upon the Duke of Bellegarde. Now she realized that by doing Henry this favour, she may well have gained the enmity of the very woman she had wished to please. She stepped back, wishing only for the floor to swallow her up.

Henriette was less easily discomforted. Knowing it was by royal command that she was even here, she placed herself at the Queen's table at supper, attempting to ingratiate herself into the court ladies' circle as if she had every right to be amongst them, even presuming to address Her Majesty directly.

'Ah, do you speak of the Savoy wars and Biron?' she asked, catching the thread of their conversation and paying no attention to the sudden tears that sprang into Marie's eyes, nor the chill condemnation of the courtiers around her. 'Dearest Henry will not tolerate such a betrayal. The Marshal will lose his head over it, mark my words. Not that he will miss it if he does, as it is as empty as a rattling drum. Mayhap it would be better to deprive Biron of other parts which he might miss more.' And she laughed, rather coarsely.

The remark was greeted in silence by the ladies. Marie stared at her rival in cold dismay. Her insolence was beyond imagining. What in the name of heaven did her husband see in this grossly rude woman?

'I assume Henry has spoken to you of this matter?' Smiling beatifically, Henriette's voice lifted at the end to form a question. One Marie had no intention of answering. 'Or mayhap you have not seen much of your husband in recent weeks? Indeed, he has been kept occupied elsewhere a good deal.' Again that throaty chuckle.

For a moment Marie was too startled to reply, but quickly recovering her self-possession, she turned to her ladies. 'I fear I must plead fatigue. I have travelled far and need rest. We shall continue our most fascinating conversation another time, when there is less . . . distraction.' So saying she rose, and calmly walked away to seek sanctuary in her own apartments.

Marie's one consolation was that, having maintained her dignity throughout, the sympathy of the court had swung very much back in her favour.

Six weeks later Marie was able to inform the King that she was *enceinte*. He was as delighted as she. Was not this the epitome of all their shared hopes and dreams? The people too were excited when they heard the news, and would run after her coach, cheering and calling their blessings upon her.

Madame de Verneuil quietly withdrew from court.

Marie smiled to herself, feeling she had won a battle, if not the war, greatly relieved to be rid of her rival for a while. She turned with enthusiasm to embrace her new life. Much work needed to be done as the court was sadly disorganized, controlled by a few great ladies who held sway. These doyens saw her as merely the daughter of a minor Italian royal, not a great sovereign, and rarely deferred to her. This, Marie decided, must change.

Nor did her husband exert sufficient influence over them. Since his accession, particularly following his separation from Marguerite, Henry had cared little about the glories of royalty. As a consequence the French Court had fallen into a sorry state, becoming one of the least splendid in Europe. In addition, it was evident that his earlier poverty had accustomed him to many privations. Nor had he been interested in the condition of his palaces, as Henry had rarely slept in his own bed, spending his time visiting the houses of the most wealthy of his courtiers, such as Zamet, Condé, and other dissipated sycophants. With them he could discard the restrictions of his royal status, and indulge his passion for gambling and womanizing.

Marie hoped to change all of that too.

As she waited patiently for the birth she began making improvements at the Louvre. She resolved to bring culture to the court. Masques and ballets were held, and the young nobles took part in a tournament at the Pont-au-Change, at which the Queen presented the prizes to the victors.

Nor did the King appear unwilling to accept these changes. He seemed anxious to improve the splendour and display of his court, perhaps to compensate his new bride for his lack of constancy in their private lives.

One evening the King and Queen were dining at the Arsenal at a banquet given by Rosny in honour of his appointment as Grand-Master of the Artillery. Perhaps carried away by his own glory that day, Rosny was overly generous with the wine. It was a Burgundy of particularly fine vintage, strong enough for the ladies to ask for water to mix with it. Unbeknown to them he instead laced the jugs of water with another wine, one of a paler colour but equal strength. The result was predictable, and Marie was furious when she discovered that her poor ladies, now very much the worse for drink, had been tricked.

Henry roared with laughter. 'It was but a jest, Madame.'

'It was a cruel insult against my Florentine ladies who are accustomed to the taste of a more refined wine. Why would such a trick be played upon them, except out of malice? Have I not attempted to bring some civilization and improvements to this dissolute court? Not least by turning a blind eye over a certain personage being presented who by rights should not have been.'

Henry looked shamefaced. 'Indeed you have been most patient, my love, and I heartily endorse your efforts.' Secretly he thought her rather fussy and quarrelsome, but could not deny that she had been sorely tested.

'Not only that but in return for Your Majesty's generosity and kindness towards me, have I not willingly taken on the nurture and care of the children of Gabrielle d'Estrées, your previous *maîtresse-en-titre*, despite their mother having been the reason for the endless delays to our marriage?'

Now Henry was almost grovelling as he hastened to assure her of his appreciation. 'Your heart is boundless in its charity.'

'Indeed that is not so; I am simply your loyal and dutiful wife. Although I confess to being particularly fond of little César. Nevertheless, Rosny has overstepped the mark. He had no right to make sport with my ladies and destroy their dignity!'

Rosny was obliged to eat humble pie and offer his most sincere apologies to Her Majesty, but the incident did nothing to further good relations between them.

Henriette was in bed with the King. Despite the Queen's pregnancy, or perhaps because of it, he could not keep away. He needed her. He lusted after her. She'd welcomed him back into her arms with a smile of pure triumph. Now, as she sat astride him, rubbing her bare breasts against the hard planes of his chest, she breathed in the acrid maleness of him. Henry always smelled vaguely of horses, or the garlic he loved to eat with every meal. Unlike many of the King's previous mistresses, Henriette had quickly grown accustomed to it and found the scent manly and intoxicating. She nibbled at his full lower lip, kissing him with a languid sweetness, and saw how his Gascon eyes darkened with desire.

'You will stay with me, will you not, Your Majesty?'

Henry was smiling, partly in ecstasy, yet partly in an attempt to reassure her, his hands caressing her breasts, thumbing the tautness of rosy nipples till they peaked with need. 'I have promised to take the Queen to meet my sister at Monceaux. I cannot dally too long. Dear heaven . . . what are you doing to me?'

She could hear how his breath was rapidly shortening, growing more ragged as she nipped at his ear with her small sharp teeth, licked him with her pink curled tongue, while her hands were busy elsewhere.

'Whatever you like, my lord. Whatever you like.' She lowered herself down the length of his lean body, savouring the tensile strength of his hips and thighs, intent on bringing him nought but pleasure. 'Do you like this . . . and this?'

Henry let out a low groan and Henriette smiled to herself, certain of her power over him. 'Why should you rush away? I'm sure your new bride can happily keep herself occupied for a little while longer, dusting and tidying the Louvre, while you and I play.'

Henriette meant to keep him with her for as long as possible. Did she not possess the power to hold a king? By rights it should have been herself wearing the crown, if only she had successfully borne Henry a son. But it was not too late. She still held his written promise, complete with the King's signature, which meant that the Italian marriage was illegal. Had not her father learned as much from the lawyers? And as she had produced a son, albeit not a live one, sadly, their judgement surely remained valid. Were she to be more fortunate next time, she would not hesitate to act.

Yet she also appreciated that in the meantime she must tread carefully. It was vital she protect herself in case the power of this new queen flourished too well and grew out of control. 'I fear that Her Majesty is determined to destroy our relationship,' Henriette mourned, sliding him inside her with liquid grace. 'How will I survive when you have cast me off?'

He gasped, a husky sound deep in his throat as he put back his head to savour the fullness of her. 'I am not about to cast you off, my sweet.'

It was vitally important that he didn't, that she held on to her power. Now that the Queen was *enceinte*, Henriette feared the Medici woman could exert an even greater influence over the King. She might even decide to have his mistress banished from court altogether. Henriette shuddered at the prospect.

It was unthinkable!

'The Queen may cast me off, even if you do not,' she said, as she rocked against him, making him cry out with agonized passion.

For a while there were no more words between them as Henry turned her over on to her back and took full control, unable to restrain himself any longer. She was a dangerous woman. He could smell ambition in her, sense it in every sleek, intoxicating encounter between them. Yet he must have her. He lived to possess her.

Later, as they lay entwined, their passion sated, he offered what reassurance he could. 'Your fears are unfounded, dear heart. Her Majesty has quite accepted the situation and will not seek to change it. She appreciates my great love for you, which is different to that which I feel towards her.'

'Oh, Henry, I do hope so. I should be desolate without you,' Henriette whimpered. 'But let us suppose, just for a moment, that she had her way. Where would I go? How would I survive, all alone, abandoned and penniless?'

Henry chuckled against her soft lips. 'I would never leave you penniless, my sweet. Do you take me for a heartless knave?'

Gently pushing him away, Henriette sat up, her auburn hair a tousled halo of fire about her head, and pouted at him. 'You should know that I have received a proposal of marriage.'

Twin furrows creased Henry's brow. 'What sort of proposal?'

'From a prince who, at this juncture, shall remain nameless. But the offer is conditional on my being able to bring with me a dowry of a hundred thousand *livres*. A not unreasonable recompense if a man is willing to take on a king's rejected mistress. Would you do that for me, Henry, to secure my future?'

'I have not rejected you, my sweet. Nor will I.'

'You may have little say in the matter,' Henriette persisted, 'once the dauphin is born. We will speak no more on the subject at this juncture, but at least think on it.' She began to kiss him again, to tease and to tantalize. The business of the bedchamber represented her pathway to success. And in that respect, Henry was very easy to please.

★   ★   ★

One morning, while the King was out hunting, Henriette was surprised to receive a visitor in the form of Galagai, the little monkey-like woman who attended on the Queen. Henriette was taking a leisurely breakfast, as she so liked to do, sipping her chocolate when the request for an audience was brought to her. Curious to hear what the woman wanted, she agreed to see her.

'Madame, I am grateful for this opportunity to speak with you.' The Italian dipped a small curtsey, as if wishing to indicate respect for the other woman's station.

'The King may return at any moment, so my time is of the essence. Pray do not waste it.'

Donna Leonora still nursed a deep resentment over not being granted the position of *dame d'atours*, and the refusal of the King to give permission for her marriage to Concini. With his full, high forehead, aquiline nose, large eyes beneath arched brows, and a slight moustache curled elegantly upward, not to mention his charming manner, Leonora remained entranced by him. They had been lovers for some time now but she longed to be his wife. They could achieve so much together.

She carefully explained all of this to Henriette. 'Unfortunately the King is not impressed by the documentation which proves that I am indeed highly connected to a notable Florentine family. He considers me to be no more than a *cittadina*, a humble townswoman of good burgher birth. This would be well thought of in Florence, but not here, in France. Only ladies of noble lineage are allowed to attend the Queen and ride in the royal coach.'

Henriette was considering the woman with a thoughtful frown. 'And what do you imagine I can do to help in this matter?'

'With respect, Madame, I believe you and I are kindred souls. Like myself, you are a woman of ambition. I feel certain we could help each other.'

'In what way could a mouse like *you* help *me*?'

'I could gain you entrance to the Queen's circle, together with the respect you deserve.'

Henriette fell silent. It was certainly true that she hated being excluded from the Queen's private assemblies, as well as not being treated with the proper courtesy and consideration her rank as the King's official mistress warranted. Only by taking a full part in court life could she carry out her long-term plan to re-establish

herself as first in Henry's life. She saw at once the benefit in such
an alliance. This ugly little woman without doubt held the Queen's
ear. The Medici may well be willing to offer a favour in return
for helping her favourite advance and achieve her heart's desire,
even if the person responsible was her husband's mistress.

The Medici was undoubtedly furious with her rival, following
the debacle of the presentation, and would do all she could to
induce the King to cast her off. But at the same time her most
treasured companion was threatened with expulsion from France,
which, if that happened, would leave the Queen more lonely and
miserable than ever.

'Very well. I will prevail upon the King to sanction your
marriage and continued residence in France, and to bestow upon
you and your husband senior appointments in the royal
household.'

The wily Italian smiled and nodded, well pleased. 'For myself
I would wish to be *Dame d'atours*, and something notable for
Concini.'

'An ambassador perhaps?'

'Perfect.'

The bargain was struck. Using all her considerable charms La
Marquise found little difficulty in persuading Henry to agree to
the intrigue, on the grounds that the deal allowed him to keep
his mistress at court, close by his side, while satisfying his wife's
request for preferment of her favourites. Thus achieving both
desire and duty.

'*Ventre Saint Gris*, what a clever minx you are,' he said with a
laugh, unaware that the idea had sprung from a different source.

They were walking arm in arm in the gardens and Henriette
cast him a sideways glance from beneath her lashes. 'My aim is
ever to please you, Your Majesty.' And leaning back against a tree
she lifted her skirts to reveal she was quite naked beneath, without
even her silk stockings.

'Oh, you do, dear heart. You most certainly do.'

He was in such a hurry to have her he almost tore his clothing
in his urgent desire to release himself. Then he pushed her back
hard against the trunk of the giant oak, lifted her against him
and took her there and then where a maid or passer-by might
chance upon them at any moment.

So well did the new arrangement suit Henry that he even gave Leonora twenty thousand *livres* on the occasion of her marriage, and agreed to consider appointing Concini as a Gentleman of the Chamber.

La Marquise took her place among the noblest ladies of the court with a self-satisfied air of triumph. She made a show of being respectful and submissive to Her Majesty, but Henriette's attitude was very much that of the cat who had swallowed the cream. She had won, had she not?

Marie was less enamoured of the arrangement, but gritted her teeth and accepted the situation for the sake of her beloved Donna Leonora. She enquired every day after the health of her rival, included her in all her assemblies and entertainments, even allowed her to take part in a special ballet she was arranging for the King's sister, Madame Catherine. A truce was declared between the two of them. The queen and the courtesan duly went through the motions of friendship and mutual respect, although it was nothing more than a façade to please the King.

And when, a month later, her rival announced that she too was *enceinte* with the King's child, it was the bitterest of blows. As Marie's uncle the Grand Duke never failed to point out to her in his constant letters, any failure on her part to provide the much needed dauphin would result in a challenge from the d'Entragues family on the legality of her marriage.

At the close of Lent, the Duchesse de Bar, the King's sister, together with her father-in-law the Duc de Lorraine, arrived to welcome the new Queen. Catherine was convalescing following a long illness, but when she and Marie met at Monceaux they liked each other on sight and became instant friends. Marie was able to pour out her troubles to a sympathetic ear, finding that even the King's sister deplored his lack of principle, and fascination with his mistress.

'Henry may seem tolerant and carefree, but he can be very stubborn on certain matters,' Catherine agreed. 'I too suffered from blighted love when he refused permission for me to marry the Comte de Soissons, the man I had loved from girlhood.'

'We princesses are ever blighted with arranged marriages. Yet I had thought myself fortunate.'

The two women smiled at each other, in perfect accord.

'I can see that you love my brother, and it must be heartbreaking having to share him with one so low, although that is not uncommon in royal circles.'

'So content is Henry with this new arrangement that he showers gifts upon us both, even expects us to share them. But worse, because she too is carrying his child, he has assigned to La Marquise a suite of apartments in the Louvre immediately above mine, and only slightly less magnificent. It is an insult too great to bear. The woman now gives herself such airs that she's formed a small rival court of her own, from which she dares to exclude me! She has gathered about her salon the prettiest women and the most reckless gamblers. The King regularly attends, of course, no doubt preferring the brilliance and dissipation of his mistress's circle, to the more formal etiquette of a queen's court.'

Catherine looked at her new sister-in-law with ill-disguised pity. 'It is most sad, but the lot of a princess is not easy. I'm sure you will find a way to win his heart. Henry is not an unfeeling man, and he does not always get his own way. No husband does,' she added with a soft sigh. 'My own is still insisting that I turn Catholic, but I remain firmly adhered to the Huguenot faith of my late mother, Jeanne d'Albret. And ever will. Now let us take a gentle stroll in the gardens. The sun and fresh air will do us both good.'

The King was in a sullen mood, worrying over Henriette's request, more generally interpreted as a demand, that she be granted a substantial dowry which would allow her to marry. To his surprise some of the nobles were actually in favour.

'You might do well to give the young lady the hundred thousand *livres* she requires,' suggested Bellievre.

Rosny, however, took a more prudent view. 'It is easier to talk of such a sum than to procure it.'

'Give the woman two or even three hundred thousand, if less will not suffice,' said another.

Perhaps they thought that by granting Henriette this huge amount of money they could be rid of her. If that was the case then they had misread his intentions. Henry listened to their arguments and did nothing. But then, he had no wish to see his mistress married. He wanted her all to himself. He strolled in the gardens with his sister and queen, and consoled himself over the muddle in his private life by the prospect of at least one son, possibly two.

Monceaux had once been the property of La Belle Gabrielle, nonetheless Marie was charmed by it and praised the beautiful gardens and parkland.

'Give me a dauphin, wife, and the château and entire estate shall be yours,' Henry recklessly promised.

'You are too generous, Sire.' Knowing that the King had already agreed that Gabrielle's eldest son should inherit the property, Marie glanced down at little César, who was even now holding her hand, as he so loved to walk with her. Did the boy understand that his father the King had just disinherited him? But she said nothing; only made a private vow to see that the child did not lose out by this unexpected gift.

Catherine, listening to these remarks with equal disdain recalled how on the death of his beloved angel, her brother had claimed, 'The root of my love is withered. Never can it revive!'

It seemed to have made a remarkable recovery.

The Queen went into labour on the twenty-seventh day of September 1601. She had stayed on with Catherine at Monceaux for some time after Henry had left for Calais. The King's presence had been required at the frontier because of the threat of further war in the Low Countries. Marie, accompanied by her sister-in-law, the Duchess of Nemours, Madame de Guercheville, and of course her loyal *dame d'atours*, removed to Fontainebleau at the end of August.

She spent her days walking in the gardens, listening to music or playing an instrument herself, and talking theology with Catherine. Her health was good but Marie was all too aware that the hopes and prayers of the nation depended upon the safe delivery of a son. An heir for France would determine a safe future for the monarchy, and peace for the nation. Would Henry then feel less need for a mistress? Indeed, she hoped so.

The pains started around midnight and continued all the next day. Marie would pace the room for a while, attempt to rest on the bed or couch, and then pace some more, biting down hard on her lower lip when the contractions threatened to overwhelm her. She was a queen, after all, and must not lose her dignity even in the throes of childbirth. She realized she would need all her strength and courage to survive this ordeal, and to successfully deliver a live child — a dauphin for France.

Yet she refused all services save for the midwife, a Madame Boursier, whom she'd chosen to attend the birth. In this woman alone did she put her trust. Out in the anteroom ministers and others of high rank huddled together, muttering on the wisdom of this decision. The royal surgeons and physicians kicked their heels with frustration while the Queen obstinately refused all other assistance.

'I am never deceived in any person I select. Let her attend me, and no other.'

Henry was by her side throughout, never leaving the room. The heir to the throne was to be born in the celebrated *Chambre Ovale*, in the great palace of Fontainebleau.

As well as the King, various other important personages including the Duchesse de Nemours, Duc de Montpensier, the Comte de Soissons, Prince de Condé, and any number of the Queen's ladies and gentlemen also crowded in to witness this momentous event. Marie felt stifled by this horde of onlookers, by the heat and stuffiness of the chamber, the shadowy darkness as the windows were all tightly shut, curtains drawn, and even a fire burning in the grate despite it being a warm autumn day.

Late in the evening, at about half past ten, just when she thought her strength would give out, Marie de Medici, Queen of France, finally gave birth to a son. Like all mothers she at once anxiously enquired after his health, waiting to hear that so essential cry. None came. The room was filled with a terrible silence, a fearful holding of breath by all present.

The King was in tears while the nobles and ladies began to whisper behind their hands that it had been a bad mistake not to allow the royal physicians to attend.

'I fear the child is lifeless,' the elderly Duchesse de Nemours mourned. 'It has all been for nought.'

Madame Boursier paid no attention to any of them. Grasping the baby, who in all other respects looked a healthy child, she tipped him upside down and gently smacked his bottom. The royal infant cried out at this outrage to his person and everyone present let out their breath on a huge sigh of relief, some sending up prayers of thanks to God, a few remembering to praise the midwife too. Marie's faith in the woman had been justified.

Henry hastened to embrace his wife. 'My love, you have suffered much, but rejoice, God has given us what we asked. We have a son!' And Marie wept in his arms.

The room cleared quickly as everyone dashed off to spread the joyous news, while the King proudly held the precious Dauphin in his arms. 'Welcome to this child who will one day wear the crown as Louis XIII.' Then placing his sword in a hand too small as yet to grasp it, he recited a short blessing. 'May you use it, my son, to the glory of God, and in defence of your crown and people.'

Marie, unable to speak for emotion, could only smile up at her husband and son with tears in her eyes.

'May I play the proud father and show him off to those who have waited so patiently outside, my love?'

She laughed. 'Of course, and tell them that their queen is well, and has survived this trauma thanks to the love and care of the King at her side.'

Henry beamed at her. 'And by the grace of God.'

The little prince was privately baptized at Fontainebleau the next day, although the State Baptism would not take place until the Dauphin was considered old enough to have some religious instructions from his chaplain, and understand the meaning of the ceremony. This was Henry's decision and none could gainsay it. The godmother was Marie's sister, the Duchess of Mantua. The Grand Duke, however, declined the honour of becoming the boy's godfather, as he was still displeased over the exchange of Saluzzo for Bresse, but he nonetheless sent warm congratulations to his niece.

Pope Clement accepted the role in Ferdinand's place, and dispatched a deputy to France to convey his blessings to Queen Marie and her infant son, together with a gift of a magnificent layette, as custom dictated.

The streets of Paris rang with joy, Te Deums were chanted, salvoes of artillery discharged, fireworks, bonfires, feasting and celebrations went on for days. Was this not the first legal heir born to the nation since Francis II? Even more auspicious, a daughter, Anne of Austria, had been born to Philip III of Spain only five days previously, surely a prophecy for the future alliance of these two great nations through marriage. Letters of congratulation poured in from monarchs and potentates of every nation. Even Queen Margot, still living in her fastness of the Castle at Usson, wrote a gracious letter of warm congratulations to Henry, and to the woman who had taken her crown and achieved what she never could.

The only person not delighted to see the new dauphin was little César de Vendôme, who, until this rival had appeared on the scene to claim her attention, had been the Queen's favourite. The boy was found one morning by Madame Boursier hiding behind a tapestry sobbing his heart out.

'Monsieur, what is wrong, what ails you?'

'Nobody speaks to me now, and they won't let me in to see the Queen.'

'Oh, my dear child.'

When Marie was told of his distress she ordered him to be brought to her at once. 'There, there,' she said, hugging him to her. 'Are you not still my precious big boy? This new little one will be fortunate to have such a fine young man to look up to and learn from. You must come to see me, and Monsieur le Dauphin, whenever you please. You need no one's permission, do you understand? Now, would you like to ride out in the forest as a treat?'

All smiles again, César eagerly nodded, kissed his beloved stepmother and went happily off with the Prince de Condé on an adventure.

A little more than a week after the Queen's *accouchement*, Henry was writing to his mistress:

> *My dear heart, my wife is going on well and my son also, praise God. He has grown and filled out so much that he has become half as big again . . . For my part I have slept remarkably well and am free from all pain save that of being absent from you, which though a grief to me is moderated by the hope of soon seeing you again.*

Good morrow, mes chères amours, *always love your* menon, *who kisses your hands and lips a million times.*

Henry at Fontainebleau

Henriette was bitterly disappointed that the Queen had produced a son. She had banked on it being a daughter, or, even better, stillborn. 'I care not whether his wife is "going on well",' she cried, tossing the letter aside with such contempt her sister Marie had to run to catch the royal missive before it fell into the fire. 'Does he never think of *me*, his *true* queen? Why has he abandoned me for *her?*'

'Give him a son, sister dear. He'll come running fast enough then.'

Three weeks later, to her great joy and relief, Henriette did precisely that. She gave birth to a fine, healthy boy, Gaston Henri, at Verneuil. 'At last I have finally achieved my aim,' she cried in exultation.

The King sent his physician, La Rivière, to attend his mistress but did not visit himself. Henriette wrote numerous furious letters expressing her displeasure at his neglect. 'Why does he not come? Have I not given him the son he wanted?'

'But sadly too late,' came the reply.

'Nonsense, it is never too late.' Henriette was already secretly dreaming of how this might change everything for her. 'I shall speak to our father and brother on the subject of a legal challenge to the royal marriage. I still have the signed document remember.'

'How could that signify now, since the Queen gave birth first?'

Henriette slapped at her sister's wrist in annoyance. 'Do not be so stupid. This promise of marriage Henry gave to me pre-dates the Italian nuptials. It is as binding as a contract. He was mine *first.*' Even if that son did not survive, this one will. Henriette made a private vow to have her son granted the position he rightly deserved. In order to achieve that, she needed to prove the Italian marriage false. She summoned Father Hilaire, a Capuchin monk she'd met some time ago when he'd acted as a secret agent for the Duke of Savoy.

'I wish you to show this promise of marriage, signed by the King, to His Holiness, and ask if this does not make the royal marriage to the Medici illegal. In which case my son, Henri, would then be the true dauphin, and not the child of the Italian woman. Bring me back proof that this document is binding.'

The moment the monk had left on his mission Henriette again wrote to the King, begging him to come to her. Seeking an excuse to quit the court, Henry came up with the pretext that the Spanish troops in Flanders might be planning a raid on northern France. Queen Elizabeth was at Dover, and it was suggested that the French monarch should cross the Channel to see her while he was at the frontier. But claiming that even Kings are not exempt from seasickness, Henry declined to make the trip. He sent Biron in his place, who was showing some signs of repentance for allying himself with the Duke of Savoy. State affairs thus dealt with, Henry rode quickly across country to Verneuil where he delightedly kissed this second son and dandled him on his knee.

'Is he not a finer child than that of the Queen?' Henriette insisted, purring with pleasure at her own cleverness. 'And all French; not a drop of Italian blood in him.'

'Certainly Louis has the look of a Medici rather than a Bourbon, being dark and plump, and this child is admittedly more handsome. He takes more after me, I think,' decided the King, on a cheerful note of self-flattery.

Part Four

Intrigue and Conspiracy

On 27 October the Dauphin made his public entry into Paris in a sumptuous cradle presented to him by the Grand Duchess of Florence. Marie felt a glow of pride that it had been she who had brought about this blessing upon the French people. Beside her in the open litter sat Madame de Montglât, her son's nurse, who lifted the child in her arms for the cheering crowds to see, some even falling to their knees in homage to the infant prince.

The only cloud over these events arose when Henry had his son's horoscope read. Superstition was always rife about court, with many courtiers having more than a passing interest in magic and sorcery. Catherine de Medici herself had been a well-known exponent of the dark arts. Now some murmured of an earthquake having taken place on the night of the Dauphin's birth. Did this mean that the nation would be plunged into yet more wars and catastrophes?

Seeking reassurance Henry commanded Monsieur de la Rivière, who professed a knowledge in the science of astrology, to draw up an accurate horoscope for little Louis. But as the weeks passed without a response, Henry grew impatient and again summoned the astrologer to his presence, demanding to know what was the cause of this delay.

'Sire,' said La Rivière, clearly shaking with nerves, 'I have abandoned the undertaking as I am reluctant to sport with a science whose secrets I have partially forgotten. And which I have, moreover, frequently found defective.'

Henry was instantly suspicious. 'I am not to be deceived by so idle a pretext. You have no such scruples. More likely you have resolved not to reveal to me what you have ascertained because you fear I should discover the fallacy of your pretended knowledge, or else be angered by your prediction. Whatever may be the cause of your hesitation, I command you, upon pain of my displeasure, to tell me truthfully.'

Still Rivière hesitated, until it became evident that it would be more dangerous to remain silent rather than speak. With reluctance he proceeded to tell what he had discovered. 'Sire, your son will live to manhood and reign longer than yourself. But he will resemble you in no particular. He will indulge his own opinions and caprices, and sometimes those of others. During his rule it will be safer to think than to speak. Ruin threatens your ancient institutions, all your measures will be overthrown. He will accomplish great deeds, be fortunate in his undertakings, and will become the theme of all Christendom. He will have issue, but after his death more heavy troubles will ensue. This is all that you shall know from me, and even this is more than I had proposed to tell you.'

Henry was dismayed by this bleak forecast of his precious son's life – not at all what he had hoped for – and coldly responded, 'I dare say you allude to the Huguenots, but I assume you only talk thus because you have their interests, and mine, at heart.'

'Interpret my meaning as you wish, Sire, you shall learn nothing more from me.' And so saying, the astrologer sketched a bow and hastily withdrew.

When Donna Leonora brought news of the birth to the Queen, as well as the King's reaction to it, Marie wept bitter tears of disappointment. 'How dare Henry prefer his mistress's child to our own precious dauphin?'

'There is more, Your Majesty. Thanks to the contacts I have made in the household of La Marquise, I have learned that the she-cat is plotting to have the royal marriage annulled on the grounds that it is illegal. She has commissioned Father Hilaire to journey to Rome and seek an audience with the Pope.'

Marie felt as if her heart might explode with anger and at once sought advice from various lawyers and canons. Their answers were far from reassuring. If the King's marriage were brought into question by His Eminence, and ultimately found to be invalid, the Dauphin's legitimacy would indeed be in doubt.

'I need help, Leonora,' she cried. 'Bring me Rosny.'

The minister was equally anxious to be rid of the Marchioness de Verneuil, fully realizing that there would be no peace in the royal household so long as Henry's infatuation for this dangerous woman continued.

'You can safely leave this matter to me, Your Majesty. The Marquise will never prove her case as this is not the first time the King has written such a letter. In fact, he tends to make a habit of it, and all have proved worthless. Nevertheless, you were right to call me, and we will take no chances. I shall dispatch Villeroy with all speed and order him to apprehend Father Hilaire before he has the opportunity to do any damage. I will also contact Cardinal d'Ossat, who protects our interests in Rome, and warn him of what is afoot. Do not fear, Madame de Verneuil will not succeed in her quest.'

Marie went next to see the King to inform him of what she had learned. 'That woman, your paramour, is threatening to declare our royal marriage illegal. She thrives on intrigue, and dares to attempt to disinherit our son.'

'Pray do not excite yourself, my love. You are but recently recovered from childbirth.'

'My health is just fine, thank you. Nor have I lost my wits and know when I am being threatened. This woman means mischief and should be charged with treason against the crown.' By the time she had related the full details even Henry could not deny a very real concern.

He was aware that he was far too tolerant of Henriette's moods and foibles, her sharp tongue and soaring ambition. Sometimes he ached to release himself from her spell, but she need only cast him a scorching glance from those bewitching green eyes and he was again in thrall. He could see now that it had been foolish of him to write her that promise. Although such a letter had never rebounded upon him so badly before, and he was a man who needed peace about him, not warring women. Why could he never achieve that? But if she was pressing His Holiness to intercede on her behalf the situation was more serious than he had realized. 'I will speak with her on the matter,' he promised Marie.

'Soon?'

'Without delay.'

As always with matters involving emotions and marital dispute, Henry shut the problem from his mind, hoping it would resolve itself without any action on his part. But Rosny soon brought him news that Father Hilaire had indeed been granted an audience with His Eminence, and Henry could ignore the matter no longer.

'Fortunately the Cardinal intervened and had him incarcerated in an Italian monastery in order to prevent him from returning to France with whatever advice he had gained from the Pope,' Rosny explained.

Henry groaned. Why was he ever beset by intrigue? 'Tell all. I need to hear the full tale.'

'The wily monk did attempt to escape but was apprehended by Villeroy, who was in regular communication with d'Ossat. The fellow was arrested and interrogated by the Papal Nuncio.'

'Was Henriette implicated?' The King asked the question with great trepidation, fearing the worst.

Rosny spared him nothing. 'Indeed she was, Sire. Father Hilaire was to inform her that the Marquise might choose her time and bring a suit for annulment, or await your death and claim her rights then, along with those of her son. Or else she could aim to take the place of Queen Marie, should she die in childbirth.'

'Dear Lord, she has betrayed me.'

Henry faced his mistress, his expression grim as he informed her of all that he had learned.

Damping down her terror over the discovery of this intrigue, Henriette faced him with stubborn pride blazing in her eyes. 'Of what am I accused? This is but court gossip which the Queen has spread against me. You have no proof.'

He regarded his mistress with sadness in his heart. 'Among Hilaire's belongings were found two compromising letters written by yourself. And letters from lawyers assuring the monk that my royal union with Queen Marie de Medici should be declared null and void. Does that not smack of treachery?'

Henriette fell to her knees, realizing her cause was lost. 'I would never hurt you, my lord.'

Cupping her lovely face between his gentle palms he kissed her forehead. 'Dear heart, I know you would never *mean* to hurt me, but this is a bad business. I cannot imagine why you felt the necessity to take such measures. Did you not trust me to protect and care for our son? However, you must always remember that Louis is the legitimate dauphin, and no letter I gave to you can ever change that fact.'

'But I am dishonoured. I lay with you only because of that promise of marriage. And you were mine *first!*'

'And if you had given me little Henri at that time, before I was married, it would have been a different matter, but sadly that did not happen. The storm took our poor child and we cannot go back and change that fact. We – *you* – must accept the reality of your situation.'

She crumpled and fell to the ground in a storm of tears. He had meant to be angry with her, to upbraid her for her mischief and interference, but nothing upset him more than to see a woman weep. Besides, fearing she might make the letter public and use it against him, it was essential he keep her content. Somehow he had to persuade her to return it. It meant no more than the one he had given to Corisande all those years ago. Why could she not see that? Lifting her in his arms Henry carried her to the bed.

'There, there, dear heart, do not upset yourself. We can still love each other. I shall still care for you and visit you.' He kissed her mouth, her throat, the soft curve of her breasts spilling out above her silk gown.

'But how can you come to me every night, as I so long for you to do, when the Queen keeps you close at court and I am stuck out here in the country. Life is so dull and lonely without you. You will soon forget me and find another mistress to please you.'

'Never, my sweet. You are my only one,' Henry assured her with the glibness of long practice. Her body was soft and warm against his, her breasts full and ripe for love. His need for her was consuming him, becoming ever more urgent by the second. Pushing up her skirts he thrust himself into her without preamble. Taking her whenever they had quarrelled always added a certain dash of excitement and danger to their lovemaking. And she was never more eager, more imaginative than when she most wanted to please him.

Afterwards, their differences forgotten, or at least set aside, Henry made her another promise. 'You shall again have rooms at the Louvre so that I may visit you whenever I choose, and no one, not even the Queen, will prevent us being together. And that, dear heart, is a promise I *can* keep.'

Henriette had the sense to realize it was the best she could hope for in the circumstances. At least for the present.

When she heard that Rosny's attempts to rid them of La Marquise had failed, Marie was filled with despair. The she-cat's scheming had resulted in reward rather than chastisement and punishment. To add insult to injury, following the delivery of her own son, Madame de Verneuil had moved back into the Louvre, leaving the Queen feeling let down and humiliated.

'I will not have your mistress treated with the same consideration that you give to your queen. I insist that you remove her.'

Henry made a feeble attempt to dismiss her hurt feelings with a pat on the hand and a soft chuckle, calling her his dear wife and telling her not to fret. But Marie remained adamant and at length the King wearied of the argument and agreed to remove her. He did not, however, as Marie had hoped, banish La Marquise back to the country, but instead installed her in the magnificent Hôtel de Soissons, which his sister Catherine had once occupied. He also paid a large sum each month towards her expenses, despite constantly crying poverty.

It seemed that the position of the King's *maîtresse-en-titre* had been elevated still further, despite an intrigue that surely amounted to treason. And just as Marie's mother Joanna had suffered by the constant presence of her father's Venetian mistress, Bianca Cappello, so would her own marriage be equally blighted.

Marie was even more distraught when, some weeks later, Henry announced that in future all his children, those of Gabrielle d'Estrées, Henriette d'Entragues, the Dauphin, and any further royal children, would share a nursery.

'It is too much to bear, you cannot do this to me,' Marie stormed. She was feeling increasingly vulnerable, as if her wishes were not even taken into consideration. 'Have you no heart, no sensitivity?'

Henry seemed dumbfounded by her reaction. 'Where is the harm? They are but children, and I, as their father, wish to see them as often as possible. It is no fault of theirs that I am also a king and therefore restricted by court duties. It will be far more convenient to have them in one place where I can slip in to see them whenever I have a few moments free.'

'But *my* child is the only legal heir,' Marie railed, stamping her foot in vexation. 'He is Louis, a Prince of the Blood.'

'I am naturally delighted to have two new sons, and in such a short time, but I trust Louis will never deny his half-siblings. What of César and Alexandre, and his sister Catherine, Gabrielle's charming little daughter? Do they not deserve love and care? I may not always be the wisest, or most constant of husbands, but do I not love all my children equally?'

Marie recognized by that certain glint in his eye that she would never persuade him to change his mind. The King's will would prevail.

The morale of the court had been so raised by the safe deliverance of a dauphin that the winter passed in a whirl of celebrations. The Queen, having made a full recovery following the birth, appeared in the royal ballet as Venus. She led little César de Vendôme, attired as Cupid, by the hand, enjoying every moment.

'Have you ever before seen so fine a squadron?' Henry proudly remarked, smiling to see his consort's happiness restored.

The only irritation, since Marie had been compelled to accept the woman's presence at court, was that the King's mistress also took part. It was perfectly plain that La Marquise was arrogantly determined not to be ousted from her position as favourite. Nor did she hesitate to comment on everything and everyone, at times even daring to criticize the Queen.

'That gown does nothing to flatter Her Majesty. Why, she looks almost frumpish. At least I have kept my slender figure following the birth, unlike the Medici who grows fatter by the hour. It is very clear to me why Henry married her. She is naught but his fat banker.'

Pretending not to hear, Marie sauntered away to speak with her friend, the Duchess of Guise. No matter how much these remarks distressed her she could do nothing but watch and smile as best she may, helpless to defend herself. For some reason the King never seemed to see the worst in anyone, certainly not that she-cat.

Later, Donna Leonora brought yet more malicious gossip to

the Queen's ear. 'Your Majesty, La Marquise is saying that the Dauphin isn't the King's child. This latest outrageous statement was apparently spoken loud enough for many of the courtiers taking part in the ballet to hear.'

Marie felt the blood drain from her face. This was too much. She could tolerate no more.

The following morning as they lay in bed together after their usual lovemaking, Marie quietly sipping her chocolate, she gathered all her courage, took a deep breath, and spoke of this latest mischief to the King. 'Are you aware, Sire, of how my rival is challenging the legality of our marriage, as well as the legitimacy of our son, the Dauphin?'

'Nonsense, I do not believe La Marquise would be guilty of such an absurd assumption.'

'I have it on good authority.'

Henry inwardly sighed, wishing his queen could simply accept his wishes and leave the subject of his mistress alone, or that his mistress could practise more restraint. But then she would not be the exciting Henriette who so fascinated him if she did. 'Gossip is rife in court circles. You should have more self-respect than to listen to the idle tittle-tattle of eavesdroppers and sycophants. You indulge your followers too much, and, encouraged by your credulity, they have become the scourge of this court. You would do well to dismiss them before I lose patience and return them whence they came.'

This threat gave Marie pause for thought. The prospect of losing Donna Leonora could not be borne, yet she surely had a right to be treated with proper respect and dignity. She was the Queen. Swallowing the tears that had lodged in her throat, she tried again. 'It is not *I* who spins this mischief, I merely repeat to you what is being said. How is it that you chastise the messenger but not the source?'

The King nibbled on a brioche, pretending not to hear.

'Henry?' she prodded, quietly setting down her dish of chocolate on the bedside table. 'This will not do. I am your wife, a mother, and a queen, and I have been insulted, the legitimacy of my son questioned and my dignity compromised. May I at least ask that you make it clear to Madame la Marquise that Louis is most definitely *your* son too.'

There was a short pause before he answered in the mildest

tones. 'I am told that you have a fond preference for your cousin, the Duke de Bracciano, that you once considered him as a husband.'

Marie sat up abruptly in the bed to glare at him in utter shock, appalled by the implication behind his words. 'Who dares to accuse me of such a calumny? No, do not tell me, I can guess. Yet more malice from that woman's vicious tongue! My cousin the Duke will arrive soon, and you can ask him yourself. He will tell you it is a wicked lie.'

'And why would I believe him?'

'Because he is a man of honour,' Marie snapped, furious that he should take her guilt for granted.

Henry half turned away from her with a weary sigh. 'I have seen too many men of honour succumb to a woman's charms and lie about it. In any case, I have no intention of waiting for the Duke's arrival. We leave for Poitiers later this day.'

Marie was dismayed. 'Oh, but when he gave notice of his visit, you promised me we would wait for him to meet us here, in Blois.'

'I have changed my mind. I now choose not to delay our journey.'

'But he is travelling all the way back from England, so how can he say with any certainty when he might arrive?'

'Bracciano may do as he wishes, I care not.'

Marie could feel herself growing hot with anger. '*I* care. He is my cousin. Then I shall wait for him here myself.'

'No, my queen, you most certainly will not. Such behaviour would only feed the fuel of these so-called rumours still further.'

'Then wait with me, Henry.'

'I have already decreed that we are leaving today.'

Marie lost her temper entirely. 'Is this because Madame la Marquise demands your presence at her château?'

'This has nothing to do with Henriette.'

'I think it does. You are trying to tar me with the same brush. She is soiled, therefore I must be too. That she-cat accuses me of being engaged in a liaison only because she is desperate to convince you that I too am without virtue. I am sick of her rumour and slander, her nasty innuendoes and malicious attempts to destroy our union. I pray you do not judge your queen by your strumpet's deplorable standards.'

Henry's face changed colour. 'I do not care for your choice of language, wife, and how do I know that she does not speak the truth? You have made enough fuss about waiting for your cousin's arrival. Why would I not suspect there is some reason beyond family loyalty?'

'If that is the depth of your opinion of me then I see no help for it, I shall return to Fontainebleau forthwith.' Marie almost went on to say – and you can go to the devil, but stopped herself just in time.

'*Ventre Saint Gris*, you wish only to return to Fontainebleau because you are longing to see Bracciano. You are panting for him. I can hear it in your voice.'

Marie swung round and slapped him across the face. There was a short, horrified silence, then grabbing her by the wrists Henry held her down on the bed, restraining her fury for some moments while Marie wept and sobbed, utterly distraught that he should think so little of her. Then pushing her from him he stormed from the bedchamber calling for his *valet de chambre* and Rosny.

For days afterwards Marie remained in her apartments. She knew Henry would accuse her of sulking but she didn't care. She felt deeply wounded and hurt by his attack, a natural reaction with which Rosny fully sympathized.

'The King makes these charges only out of jealousy. He cares for you, truly he does.'

'I have given him no reason to be jealous. He listens to evil tongues.'

Marie refused to emerge, having her meals brought to her, and keeping all three of Gabrielle's children, and baby Louis, by her side in her seclusion. Meanwhile the King's favourite minister flitted back and forth between the two royal chambers, begging first the King, then the Queen to resolve the dispute, but to no avail.

'I am considering confining the Queen to one of my castles,' Henry coldly informed Rosny. 'In the meantime I shall exile those personages who have formed such a clique about her that they carry every bit of malicious gossip, quite unnecessarily, back to her.'

Rosny was appalled. He loathed La Marquise with a vengeance, and was personally very much on the Queen's side in this matter. As the mother of Prince Louis of France, their precious dauphin, she was above reproach in his eyes. It had been a bad mistake on the King's part not to banish La Marquise from court, particularly after the Father Hilaire intrigue. Henry's soft heart and love of women was ever a flaw in his pragmatic nature. Now his over-ambitious mistress was starting a whispering campaign against the infant dauphin. Was it any wonder if the Queen had taken offence at such a calumnious charge? For the sake of France, Her Majesty must, at all costs, be protected.

'Sire, I counsel patience and moderation. You would do well not to aggravate matters. Your proposal might be feasible if the Queen had no children, but since God has graciously given her a son, beware of committing such folly.'

'She is a difficult, quarrelsome woman,' Henry stormed.

'A woman of spirit, certainly, one able to stand up for herself in what she finds to be most trying circumstances.' Rosny struggled to disguise the admiration in his tone.

'That harlot's insolence is beyond bearing,' Marie was even now saying to her stalwart companion. 'Why does the King see no wrong in *her*, and force *me* to endure her constant presence?'

'He can refuse her nothing,' Donna Leonora agreed, still managing with consummate skill to remain on friendly terms with the King's mistress whilst giving every impression of remaining loyal to her own. 'The latest rumour is that her half-brother, the Comte d'Auvergne, is working with Biron to form a new league which reportedly has many grievances. They are said to be against the charter of Huguenot liberty, urging citizens not to pay the latest levy, and they are growing in strength daily. I believe the King has been informed but has chosen, as yet, to do nothing.'

'Auvergne is weak and overambitious,' Marie scoffed. 'And no doubt out for revenge for the supposed slight against his sister when Henry chose to marry *me*, a royal princess, rather than that cheap trollop.'

Donna Leonora continued to brush the Queen's luscious brown hair, calming her by the measured strokes, as always. Best to keep off the painful subject of La Marquise, she decided. 'Monsieur

Biron is certainly boastful of his influence and power with foreign potentates. Concini tells me that the Marshal is now conniving with Spain as well as Savoy.'

'I think we should take care, dear friend, that we do not help to spread these dangerous rumours. I have no wish to upset the King further.'

At length, thanks to the patient auspices of Rosny and his good wife, the Queen was persuaded to continue with the royal progress to Poitiers, and the King grumpily accepted that he had no just cause for jealousy.

So it was that in April the court left Paris and removed to Fontainebleau. Finally losing patience the King instructed Rosny, together with Villeroy and Bellièvre, to investigate the intrigue concerning Marshal Biron. Being naturally austere the minister had quickly grown tired of the banquets and revels, and was more than ready to put his time to better use. The investigation took some weeks, but the outcome was that incriminating documents were found that appeared to prove Biron's connivance with Spain and Savoy, which was surely evidence of high treason.

'Can I trust no one, not even my once most loyal supporter?' Henry mourned to the Queen. 'Rosny urges me to arrest all the perpetrators of this alleged crime. He tells me that the Sieur de La Fin, the former agent of the Duke of Savoy, has confessed, yet the Marshal continues to prate his innocence. Can I trust his word or no? What is the truth of this?'

Hating to see the King so dejected, particularly now they were again reconciled, Marie made a tentative suggestion. 'Why do you not ask him?'

Henry looked at her in some surprise. 'As always, my love, you give good counsel. Why do I not?'

Marie was delighted. Loving Henry as she did, it was a relief to be of genuine assistance to her husband for once, and after being so sorely tried with the goings-on of La Marquise.

Biron was summoned to Fontainebleau. Bowing low he kissed the King's hand, and Henry felt so deeply moved to see his old friend again that he embraced him. 'You have done well to come, *mon ami.*'

Dismissing his attendants Henry grasped him about the shoulder in that familiar way of his, and begged him to tell all. 'Confide in me, my friend. If you disguise nothing I give you my royal word that I will, with all my heart, accord you a free pardon.'

With barely suppressed irritation Biron haughtily denied any wrongdoing. 'In short, Sire, I am not here to justify myself, but to learn from you who are my accusers. That is the sole object of my journey.'

The Marshal continued to profess his innocence in the days and weeks following, quite certain that La Fin had already destroyed all documentary evidence against him. Too late he realized this was not the case, but his attempt to flee only resulted in his arrest and incarceration in the Bastille, of which Rosny was now governor. In July, Marshal Biron was tried and found guilty of high treason. Falling on his knees before his accusers he fiercely denied any part in a plot to have the King assassinated.

'False!' he cried. 'Efface that charge.'

His defence was that he had sought only marriage with a daughter of the Duke of Savoy. No one believed him. Henry wept when he heard the news, but could do nothing to save his erstwhile friend and comrade.

Marie courageously attempted to intercede, suggesting His Majesty might at least spare the traitor's life.

'Madame, I have too great an affection for you and your son to grant your request. I cannot leave in the heart of my realm so sharp a thorn, when I have the power to extract such.'

For all her deep sympathy and longing to ease her husband's pain, Marie understood. Should anything untoward happen to the King, then her own position, and that of the Dauphin, might be put at peril by such an intrigue.

The Marshal was led at last to the scaffold, still proclaiming his innocence, where he resisted to the last the efforts of the executioner to remove his head. All dignity and arrogance gone, he tore off the blindfold time and time again, suffering a pitiful and ignominious end to his ambitions.

The charges against Auvergne were weak, as was the man himself. But Henriette was in a lather of fury that they should have been brought at all. 'My brother is not a traitor!' she screamed at the King. 'I cannot bear to see him imprisoned in that grim fortress, the Bastille. Every time I visit him he looks more shrunken, as if he is dying before my eyes.'

'Dear heart, your brother was spared the ordeal of a trial with Biron. I agreed to exempt him, as an indulgence to you, until proof positive of his guilt has been found. But sooner or later he must face his accusers. If he is innocent he has nothing to fear.'

Throwing herself at his feet Henriette burst into floods of tears, for once genuine. 'You know that is not true. You must save him. He is my *brother*! If you loved me you would have him released.'

Henry stifled a sigh. 'I must indeed love you, otherwise I would not tolerate these endless tantrums. And if he is innocent, why did he attempt to flee?'

'Because he is a fool. If he lent his name to this intrigue it is because he understood little of its aims. He was a milksop in the hands of the clever marshal. Reckless, yes, and light-minded, but not with any evil intent. Rather he is young and weak. Grant him audience, I beg you, Sire. Listen to what he has to say.'

When the Count stood before his sovereign, Henriette beside him as support, his first words did nothing to reassure Henry of the young man's innocence.

'Sire, as the price for my liberation, if you would allow me to continue my relations with Spain I would willingly divulge the plots and secrets of the cabinet of Madrid to Your Majesty.'

Henry looked at him with disdain. 'You would wish me to allow you to be a traitor twice over? Or do you choose to spy for both Spain and for France?'

Henriette hastily intervened. 'My brother is but offering you his loyal services. He would reveal nothing of your own plans to Spain. You can trust him in that.'

'Is that so? He has proved himself to be trustworthy, has he?'

Henry's glance quelled her and she stepped back, suitably chastened. Henriette was beginning to learn that you could push this king only so far.

'All I ask,' Auvergne continued with growing confidence, 'is that Your Majesty demonstrates neither surprise nor anger over my liaison with the Spanish ambassador, nor seize certain packages which may from time to time be transported from Madrid.'

'I think you ask a great deal,' Henry said, unable to disguise the contempt he felt for the Count. The man's arrogance was offensive, his proposition outrageous. He deserved to lose his head for that alone. Yet Henry kept reminding himself that this foolish half-brother of his mistress was a Valois, the son of Charles IX by Marie Touchet, and the uncle of his own children by Henriette. 'The machinations of the Spanish cabinet can be dangerous,' he reminded him. 'They are not to be taken on lightly.'

'Therefore, would it not serve Your Majesty well to have me accepted there, to give me leave to correspond with Spain?'

Henry pardoned Auvergne. He found he did not have the stomach to see the young idiot lose his head. And if that was partly because he realized he would then lose the heart and favour of his fascinating sister, so be it. He would take the risk.

The following year Henriette was again *enceinte*, and the Queen gave birth to a daughter. Marie was so disappointed that she burst into tears and refused to even look at the child.

'Take her away,' she told Madame de Montglât, the children's nurse. 'I was assured by the seers that I would bear three sons. The King will despise me for this failure.'

'I'm sure His Majesty will be delighted.'

And indeed, when Henry came, he took the newborn princess in his arms and kissed and cuddled her with great affection before carrying her to the Queen. 'My love, let us thank God for the blessing of this daughter.'

'A boy would be of greater value,' Marie wept.

'How so? Did not your own mother give birth to a fine daughter who became Queen of France?' he teased. 'Daughters are necessary to royal houses in order to form foreign alliances. Now what shall we call this one? Elizabeth, I think, after the great queen of England. And our little princess too will one day be a great queen. Now kiss her, my love.'

Marie obediently took her daughter in her arms to kiss her at the King's bidding, and instantly fell in love with the child. 'You are so good to me,' she told him, her tears now sparkling with joy.

The King was attentive, even loving, and she had proved herself fecund. Perhaps she would produce a son next time. Marie was content.

But she remained troubled by the constant presence of La

Marquise. Every now and then Leonora would bring her titbits of gossip, saying that the she-cat was secretly receiving Bellegarde, or some other *chevalier*. Marie drank it all in, would sometimes suggest to Henry that his *maîtresse-en-titre* was not so faithful to him as she might appear. But without exception he always laughed off such charges, which was immensely frustrating.

Marie knew that her own constant jealousy often resulted in her appearing cold and somewhat haughty. Had not her own mother suffered from a similar trait? It was but hurt pride and wounded feelings, yet she must do her utmost to guard against this tendency, however justified.

Henriette was beginning to feel a little less secure. Her attempts to further the interests of her own treasured son had met with failure, which was a great disappointment to her. It may well amuse the people of Paris to have the King's wife and his mistress pregnant at the same time, but of what benefit was it to her? She even noticed a slight change in Henry's attitude towards her. He visited her less often when she was in this condition, which was deeply worrying. Henriette resolved to improve her situation.

'Even if we cannot marry, I beg you, Sire, to at least legitimize our son. You could remove the stigma of his birth.'

'And would you then return my promise of marriage?' Henry had hoped to put an end to this issue years ago, never having expected it to be a problem in the first place, since he'd most carefully put a time limit of six months on his promise to wed her. Unfortunately, he'd not insisted that the child live, and Henriette was growing increasingly stubborn on the matter. If he removed the stigma of birth on her second son, would that not make her even more demanding?

Henriette cast him a teasing glance. 'One day, when I feel sufficiently secure.'

Two months after the Queen's accouchement on 21 January 1603, she gave birth to a daughter. The child was christened Gabrielle Angelique, the names again chosen by the King. Three days before the birth, Henry instructed Parliament to register letters patent to legitimize her brother, Gaston Henri. He also promised Henriette that this child too would later be granted the same benefit.

But this was not enough for Henriette. She was beginning to think that it was time to look for a husband.

'Who will you choose?' asked Auvergne.

'I was thinking of the Prince de Joinville. We once enjoyed a short *affaire*. In fact, he offered for my hand but the King would not hear of it.'

Auvergne was almost salivating with excitement. 'Joinville is of the House of Lorraine, a Prince of the Blood, which would make you a Princess, sister. Should I speak with him on the matter?'

Henriette gave her catlike smile. 'I shall write him a letter which you can deliver for me.'

Many letters were exchanged between the pair. Joinville was at first cautious, having been rejected once already, but it did not take long before he was entirely smitten by her charms and again offering for her hand. He begged an audience with the King in order to seek permission.

Henry was not amused. Overwhelmed with a fierce jealousy he glared at the young prince, rejecting his request with the same resolve he'd once used against Bellegarde when the Grand Equerry had pressed his suit to marry Gabrielle d'Estrées. That unfortunate young man had found himself banished from court for the crime of falling in love with a woman the King desired. Was history about to repeat itself?

'You get above yourself, sir. Did you not learn your lesson when I stopped your fight with that troublesome knave, Bellegarde? Be warned, I will not tolerate interference in my affairs. Find yourself another wife to espouse.'

The Prince de Joinville had more sense than to challenge the King, and gracefully withdrew his suit. But having been rejected a second time, he took out his disappointment by indulging in an affair with Juliette. She was the sister of the late Gabrielle d'Estrées, and almost as beautiful. He soon forgot all about Henriette.

In truth, Henry cared little about whether or not Henriette was married. A husband could be useful if a mistress was reluctant to succumb to his charms, or he had grown tired of her. The King asked only that the marriage be in name only for as long as he desired the wife in question. But this particular union would bring Henriette uncomfortably close to the crown, perhaps handing her too much power. Worse, it could detrimentally affect Henry's private life. He suspected that were he to agree, Joinville might well insist on becoming a husband in every way, and Henriette would be obliged to withdraw from court. Such a prospect did not bear contemplating.

'I would never abandon you,' Henriette said, attempting to reassure the King when she found her cleverly laid plans again falling to dust. 'It is *you* that I love, but I must needs have protection for my children, and for my future when you fall out of love with me.'

'I shall never do that,' Henry smoothly insisted, as he was wont to do with all his mistresses. 'You are everything to me.'

Irritating and meddling though she might be, he needed her. And fond as he was of his wife, Marie was turning into a veritable harpy, constantly complaining and nagging him about La Marquise. On more than one occasion he'd been driven to leave her bed in order to avoid yet another lengthy lecture. Why could she not learn to turn a blind eye? No, no, he needed the excitement that Henriette had to offer, her indiscretions still fascinated him, and she still set his pulses racing despite the risks she presented, or perhaps that sense of danger only added to his pleasure. Whatever the reason, he would keep La Marquise exclusively for himself, and well away from the crown.

Henry had hoped to keep this latest concession private, but the Queen's spies were too clever for him, and Marie was again furious, entirely forgetting her resolve to remain calm and controlled, and not allow the she-cat to upset her. 'You are so weak! Why can you not learn that the harlot is manipulating you? How could you think to legitimize her son when you are not, and never will be, married to her.'

The very lectures and storms that Henry so dreaded started all over again, the royal couple's brief harmony utterly destroyed. How he longed for domestic peace, but his wife's tongue was becoming almost as sharp as that of Henriette's. Was any man more plagued than he? He felt at a loss to know how to pacify and silence his irate and nagging consort.

'If only I could find some way to separate the she-cat from

the tabby,' Marie cried, wringing her hands in anguish after Henry had hastily withdrawn.

'An opportunity will arise to rid us of La Marquise, I am sure of it,' Donna Leonora consoled her. The Italian had no further need of her former co-conspirator, not now that she had achieved her object. She'd married Concini, and the pair of them had been granted the promotion they'd both desired. All that mattered now was the security of her beloved mistress, for in that lay her own.

Some short while later, when the Queen was convalescing at Fontainebleau, a young woman called, begging leave for an audience, claiming she possessed information which may be of interest.

'May I remind Your Majesty, in case you have forgotten, that I am Juliette, the sister of Gabrielle d'Estrées, now the Duchesse de Villars, and I too have no reason to like La Marquise, for reasons we will not go into.'

Marie accurately guessed that the young woman had hoped to take her sister's place on Gabrielle's death, until Henriette had stepped in. Yet Marie was not against a little intrigue which might successfully pluck this thorn from her side. 'And what is it you have to say to me?'

'Some letters have come into my possession which I considered so shocking that I brought them to you with all speed. It is for Your Majesty to decide how best to deal with them.'

'What kind of letters?' Marie remained cautious, not wishing to commit herself to any idle remark which, in this court of wagging ears, might be relayed back to the King by some circuitous route or other.

'Love letters, Your Majesty, between La Marquise and the Prince de Joinville. I confess he and I have enjoyed a short dalliance and he boastingly showed them to me. Your Majesty will no doubt be aware that he had ambitions to marry Henriette, and these documents speak of their love for each other. Some, I should warn you, also contain remarks by Madame de Verneuil about Your Majesty, which are less than complimentary.' Juliette handed them over.

Marie felt a rush of heat to her cheeks as she read the letters, but it was joy not embarrassment which caused the colour to rise. This was the very material she needed to blunt the she-cat's claws once and for all. She handed the documents back. 'It is your duty to take them to the King.'

Juliette paled. 'Oh, but will His Majesty not be angry?'

'I'm sure he will not blame you. And it is not for me to decide on such matters. The King should be told.'

Still the younger woman hesitated. 'I would not wish there to be repercussions for members of the Prince's family, for Mademoiselle de Guise, his sister, whom Your Majesty is so fond of. I beg Your Majesty not to reveal to her my interference in this matter. Were she to discover my part in it, she may seek vengeance.' Juliette trembled at the prospect of upsetting so great a house as that of the Princes of Lorraine. Confronting the King with evidence of his mistress's infidelity had not been part of the plan.

Marie smiled and offered her hand. 'It shall be our little secret.'

Rosny championed the Queen in every respect, and, forewarned, he brought the lovely young woman before the King. 'The Duchesse de Villars, Sire, seeking an audience.'

Henry was intrigued. With Christmas and the festivities of New Year long since behind him, he had repaired to Paris to confer about problems that had arisen in Metz. The deputy-governor had been obliged to lock himself into the citadel, where he was under siege from the citizens who for some reason had taken up arms against him. A visit from a young, beautiful woman would certainly enliven a long, dull day. Besides, he had a fondness for pretty young women, and at one time had felt an attraction to this one in particular. Until he had met her sister, that is, his darling Gabrielle. How he missed his angel, and how different she had been from Henriette, so much easier to live with. But her sister too was beautiful. His curiosity piqued, the King readily agreed to meet her privately in the side chapel of the church of Saint Germain l'Auxerrois.

Having swept a deep curtsey, Juliette hastily embarked upon a lengthy affirmation of her family's loyalty to the crown. 'But the obligations which my family owe to Your Majesty prevent me from witnessing unmoved a deceitful outrage.'

Henry frowned, dejection at once setting in as he sensed trouble. 'Of what deceitful outrage do you refer?'

Juliette answered by handing the letters to the King. Dropping another curtsey, she quickly withdrew.

It took a matter of minutes for Henry to learn the unpleasant truth, and he called sharply for Rosny. 'Do you know of this?'

Rosny professed ignorance, even though the matter had been fully explained to him by the Queen.

'These documents suggest that La Marquise sees the Prince de Joinville.' He thrust the papers into the minister's hands. 'Learn the truth of this rumour, and let me know what you find.'

Henry was beside himself with anger and jealousy. 'I have been too lenient with her, too forgiving, and this is how she repays me.'

'Sire, pray keep your composure. Perhaps you should hear what Madame de Verneuil, and Joinville, have to say on this matter before making up your mind to condemn them as guilty.'

'What could she possibly say in her own defence?' growled the King. 'Her tongue is so clever that she would easily prove herself right and I to be wrong. Nevertheless, I will repair at once to the Hôtel de Soissons and confront her with this evidence.'

Henriette lifted her chin in defiance and denied, absolutely, all charges. 'How can you accuse me? I am innocent. Do you still not believe how very much I love you? These are all lies, false documents no doubt forged by the Prince's own hand.'

'Why would he go to such lengths to discredit you if there was no affair?'

Henriette thought quickly. 'Because even though I refused him, he still wanted me. He would stop at nothing to take revenge for my twice having rejected him, even to making Your Majesty appear a cuckold.'

Henry scowled. 'Take care what you say.'

Henriette was too angry, and too desperate, to choose her words with care. 'As for the Duchesse de Villars, she would willingly be his messenger. Madame Juliette has always resented me for winning your favour because she wanted Your Majesty for herself. But she would not risk your royal displeasure without the consent and connivance of the Queen.'

The King's expression hardened, the usually merry eyes turning ice cold. Aware suddenly of the risks she ran in challenging her sovereign, let alone a Prince of the Blood, a son of the influential Guise, Henriette quickly tempered her accusation. 'What else am I to surmise? I swear I have never written any love letters to the Prince de Joinville. Why do you not instruct Rosny to investigate the matter, and whatever he discovers, I will abide by it.'

Without another word, Henry strode from the house.

The moment the King had gone Henriette ran to find her brother, and quickly informed him of what had occurred. 'Find Joinville, and beg him to insist the letters are mere forgeries, written by Juliette d'Estrées out of revenge. Tell him to stick to this tale or we are both done for.'

Once more the Prince faced the ire of his monarch. Henry listened largely in silence to the story that Joinville had never written such letters, that he had not only abandoned his suit to marry the Marquise, but had indulged in an unfortunate affair with the Duchesse de Villars, and by rejecting her, had incited her wrath.

'Am I expected to believe in your innocence?'

'I speak true, Sire.'

The King read the report submitted by Rosny into the case, then interviewed several family members of the House of Lorraine, including his brother the Duc de Guise, and the Prince's grandmother, Madame de Nemours.

'Behold your prodigal, Madame, who has been guilty of innumerable follies.'

'He is but young still,' the old lady gently pointed out, feeling the full brunt of the King's ire. 'And foolish. He will grow in wisdom, given time.'

'If time he is allowed,' Henry coldly responded.

Rosny stepped quickly forward to quietly whisper in the King's ear. 'Sire, infidelity is not an offence against the crown. The boy has not committed treason.'

Henry drew in a sharp breath at this interruption, but then let it out slowly, attempting to ease his temper, for the minister spoke naught but the truth. 'Because Monsieur de Rosny intercedes for him, and because of my great regard for you, Madame, I shall treat him as a boy and pardon him. This time. But you will answer for his prudence.'

The young Prince was banished from court, his brother and grandmother undertaking to guarantee his good conduct. Joinville found the old castle at Dampierre lacking in the comforts to which he was accustomed, but once he had cooled his heels a little the King sent him off on campaign to Hungary, which did not please him any greater. But at least he had escaped incarceration in the Bastille.

The Duchess de Villars received a *lettre de cachet* and found herself banished to a distant château. She too was thankful to escape a worse fate, as the whole matter had run completely beyond her control.

Henriette, sunk in deep depression, shut herself up in her Hôtel and continued to swear her innocence. 'This is all a fabrication on the King's part, devised out of jealousy to prevent me marrying Joinville.' And although Henry called frequently, hammering on the door, she absolutely refused to admit him, swearing she would take herself off to a nunnery if he dared to suggest, or even to think her guilty of betraying him.

Henry felt bereft. Had he successfully quashed a dangerous affair, or simply made himself appear a jealous fool? Either way his life was certainly the poorer without the sensual titillations Henriette had provided.

Rosny, as always, came to Henry's rescue. In a bid to lift the King's spirits, he made a suggestion. 'You would do well, Sire, to ride out and quell the rebellion in Metz yourself. Take Her Majesty with you. You know how much you like company on a campaign, and the change of air would do you both good.'

Henry approved the idea. 'Well said, Rosny. I could call upon my sister in Nancy afterwards. See how she fares, if her health has improved.'

Marie was thrilled at the prospect, and could think of nothing better than spending some time alone with her husband, leaving the she-cat behind at court to brood.

'We shall be all in all to one another,' she said, clapping her hands in delight at the news. 'And I shall be delighted to see Catherine again.'

Marie greatly enjoyed her stay with Catherine, the two women sharing their domestic tribulations and their needlework with equal fervour. 'I envy you your ability to bear children,' Catherine confided. 'I thought for a time that I was *enceinte*, but sadly I was mistaken. I have a malady – dropsy, the physicians call it. I'm a great disappointment to my husband as I will not even accept his religion, let alone provide him with an heir.' She smiled, but there was a bitter sadness behind her careless words. 'How fortunate you are, dear sister.'

Marie saw that perhaps she was luckier than she had realized, having her two darling babies, and warmly embraced the other woman. 'You must do as your conscience bids, and you cannot be blamed for any failing in your health.'

'The Duke, my husband, considers me obstinate, accusing me of refusing to take the remedies which might help to produce a child, because it would be brought up a Catholic. As if I would go to such extremes simply in order to keep my faith? Do I not ache to hold a child of my own in my arms? Men have to blame someone, and it is never themselves. But enough of me, how does my brother?'

Marie gave a wry smile. 'He does not change. He is a good king, the people love him as he thinks always of what is right for France, far more so than his predecessors. His latest scheme is to encourage the rearing of silkworms for the silk industry. He is taking over entire chambers at Fontainebleau to hatch eggs, and also Queen Margot's château in the Bois de Boulogne.'

'Henry was ever one for his enthusiasms,' Catherine remarked, and both women laughed.

'But Marguerite is complaining that if her property is taken over by worms, where could she stay if she came to Paris?'

Catherine raised a questioning brow. 'Is the Queen considering returning to Paris?'

'I trust not,' Marie tartly responded. 'Have I not enough of the King's women to contend with? He has even now made some excuse to return to Paris on the pretext of state affairs. More likely he is paying a call upon Madame de Verneuil.'

But within days a messenger rode breathless into the courtyard at Fontainebleau with the news that the King was ill.

Marie wasted no time and at once rushed to her husband's side. Although he led a full and active life, rising early to walk in the park each morning, riding or hunting every day, Henry was over fifty and the maladies that had troubled him on and off since his younger days now took a greater toll upon his health. On this occasion he'd caught a chill which led to a urological disorder, and the royal physicians were concerned.

'*Mon ami*, I feel so ill that in all probability God is about to summon me,' Henry informed his favourite minister.

Rosny could not hide his anxiety when he relayed this remark to the Queen. She had been seated by his side for some hours, holding his hand while he slept. The minister leaned close to whisper in her ear. 'His Majesty is concerned for the succession, and for the children. There will need to be a regency.'

Marie's gaze flew to his. 'I am ready for whatever task the King deems me worthy.' Henry stirred in his bed, and quickly she kissed his hand. 'My love, you are awake. Are you feeling better?'

'I am marvellously glad of your presence. Seeing you beside me brings singular relief. And Rosny too. Madame, in the event of my demise this is the servant who will serve you and your children best. He knows my affairs, and possesses all my confidence. His temper is hard and austere, and sometimes he speaks more freely than he should, but if you neglect him it will be to the perdition of this crown.'

'I will lay in him a trust to equal your own, dearest. But Henry, pray do not distress yourself with talk of your demise. You must rest and recover your strength.'

Tears rolled down the King's cheeks as he looked at the miniature portrait of his son which lay beside him on the bed. 'Poor little one, evil days are at hand if it be the will of God to take me.'

Marie soothed him, urged him to drink the wine and water she had prepared, then sat with him till he slept again.

'You too should take rest, Your Majesty,' Rosny urged her.

'I do feel rather weary; you will call me if there is any change?'

'Of course.'

Leaving the devoted Rosny by the King's side, Marie retired to her room, attended by Donna Leonora. Later, it was her *dame d'atours* who brought her the news that Madame de Verneuil had arrived. 'La Marquise begs an audience with Your Majesty. Shall I send her away?'

Marie was thoughtful. Were the worst to happen, the she-cat's position in court, the woman's safety and security, and the well-being of her children, would be very much in the Queen's hands. 'No, let us see what she has to say.'

Henriette sank into a deep curtsey before her rival, head low, then brushing aside a stray tear she lifted her lovely face to the Queen's. 'Your Majesty, I am distraught. Is it true what they say that the King is unwell, that he might . . .' It was forbidden to speak of the death of a king, so she left the sentence unfinished.

'The report of the physicians is not unfavourable. We must hope and pray for the best.'

'With all my heart and soul I will do so. Madame, I wish you to know that if in the past I have in any way offended you, it was not my choice so to do. I obey the King's will, as do you. He would not allow me to leave his side for anything.'

Marie said nothing, knowing the woman had used all her wiles to make herself indispensable to Henry's happiness.

'But having said that, I swear I will give you no such offence in future. If Your Majesty will only allow me to remain at court, I will break off my connections with the King.'

The Queen walked to the window to look out across the magnificent gardens, in full bloom in the May sunshine. Much as Henry's condition distressed her, Marie almost smiled to think of the power she now held in her hands. Clearly the she-cat was anticipating the possibility of a regency, perhaps while the King lay too ill to govern. She clearly dreaded the prospect of exile, or that the Queen may seek revenge for past slights. Marie remained silent for some minutes while she considered how best to respond. At her most regal, Marie turned at last to hold out her hand to be kissed. 'Keep your word in this and we will draw a veil over the past, Madame, and proceed anew from here. Better to be the Queen's sister than the King's . . .' Now it was she who left the sentence unfinished, but the unspoken, vile word, hung between them like a dark shadow.

Biting back the sharp rejoinder she would so love to have given, Henriette kissed the proffered royal ring, and after a second deep abeyance, silently withdrew. Difficult as it had been to humble herself before Henry's fat wife, she must think of her children's future.

But nothing and no one, certainly not an ambitious queen, would prevent her from fighting to have her beloved Henri rise to the position he deserved, no matter how long it might take.

Meanwhile, in the King's chamber, Henry was expressing his concerns on the very same subject to Henriette's brother, Auvergne. 'I do not believe the Queen is a vindictive person, or will seek to persecute your sister, but we must needs make some provision for Henriette in the event of my demise. I give you leave to speak to the Spanish ambassador to request that she be offered the protection of Spain. I shall also ensure that she is granted the Château de Verneuil for herself and the children.'

Auvergne was thoughtful for some moments. Having drawn a piteous picture of the desolation his sister would suffer, in the event of the unspeakable happening, he dare not press further his lack of faith in the Queen's goodwill. Nevertheless, he was unwilling to commit himself to what might be a dangerous assignment.

'Sire, the Bastille has taught me prudence. In the event of such a calamity to which you allude, and from which we pray God will yet deliver us, the anger of the Queen would focus upon myself, and the entire Balzac family. I would need to prove that I was but obeying your will in this matter. I beg you to grant a written warrant ordering me to carry out the mission.'

Henry was too ill to argue. He had the paper quickly drawn up by his secretary, which he willingly signed, and having now ensured the safety of his wife and children, and that of his *maîtresse-en-titre,* perhaps he might be permitted to concentrate on making peace with his maker.

But when Auvergne returned some days later from making the necessary arrangements with the ambassador, it was to find the King sitting up in bed partaking of a hearty breakfast.

'How glad I am to see you, Auvergne, for the doctors are now telling me that I should make a full recovery.'

The Count was slightly taken aback, having already begun to secretly dream of putting his nephew, young Henri, on to the throne, with himself as regent. 'I am delighted to hear it, Sire, as no doubt you will be relieved to hear that the Spanish ambassador willingly agreed to help you in the delicate matter of which we spoke earlier.'

'Then I shall write a note expressing my gratitude, despite his assistance being no longer required. You may also return to me the document I gave you.'

There was a slight hesitation before Auvergne continued, 'Sire, I understand that Her Majesty is nonetheless to be proclaimed regent and a council of regency nominated, of which Rosny will be president, in the event of such a disaster ever occurring. I beg leave, therefore, to retain the document for the same reasons for which you issued it.'

The King, still not fully recovered, attempted to consider the implications were he to comply with this request. He most certainly wanted Henriette to be safe, were the worst ever to happen. And not even a king was immortal. Nevertheless, he had no wish to incite the ire of his consort. 'I would have no wish for the Queen to hear of the purpose of your visit to the Spanish embassy.'

Auvergne bowed low. 'She shall not hear of it from my lips. I beg you, Sire, to allow me to continue to protect my sister, and my family, as Your Majesty suggested.'

Henry saw no reason not to agree.

He was less happy though when, fully recovered, he again found his mistress's door closed to him.

'I cannot see you! I promised the Queen,' Henriette wailed. She had practically prostrated herself before the Medici woman, and now that the King was fully recovered, the humiliation had proved to be entirely unnecessary.

But Henry was not to be denied entrance. Was he not a man who needed his comforts? 'Do not dare to blame Her Majesty for what is plainly your own perfidy. Where is he?' Henry shouted as he burst through the door on a tide of fury.

'Where is who?'

'Your lover. Bring him out so that I can run him through.'

Henriette cried out as she heard the scrape of metal. But then remembering that on this occasion at least she was innocent, she drew herself up proud before him and looked Henry straight in the eye. 'Search every corner of my house, but you will find no lover hiding in a closet, nor under my bed. Should you do so, then you have leave to run me through with that sword for being so foolish as to betray my dearest love.'

Her words gave him pause, and finally, a satisfactory search having been made, Henry sheathed his weapon and took his mistress to bed. 'I will not be denied you,' he cried, ripping aside her bodice to suckle her breasts.

Hiding a smile of delight, Henriette lifted her skirts and happily broke her promise to the Queen.

Part Five

JEALOUSY AND REVENGE

1604

The scare over the King's health had only increased Henriette's fears about her own situation. If Henry would not grant her permission to marry, then other steps must be taken. She needed security for the future, and for her children. So when one day the Comte de Soissons came asking for her support in a financial project, she snatched at the opportunity. They were both in need of a larger income and the Count intended to request the privilege of levying a small tax on bales of linen cloth at the frontier.

'Is it likely that Henry will grant such an edict?' was the only question Henriette asked.

'Am I not his cousin? Besides, he owes me some recompense for having married his sister off to the Duke of Bar despite her protests of undying love to me, the woman I have loved all my life.'

The King did indeed grant permission, although prudently insisting that Rosny's signature must still be obtained as his favourite minister was in England arranging a treaty. When he returned, the Count told Henriette that Rosny was opposed to the plan and had refused to sign.

'He had the temerity to say that he could not presume to allow such a benefit when the finances of the realm are so embarrassed.'

'How dare he refuse when the King has already given his word?' she furiously retorted. 'The fellow gets above himself.'

'I told him that money has never been grudged to near relatives of a king in the past. Rosny's response was to say that the King's relatives were those persons whom His Majesty *chooses* to acknowledge. Evidently meaning that he has no wish to acknowledge my kinship.'

'I shall speak with him myself on the matter,' Henriette said, with a toss of her abundant curls. 'Rosny will not dare to refuse *me*, as that would risk a fall-out with the King.'

Rosny was about to leave for the Louvre when La Marquise came striding into his room, skirts swishing angrily upon the tiled floor and his secretary scurrying behind in a feeble effort to restrain her.

'Madame?' He sketched a bow only just short of insulting.

Henriette's gaze fixed at once upon a roll of paper in the minister's hand. 'May I know the contents of that document?'

'It relates to an affair in which you bear no small part.' Rosny unrolled it and began to read. 'These are the sums allegedly conceded. However, I have amended them with the true figures.' That such a tax should benefit Soissons, let alone for Madame de Verneuil to take a share of the plunder, was, in the opinion of the prudent minister, quite outrageous.

Henriette met his disapproving glare with audacious impertinence, holding on to her temper with difficulty. 'And what, Monseigneur, are you about to do with that document thus amended?'

'I am even now on my way to the Louvre to make suitable representations to His Majesty.'

'Upon whom would you desire that a king *should* bestow his favours, if not on his relatives and his mistress?'

Rosny bestowed his coldest glance upon this woman whom he loathed even more than he had hated Gabrielle, whose life had ended so tragically and so mysteriously. 'Your remark, Madame, would be reasonable if the King took this money from his privy purse, but to burden poor tradesmen, artisans, labourers and farmers, is without excuse. They, poor creatures, have enough to do to pay tribute to one master, without the burden of relatives and a mistress!' So saying, he rudely abandoned her and left for the Louvre.

When Henriette reported her failure to the Count she over-dramatized the minister's reaction somewhat, as was her way, for added effect. 'Rosny will not sign. He says that the King has too many relatives, and would be glad to be rid of such personages altogether!'

Incensed beyond measure, Soissons requested a further audience with the King and demanded satisfaction.

Henry looked at him askance. 'Are you challenging my minister to a duel?'

'If he is man enough to accept.'

'And how do you know that he made these remarks about you? Who was your informant in this affair?'

'I cannot say, Sire. But the insolence of Rosny was a dishonour to the blood royal. I *will* have satisfaction. At the very least the fellow should be exiled.'

'*Ventre Saint Gris!* Cousin, since you refuse to divulge the name of the person who spread this mischief, then I can only believe what Monsieur de Rosny tells me. What other proof do I have? And his veracity has always been without question in the past.'

Nevertheless, Henry was sufficiently fearful for the life of his favourite minister to take him under royal protection, and confined Soissons to his Hôtel until he agreed to a reconciliation.

Henriette came to Henry the next day in a fine temper. 'Why do you refuse this most modest request? It is not right that a king should go back on his word. You promised!'

'I might ask why you support the Count in this, and not your sovereign?' Henry's jealousy was again aroused.

Henriette tilted her chin in open defiance. 'Do not think to win me round with soft words. I am indifferent to you now. I have promised the Queen that in future I will resist your attentions.'

Henry laughed, and grasping a lock of her wild auburn hair tugged her closer to within inches of his lips. 'You cannot possibly resist me.'

'Indeed I can! If I had my way I would leave for my estate at Verneuil this very day and have done with this pernicious, insecure life.'

She spoke with such conviction that Henry's worst fears were confirmed. 'Dear heart, you must understand that I only agreed to the scheme being imposed in the first place on the condition that the total amount levied should not exceed fifty thousand *livres* per annum. Rosny estimates the tax would yield more like three hundred thousand, and be most prejudicial to trade in several provinces. Soissons has duped me.'

'Rosny is the one who has duped you. The Count is seething. He refuses to comply with Your Majesty's request, and here lists the wrongs and insults he has suffered at the minister's hand.' Henriette thrust a letter into the King's hand.

Scanning it quickly Henry tossed it aside with a careless shrug. 'Let the fellow seethe, it will do him no good. But enough of this, you do not truly mean to obey the Queen and shun me, do you? What is all this about your being indifferent to me now?' He slid a hand down her bodice and began to fondle her breasts as he so loved to do. 'Are you indifferent to that?'

Henriette instinctively arched towards him, eyelids fluttering close. 'Entirely,' she murmured.

'And what about this?' He was lifting her skirt now, his hand sliding over the silk of her stocking, seeking bare flesh.

'You mean nothing to me,' she gasped, nibbling at his smiling mouth.

'Therefore I must conclude that you no longer love me. Would you abandon me to the mercies of my wife? How shall I survive?'

Henriette slapped his probing fingers away and adjusted her clothing in a huff of indignation. 'Since you clearly mistrust me, Sire, searching my house, accusing me of having a lover, and now of being party to fraudulent practices, I am quite indifferent to whatever Your Majesty chooses to do.'

Her sudden change of mood irritated and enslaved him all at the same time, but he would not beg. 'So tell me why you would ally yourself with such a scheme? Do you not already have a king in thrall to you?'

'Since you refuse me the benefit of a husband I must needs protect my own future.'

'Dear heart, have I not promised time after time to look after you, and our children? Do you not trust my word?' Henry asked, holding out his hands in a gesture of humility.

'How can I believe your word when you so easily break it? I must make my own arrangements.' Henriette stamped her foot in annoyance. 'I want to look after myself and not be humiliated by constantly having to beg Your Majesty for favours.'

Henry folded his arms and stood, legs astride, to consider her. 'Ah, so it is independence you crave, is that it?' His tone had cooled considerably. 'Very well, then I assume you will no longer require the sum of one hundred thousand *livres* which I'd promised in order for you to purchase the county of Joigny.'

Henriette regarded him in horror. 'You become insufferably

more jealous the older you get. There is no longer any means of pleasing you.'

'As I am such an old nuisance then go home to Verneuil, if that is what you wish.' And turning his back on her he strode away, leaving Henriette almost foaming at the mouth in fury.

Unfortunately, the King had called her bluff and she had no choice but to obey. Before the day was out Henriette packed her belongings and reluctantly set off back to her own château, deep in the quiet of the countryside, far from the gossip and political goings-on of court life which was her lifeblood.

But, as always in this volatile relationship, Henry could not bring himself to cast her off completely. Within weeks he was riding out across country to meet up with her again in secret. The truth was that while he could not live with her, no more could he live without her.

Marie had escaped to Compiègne to avoid the stress of these disputes, as well as the sight of her husband sinking into depression because he was again at odds with his mistress. Was ever a queen more slighted than she? Bad enough to be compelled to suffer the fact her husband had a mistress at all, but to have one who possessed a promise of marriage in his name, and refuses to relinquish it, was unconscionable. Were Henry to die then the legitimacy of the Dauphin would immediately be brought into question. It was not a prospect conducive to inspire security in any consort.

How she wished she saw more of her sister-in-law and dear friend, the Duchesse de Bar, in whom she could so easily confide her troubles. But she feared for the Duchess's health for it remained poor. In one of her frequent letters Catherine was hopeful that she was at last pregnant. Marie had written to congratulate her on this joyous news, if it was indeed true, and to commiserate on a persistent cough.

Marie met up with the King again at the house of Rosny, and not only was Henry distant towards her but storms and a flooded river quite ruined the feast. It was a damp and dispiriting evening with barely a civilized word exchanged between them. Marie felt close to tears, and did indeed weep when Henry briefly referred to these outrageous allegations about the Dauphin, as if it were of no great moment.

'Since Madame de Verneuil refuses to return my promise of marriage, His Holiness will retain the power of pronouncing the lot of my son, my own fate, and the destiny of this realm.'

'And you can do nothing to force her to relinquish it?'

Henry shrugged. 'I cannot, though I doubt she would act upon it.'

Marie had to bite her tongue to stop herself from screaming at him. She so longed to say more but, in view of the precariousness of her own position, dare not. And she saw by the weary resignation in Rosny's eye that he shared her exasperation with the King's weakness.

'His Majesty turns deaf, dumb and blind whenever he suspects a friend might have betrayed him,' Marie complained bitterly to her *dame d'atours* later that night as she prepared for bed, hoping in vain that her husband would join her. 'Henry does so hate to face unpleasant truths.'

'I doubt His Majesty realizes that Auvergne and his father are in league with the Spanish ambassador,' Donna Leonora casually remarked as she helped her mistress into her nightgown.

Marie felt a shiver of alarm at hearing this concern so calmly articulated. Her knees suddenly giving way, she sank into a chair. 'My uncle too has written of his suspicions in that respect. And were the unthinkable to happen, and the she-cat to challenge my son's right to reign, then there would be civil war in France all over again.'

The two women looked at each other, both careful not to speak of the King's death out loud, yet needing to express their fears and consider the consequences of such a catastrophe.

Donna Leonora lowered her voice as there were other maids of honour present in the bedchamber. 'I have heard it whispered that Balzac and Auvergne seem determined to ally themselves to the machinations of the Spanish Hapsburgs. They enjoy basking in the sun of their ambitions, so who can say what the outcome might be.'

'Should I speak to the King of these suspicions?'

Donna Leonora hesitated for a second while she tucked the Queen's hair into her nightcap, then slowly shook her head. 'It is not my place to offer advice, Your Majesty, but I believe you should not be seen to challenge the King's judgement in such matters.'

'That was my view too. The she-cat has insolently ignored the promises she made to me when she thought His Majesty at death's door, and taken up with him again. Would that I could have my revenge for such arrogance.'

Donna Leonora was anxious to keep on good terms with the King's favourite, since being able to visit La Marquise allowed access to all manner of snippets of gossip useful to her beloved mistress. She therefore advised caution. 'Your time will come, Your Majesty. Concini too agrees that you should bide your time until you're in a stronger position to make demands.'

The wily *dame d'atours* always kept her husband fully informed of conversations she enjoyed with the Queen, but she was never too sure how much he confided in the King, nor whether that was a good or a bad thing. She was not afraid of stirring up mischief between the royal pair if the end result was beneficial to their own position. But for once she was opting on the side of prudence.

Marie was almost in tears as she climbed between the sheets, finally admitting that Henry wasn't coming to her tonight. 'And while I await the King's attention, nibbling sweetmeats to console my loneliness, and growing plumper by the day, La Marquise remains triumphantly radiant. She is bright and clever, witty and charming, and Henry sees me as dull and plain.'

'She only sparkles when she chooses to, Madame. At other times she can be wickedly caustic, or engage in childish tantrums.'

'But even at her most insolent and abrasive, the King does nothing to reprimand or punish her.'

Marie was obliged to watch in silence as events unfolded, nursing a private desire for vengeance that ate into her soul and filled her with bitterness. She saw how her husband's spirits rose or fell according to whether he had recently ridden out to visit his mistress, or the woman had again banned him from her presence.

She was in despair that Henry should so weakly capitulate to his mistress's litany of demands without demur. However flagrant, however grasping, however outrageous the she-cat's efforts to claw money out of him, he would always pardon and forgive her, then be panting at her door like a whipped lapdog the next instant.

La Marquise led the King entirely by the nose, and his own wife could barely capture his attention for more than a moment.

★   ★   ★

'I believe the Queen would like to see me dead,' Henriette announced to her father one day. 'Much as I miss being in court, I no longer consider it safe for me to live there.'

'It would be a bad mistake,' Balzac told her, 'for you to stay away too long.'

They were at Malesherbes, where Henriette had arrived on a visit with her family, seeking their support in her troubles. Her mother, of course, took a different view.

'It may well be wise for Henriette to stay away if the situation is as dangerous as she suggests,' Marie Touchet said. 'Could we not still find her a husband, Balzac? Mayhap, the King would agree if we asked politely.'

'Silence, woman, these matters are beyond your comprehension.'

'I would not be against marriage with the right man,' Henriette protested, for once agreeing with her mother. 'But as the King is unlikely to accept any husband who might claim his conjugal rights, I doubt we will ever succeed in finding one he'd agree to. Nor will he allow me to stay away from court for too long.'

Auvergne, who had recently ridden in, now joined them, striding in on a blast of cold air. Drawing off his gloves he tossed them on to a side table, and gave a wry grin of satisfaction. 'The Spanish ambassador has offered me a pension of ten thousand *livres* for a copy of the marriage document. What think you of that?'

'We will not accept,' was his stepfather's immediate response.

Auvergne looked astounded. 'Why ever not? Ten thousand *livres* per annum is no small sum. He asked if the promise was conditional and I admitted that it was.'

'But only on Henriette producing a son, which she did. It was no fault of hers that the child died.'

Henriette stiffened her spine with pride. 'You are right, Father, the fault was not mine. And why accept such a trifling sum when we can have the crown? All we need do is to hold fast to our patience until the unspeakable happens and France looks to a new king. The only danger is the moment that day dawns, the Queen will have me arrested and thrown into the Bastille. I truly live in fear of my life.'

'There is no reason to feel threatened, daughter, not when you have a brother and father to protect you. And perhaps the Queen does not have quite the power she imagines. Just remember that we hold all the cards, or rather the key to challenging the legitimacy of France's future King. We will never voluntarily surrender that document.'

Henriette showed her father a letter. 'See, the King asks that I send my son to be educated alongside the Dauphin. He says he makes the offer out of love for our son, and if the boy is at court then his mother − myself − will surely follow.'

'Will you accept?' Auvergne asked.

'I have already declined his generous offer. I told His Majesty that I would not allow my son to be educated with the royal bastard, son of the Florentine.'

'Well spoken,' Balzac agreed, and Auvergne laughed out loud.

'That will show him what he is up against, that you are not a woman to be lightly set aside.'

'Is she not the most exasperating of women?' Henry asked, as he slammed Henriette's response down on the table before his minister.

'I trust you will call her to task over such insolence?' Rosny said.

Henry sighed. 'How can I? She has her own view of these matters and I cannot persuade her to abandon them. Nor do I wish to take the risk of her escaping to England. No, no, I shall pardon her, as always. Am I not weary of squabbles, and seek only peace?'

Rosny was privately incensed by the King's folly. 'I beseech Your Majesty to terminate this liaison which is degrading to yourself, and humiliating for the Queen. Why not allow Madame de Verneuil to marry the Prince de Joinville, or if not him, then some other suitable person of your choice, Sire. Or settle a liberal income on anyone willing to espouse her. She constantly claims that this is what she wants, or else to retire to a nunnery. Why not let her do one or the other. Take her at her word.'

'Would she then voluntarily surrender the marriage document, do you suppose?'

'It would have to be a requirement.'

Henry considered this excellent advice for all of half a second, but it really was too painful for him to contemplate for too long.

Life without his captivating Henriette was unthinkable. 'If only the Queen were not so set against her, so resentful of her presence at court. Why cannot Marie accept that a king is entitled to one mistress, at least? How can I live with such discord between them? My wife shows me no respect.'

'Sire, the Queen worships you, but she has been greatly provoked by the fact that this particular mistress has spread scandalous mischief that it should be her own son who claims the throne, and not Louis, our little dauphin. How is she supposed to deal with that?'

'*Mon ami,*' grumbled Henry. 'I find the society of my wife neither a solace, an amusement, nor a contentment to me. She is not gentle, nor does she possess the facility for gliding smoothly over trifling differences. She does not try to accommodate herself to my temper or my habits. When I enter her saloon and approach her for a conversation, or perhaps acknowledge her with a kiss, she receives me coldly, so that I soon hurry elsewhere.'

'But if Your Majesty were to dismiss La Marquise from court, I'm sure the Queen's coldness would thaw.'

'Never! Would to Heaven, Rosny, that she had never come, but it is too late for such regrets. If you could but induce the Queen to become more amenable to my wishes, and more indulgent to my errors, *Ventre Saint Gris,* then I would be forever grateful! Pray tell her to behave with better manners, that the King demands it.'

'The King demands *what?*' Marie clutched one hand to her breast at the pain caused by these words. 'I shall *never* submit to that *she-cat* while she continues to malign my son. She is greedy and overambitious. Why cannot His Majesty see that?'

A question Rosny wisely did not attempt to answer.

'The woman constantly sets out to humiliate me at every turn. I am the subject of endless pity and speculation by the courtiers, and live in dread of her plotting. Yet the King takes *her* side against *me!*' Tears shone bright in her dark eyes, and slid down her pale cheeks.

Rosny stifled a sigh. The Queen's response was exactly as he'd expected, and she had his full and profound sympathy, but that made it no easier for him to cope with. He must carry out the

King's orders, although not quite using his choice of words. As tactfully as he could he made his suggestion. 'Perhaps if Your Majesty were to be a little less confrontational, more demonstrative in your loving, then the King might not feel the same need to visit Madame de Verneuil.'

Marie's patience snapped. 'How he can think so much of her defeats me. The woman is a traitor to the crown. She has betrayed the secrets of this country, which the King will one day discover to his cost.'

There was a small startled silence while the minister considered this remark, a frown puckering his brow. 'Are you in possession of facts to that effect, Madame?'

What had she said? Marie's heartbeat quickened as she pondered on the wisdom of speaking out. Beyond the gossip that Donna Leonora relayed to her, she had only the warnings from her uncle, the Grand Duke, that some intrigue was going on with Spain. Unfortunately, neither source could back up their fears with sound evidence. Yet Rosny had shown himself to be supportive. Glancing about to be sure they were not overheard, she lowered her voice and told the minister swiftly what she had heard. 'But I have no proof. It may all be malicious gossip.'

Rosny's interest sharpened. There was nothing he wanted more than evidence to rid the court of that meddlesome strumpet, and her pestilential father and brother. 'Nevertheless, the matter should be investigated.'

'I would not have the King think that I intrigue against him,' Marie said, instantly alarmed.

'The task will be carried out with the utmost discretion. His Majesty shall hear nothing of it until we have the full facts. Know, Madame, that you have my full support in this matter.'

'Thank you, and it is greatly appreciated. Trusty friends are rare in this hothouse of gossip and intrigue.'

Remembering his purpose for calling, Rosny again made a feeble attempt to obey his master's orders. 'It should be remembered that His Majesty is of an easy-going nature, and asks only for domestic peace, Madame.'

'Well, he will get no peace from me, not while his whore plots to have my marriage annulled and my son branded illegitimate. I shall make his life a misery until he banishes her for good.'

Rosny quietly left, unsure whether his visit had promoted success or failure, but he was certainly now in possession of some interesting information.

On 13 February 1604, Catherine of Navarre, Duchesse de Bar, succumbed to her ill health and died. Her last words were 'Save my child!' Tragically there was no child, no pregnancy, only the severe symptoms of the disease that had devastated her.

When the news was brought to the King he withdrew to his bedchamber, behind closed doors and shutters, and gave himself up to inconsolable grief. Despite their differences in recent years, he still loved his sister as much as ever. He looked back with painful nostalgia to a childhood when they had been close companions. Yet in adult life, with all the responsibility of kingship upon his shoulders, he had ignored her pleas for love and happiness and used her as a political pawn in the game of power.

Even when he had failed to win her the throne of Scotland, when she had begged him thereafter to allow her to marry Soissons, the love of her life, he had chosen instead the Duc de Bar for diplomatic reasons. The marriage had been one of untold misery and dispute, and Catherine never had converted to her husband's religion. She had remained, in the hour of her death as in life, true to the Huguenot faith of her mother. He wept for her now, and for himself at the decisions he'd needed to make. Such was the lot of kings.

The Queen too was equally distraught. She not only sympathized with Henry's sufferings, but shared his grief as in Catherine she had lost a most dear friend. Full court mourning was put in place and Marie also insisted that all amusements be forbidden. The entire court grieved, save for the papal legate who dared to rebuke the King.

'Consider, Sire, that you grieve only for the bodily demise of Madame la Duchesse de Bar, but I deplore the loss of her soul.'

Henry, who had never shown much patience with religion, and had changed it more than once, was deeply offended. 'Your words, Monseigneur, savour little of Christian reverence. We know that a last wish, a pang of remorse, can send a soul heavenward. I therefore firmly believe that my sister is saved.'

Henry also ensured that the body of his beloved sister was

conveyed to Vendôme and buried beside that of their mother. It had taken a dispensation from the Pope to achieve it, but he knew this to be her dearest wish.

In addition to all of this trauma, his domestic turmoil continued.

Henriette persisted in declaring that she felt threatened by the Queen. 'Not only is my life in physical danger, but so is my soul. I have been dishonoured by lying with Your Majesty unwed.'

In truth, such a thought had never seriously troubled her, but she was fearful of the King discovering the intrigues of her father and brother. Henriette was also anxious to win the sympathy of the people, which might be important in the future. Affecting a deep and bitter repentance for her past errors seemed an appropriate stance to take, and suited her dramatic nature, particularly in the current climate of deep mourning. 'I request that I be granted a place of safety, and time alone to pray to God for grace and forgiveness. I feel I should withdraw, perhaps even leave France altogether and live a life of retirement and piety.'

It was the last thing she wanted, but Henriette hoped that by threatening to leave, the King would see how very much he needed her.

Henry hid a smile, for once not so easily fooled. 'You are of course at perfect liberty to withdraw whenever you see fit to do so. However, I will not permit you to take my children. And before your own departure you must deliver into my hands the written promise of marriage. According to all the high ecclesiastics of the kingdom it is totally without merit or value, but nevertheless a source of unease and annoyance to the Queen.'

Henriette was shocked. This was not the response she had hoped for. 'I will neither part with my children nor with a document that renders me the legal wife of a king. Do you not care that my life is in danger?'

Henry sighed, struggling to maintain his patience when he had so much more serious matters on his mind. 'Very well, you can use the Castle of Caen, which was once in the appanage of my sister.'

Henriette wrinkled up her pretty nose. 'Perhaps the castle at Poitou?'

'I think not. The area is rich in plotters associated with your father, your brother Auvergne, and Biron.'

Henriette found herself flushing, and flounced away as the conversation had taken a dangerous turn.

Henry ordered Rosny to conduct an inventory of Madame Catherine's property and belongings. He felt obliged to sell his sister's Paris home, the Hôtel de Soissons, to pay off her debts, although he later regretted it when he discovered these were not as bad as anticipated. Her jewels he gave to the Queen, together with a house at Saint Germain. The one at Fontainebleau he gave to Madame de Verneuil.

'There can be no safer place for you to retire to,' he told her, and she purred with pleasure since it excelled even her wildest dreams.

'How good you are to me, Henry. I shall make you a happy man this night by way of reward.'

Henry smiled dotingly upon her, even as he led her towards the bedchamber. 'I always prefer a night of lovemaking, dear heart, rather than a war of words. I am glad we are friends again.'

But in pacifying one of his women he had succeeded only in offending the other.

'How dare you treat your mistress with the same consideration as your wife?' Marie stormed at him when she heard the news. 'A house for each of us? It is insufferable. Your Majesty treats us as if we were equals, and we will never be that. How many insults must I endure while you meekly indulge her greed? My entire married life has been embittered and blighted by that woman.'

'My love, if you would but—'

'*No!* I will listen to no more blandishments from Your Majesty. I refuse to agree to any further compromises until that obnoxious promise is returned.'

Henriette was ostentatiously frequenting churches and confessionals, publicly bewailing her past sins and declaring how she had been fooled by the King. Outwardly she appeared as confident as ever, but inside was a growing fear that the Queen might win, that she may never see her own darling Henri on the throne. For this reason she welcomed her father and brother's plan to seek help from Spain. She had even engaged a new lady-in-waiting who was teaching her the Spanish language. If she was forced to escape, Spain would be as good a place as any to retire to.

'We should also secure family connections in England,' Balzac told her. 'They may prove useful. My sister's son, the Duke of Lennox, is advocating your cause to King James, and has even enlisted the sympathy of Anne of Denmark.'

'I welcome his support but have no real wish to go to England, Father, and pray it won't be necessary.'

They were walking in the gardens of the Louvre, as it was never safe to conduct such dangerous conversations indoors. 'Do not fret, my dear, if all goes according to plan it will not be necessary. Your brother is in close communication with Spain, using Morgan to act as emissary through the Spanish Ambassador. Philip III is ready to assist if it means he can gain more power in France. We also have won the support of Bouillon, La Tremoille, L'Hoste, Father Hilaire and other disaffected nobles who were once important members of the League.'

'Why would they choose to risk all to help *me* against the King?'

'Some have never trusted Henry's conversion to Catholicism, others seek to reduce the royal authority and increase their own.' Balzac gave a wry smirk. 'While many are simply anxious to replace what they lost in the civil wars with Spanish gold. And there is always the hope that other discontented French subjects might be induced to join the cabal.'

'I am aware there is no love lost between Henry and Spain, but will Philip fully support us in this?' Henriette asked, feeling a stir of excitement at the prospect of a successful intrigue, with the crown as the prize.

'He has agreed to recognize your son, Henri de Bourbon, as dauphin of France and legitimate heir to the throne. Asylum would be offered to you, dearest daughter, in Madrid, together with five hundred thousand *livres*. The King of Spain will despatch the troops which are currently occupying Catalonia. Once we have achieved our object, the country will be divided between the chief conspirators, under the auspices of Spain, of course. Philip would hold the real power.'

'Would that not be bad for France? Would it not result in further war?'

'The odd skirmish, maybe,' Balzac agreed, somewhat dismissively. 'But these men are not concerned about the interests of the realm, only with their own – a desire we can use to our advantage. Never forget that your son would then be King. For my part, I welcome it. Henry of Navarre and France has dishonoured our family name,' he finished, blithely forgetting that he had himself married a woman whose reputation had been ruined by a king.

Almost as if she followed this thought, Henriette asked after her mother. 'Is *Maman* aware of what we are about?'

'I believe she has a suspicion, for she has railed at me enough of late.'

Henriette received a letter from her mother the very next day warning her not to involve herself in any designs upon the throne. 'Your father's ill-conceived plan will be the death of us all.' Marie le Touchet's fury came over in every word, but her daughter laughingly tossed the letter into the fire, paying it no heed. Ambition was far too strong in her.

'I will have what is rightly mine, at whatever cost,' Henriette wrote to her brother, who was far more reliable, as he was utterly devoted to her. She warned him of her mother's rage, and also urged him to do all he could to secure her a foreign refuge.

'If you are what I deem you to be, you will never cease until you obtain for me this boon. Your interest is bound up in mine, and I am compelled to contemplate this step, principally because *his* health appears to indicate such a necessity.'

The King had suffered from bouts of ill health all his life and was even now enduring yet another attack. Henriette was certain it would not be long before he succumbed, in which case it was essential she be in a safe place before making a claim for the crown.

Auvergne being notoriously careless with his belongings, Henriette's letter soon fell into Rosny's hands. The minister showed it at once to the King. It wasn't quite the evidence he'd hoped for against La Marquise, but it hinted at intrigue as well as a firm determination to leave France, at least temporarily. 'Were Madame de Verneuil to depart without first relinquishing the marriage document, the danger for Her Majesty and the Dauphin would intensify.'

'She would never leave. She has no wish to leave. She is but posturing.'

But by the time Rosny had finished outlining his suspicions, without any mention of the Queen's input on the matter, Henry was convinced that some mischief was afoot. Seeing that he had no alternative he summoned all his courage, every scrap of his regal authority, and ordered Henriette to deliver the promise of marriage without delay. With these words ended an uneasy truce as Henriette turned on him, spitting with rage.

'I see no reason to return it. The document was freely given, and the birth of my son rendered it valid.'

'It is absurd to claim it as such, when, tragically, the child died.'

'I pity Your Majesty if you would deny *me* in favour of a fat Tuscan princess, whose gestures and language are the jest of the whole court!'

'That is a gross impertinence upon the dignity and bearing of my royal consort. I warn you to silence your insolent tongue.'

'Do not dare to criticize *me* for speaking no less than the truth. *I* have not broken any promises. It is Your Majesty who has done that, and your so-called royal consort who swore to accept me into her circle without argument or disfavour. Yet she brands me as a traitor, and my children as a disgrace to the realm. I can only reiterate my demand for permission to leave the country for a safe haven with my son and daughter. My family have offered to come with me, as they are willing to share my misfortunes, gloomy as they might be. My fear of God will not permit me to repeat the errors of my past without the most profound repentance.'

Henry listened to these arguments with some cynicism and a great deal of irritation. Not for a moment had he ever thought of Henriette as devout, and knew she was adopting this guise only as a ploy, and so for once he held fast to his resolve. 'If you insist, Madame, then you are at liberty to retire to England whenever you think it proper to do so, and place yourself under the protection of your kinsman, the Earl of Lennox. However, I repeat that I will never suffer our children, nor any other member of your family to share your exile.'

Henriette picked up a figurine and threw it at the King, who neatly caught it as he might a tennis ball and set it gently down on a side table.

'Nor will you be permitted to reside either in Spain or in the Low Countries, where the treasonable practices of your brother, the Comte d'Auvergne, and the party of the discontented nobles with whom he has allied himself have already given me cause for displeasure,' he quietly continued. 'Do not take me for a fool. Others have made that mistake in the past and regretted it. If you insist upon an estrangement from me, then you must face your exile alone.'

'I care not for our estrangement!' Henriette shouted, not really meaning it, but quite beyond reason now as terror gripped her heart. *How much did he know about this latest intrigue?* She lashed out in the only way she knew. 'Your royal presence has long since ceased to be a subject of joy to me, since you became so distrustful, and suspicious, and stupidly *jealous.* I feel myself to be an object of revulsion in the eyes of the court and shall be only too glad to leave.'

Henry breathed a heavy sigh of despair. Yet even as he furiously argued with her, he could not help but be filled with admiration at her daring, her courage to treat him as she would any other man. He should feel naught but disgust for this woman who, in every respect, had insulted the person and decency of the Queen. But no matter what he ought to do, both as monarch and as a man, Henry knew he could never overcome the attraction he felt for her.

Yet again Henriette withdrew from court, and Henry stubbornly looked elsewhere for the sensual excitement he craved. He did not find any.

'Every other woman is pale and insipid by comparison,' he mourned to Rosny. 'They are meek and agreeable. *Too* meek, *too* agreeable. They show no sign of her wit or vitality. They possess no fire, no spirit, not a trace of excitement in their lovely bodies. Unlike the fascinating La Marquise, who might well be outrageously bold and grossly impertinent, but at least she makes me feel alive. Do you see?'

Rosny saw that, sadly, their separation would not last long. 'Never forget, Sire, how you are blessed with good fortune in your wife and family, the Dauphin and little Princess Elizabeth. Her Majesty is a handsome woman still, for all she has grown a little plump of late, and would be a loyal wife.' If she were so allowed, he might have added.

Henry looked at his advisor as if he were speaking some foreign language he did not quite comprehend. 'But how can you compare the two? The Queen and the Marquise are different in every way. While Marie de Medici is cold, Henriette is warm and full of teasing vivacity. My mistress possesses wit while my wife is haughtily supercilious.'

'Her Majesty may consider that she has reason to be so, Sire, as I have said before. It is good that the Marquise has left court. Let her stay away, and concentrate on rebuilding your relationship with your consort.'

Henry mumbled an agreement that he would try, but the moment Rosny departed, he sat down to pen Henriette a letter.

If your words were followed by effects I should not be so dissatisfied with you as I am. Your letters speak solely of affection, but your behaviour towards me is nothing but ingratitude . . . It is useful to you that people should think I love you, and shameful to me that they should see I suffer because you do not love me. That is why you write to me and I reply to you by silence. If you will treat me as you ought to do I shall be more than ever yours; if not, keep this letter as the last you will ever receive from me, who kisses your hands a million times.

But it was not the last. When this letter elicited no response Henry wrote again, in a softer, more persuasive tone, suggesting that she may stay at the house at Fontainebleau which he had given her, if she wished.

And bring the children, whom I miss sorely, as I do their mother. I wish to carry out my intention of having them brought up with my wife's.

'How can I resist him when he writes such loving letters?' Henriette cried, showing the latest missive to her sister. 'Let us start packing at once. We can be in Fontainebleau by noon on Friday.'

Queen Marie was not pleased when she heard of the she-cat's return. 'I refuse to receive her,' she told Henry, her cheeks afire with outrage.

'You will do as I ask, as a duty to me, your husband and king.'

'I will *not*! I will hold on to my pride and dignity, since nothing else is left to me.'

Henry rode off in a temper to meet with his mistress. 'I trust that when, *if*, I return, you will be in a better frame of mind, wife.'

Donna Leonora was greatly alarmed by this display of reckless independence on the part of her mistress. She was happy enough to stir things politically, but if the Queen grew too quarrelsome they would all be the losers. 'Would it not be wise to write and apologize?' she humbly suggested.

Concini, the Italian's equally devious husband, fearful for his own ambitions, also advised caution. 'Your Majesty does not wish to risk losing all influence over the King,' he warned. Being the Queen's equerry was all well and good, but he had his sights set on higher office.

'I have no influence. The King ignores me.'

'But you are still his queen. For now,' Concini shrewdly added. 'It would be wise to remember that His Majesty has already disposed of one wife, Queen Margot, who was a trouble to him. He would not hesitate to discard another, were it politic to do so.'

Marie was shocked by this thought, which had never before occurred to her. Now she considered the possibility with a flutter of unease. Perhaps she had grown a touch strident in her jealousy, and should guard her tongue better, as she was ever telling herself. Ever since the affair of Father Hilaire she had kept a close watch on her rival, fearing further intrigue, which helped her to feel a little less powerless. For it was true, she had neither influence, nor proper support from her uncle.

The Queen found the endless stream of letters from the Grand Duke trying in the extreme, as if she were incapable of organizing her own life. She knew that Concini disliked the way the Tuscan envoy ignored him, as if her equerry's presence in the French Court were of no account. Don Giovanni was also her uncle, as an illegitimate son of Cosimo he was the half-brother of the Grand Duke Ferdinand, but Marie disliked him with an equal intensity, finding him supercilious. When once she had written demanding Don Giovanni be recalled as he was creating difficulties, Ferdinand had responded most disagreeably. He had found her request to be so disrespectful that he'd complained to Henry about the lassitude he allowed his wife. He considered the court of France a disgrace to a hero who had conquered France inch by inch but could not control two unruly women. Marie had been shamed by those remarks, and furious that her uncle's refusal to recall the hated envoy meant that she was unable to grant the position to her favourite's husband.

'What value do I have if I am not allowed any say over my own household? Yet I have given the King a son, a dauphin.' She gazed at her loyal equerry with dark, troubled eyes.

'Unfortunately there is a rival for that post.'

'Of that I am fully aware,' the Queen bitterly replied.

'Your Majesty must know that my wife and I will do everything in our power to assist you.' And also improve our own situation, he thought, but did not say as much.

Marie could only smile with warm gratitude at these, her most loyal supporters. Being Italian they shared a love of their home-land, could converse quickly and easily together, and therefore felt united in this foreign land. Above all, she trusted them. And if, as the Grand Duke claimed, she spent too much time conversing with them and her other Italian supporters, and had lost some of her facility with the French language, she cared not. Why trouble to please a husband who made no attempt to please her?

'My life is a complete misery,' Marie mourned.

'Then we must make every effort to improve it, and win the result Your Majesty craves,' Concini said.

'But first write the letter.' Donna Leonora handed the Queen a sharpened quill, and Marie was inveigled upon to write to her husband with every show of affection and humble apology, begging him to return to her. Which, thankfully, he did.

A matrimonial truce had been declared. The Queen was doing her utmost to be all that Rosny had asked her to be, and for a time there was genuine contentment between the royal couple. Marie organized entertainments to amuse the King, and made no complaints about La Marquise. All was going well and then one afternoon Rosny walked in to the Queen's closet, obviously with some important purpose in mind, and found her deep in conversation with Concini.

The minister's expression was forbidding. 'I trust this fellow is not brewing more trouble for Your Majesty. I heard of his recent fight with the Tuscan envoy.'

The Queen flushed, as it did look very much as if they were hatching some plot together, which perhaps in a way they were, albeit of a minor nature. 'I was merely saying how weary I was of my husband's affairs, and wondering whether or not I should feign some of my own,' she admitted. 'I could tell Henry that I too might take a lover. How would he react to that?'

Rosny looked startled by this suggestion, but while he swiftly assessed how best to reply, Concini rashly intervened.

'Would it not be a good ploy to make His Majesty jealous?'

Having collected himself, Rosny rewarded the arrogance of the Italian with a condemning glare. He disliked these hornets of the Queen's household with a venom, and would as dearly love to be rid of them as would the King. They were forever dipping their sticky fingers into the treasury, as well as stirring up mischief at every opportunity. 'It is not for me to advise on such delicate matters,' he tactfully remarked, 'but I would say it is a risky device. The danger is that the King will assume that you only tell him this because you are already guilty of the offence, and have been discovered. What then of the provenance of the Dauphin?'

Marie was stunned into silence for some moments, but when Concini would speak again, she dismissed the equerry with a flap of her hand. 'I beg your forgiveness, Monsieur Rosny,' she murmured when they were at last alone. 'Sometimes my supporters do not always think matters through clearly.'

'We could find you wiser advisers.'

'No, no, I need my friends about me.'

'So long as they are trustworthy.'

She stiffened, adopting that familiar haughty expression which she used as a defence to protect herself. 'May I ask why you chose to call upon me today?' Marie wanted to make it very clear, by the coolness of her tone, that she would not tolerate any interference over the choice of her attendants.

'I fear I must query Your Majesty's expenditure.'

'Are you suggesting that I am profligate?' Marie was shocked, yet only too aware that she could be a little reckless in her expenditure. It was very much a family flaw. But then it was such a relief to be free of the parsimony of her neglected childhood. Rosny, ever the prudent minister of finance, disapproved, and had become somewhat dilatory in the payment of her allowance of late. Marie at once went on the attack and took him to task over the matter. 'I admit that I am somewhat generous to my favourites but that is no reason to withhold my allowance, sir.'

Rosny cleared his throat, again finding himself playing devil's advocate. 'I apologize and will look into the matter. Nevertheless, the expenses of Your Majesty's household exceed three hundred and fifty thousand *livres* a year. No small amount. It has also come to the King's attention that eighty thousand *livres* has been offered to you in return for an edict granting certain privileges to officials of the salt-works in Languedoc.'

Marie looked at him in dismay. 'I am not alone in accepting such sums. It is normal practice.' These gifts, as she termed them, were an essential part of her income. Henry was not a particularly generous husband, although even more parsimonious with himself.

'In this instance the privilege will be allowed, but the King merely asks that you curb your excesses, and do not dispense too many favours or gratuities created in your favour. These tend to offend the people without any benefit to the realm, and I would then be obliged not to countersign such documents.'

Deeply offended, Marie went at once to see the King. 'Do you accuse me of overspending?'

'My love,' Henry wheedled. 'I ask only for a little prudence, and a curtailment in your generosity towards Monsieur and Madame Concini, who are preening themselves somewhat.'

Marie was at once filled with fear, remembering Rosny's hints on the very same subject. 'Do not ask me to part with them, for I shall not. I could, of course, pawn the jewels which I brought as part of my dowry,' she suggested, a neat reminder of her own contribution to the French treasury.

'True, Madame, your uncle purchased the alliance of France, and, having done so, his munificent donations to me now consist of cargoes of lemons and oranges.'

She said no more on the subject of finance, and put into effect a more thrifty budget.

★   ★   ★

The King and Queen returned to celebrate Easter 1604 at the Louvre in reasonably good humour, and the court proceeded to celebrate the season with an almost festive joy. It felt good to be in perfect accord with her husband again, to have Henry come regularly to her bed, and see him smile and jest with her. They could have been such a loving couple had it not been for La Marquise.

There was one amusing incident concerning the she-cat which greatly delighted Marie. She and the King were in church, seated on their usual beautifully carved and gilded fauteuil, when La Marquise and her sister came bustling in. It was unheard of to arrive after the King and there was a shocked silence as the late-comers took their seats, their rustling skirts and stifled giggles the only sound in the hushed chapel. The behaviour of La Marquise worsened as she kept wriggling her fingers at the King, sending him little signals, and winks and gestures throughout the service.

'Their indecorum was shocking,' Marie was moved to say to Henry as they strolled from the church, her hand on his arm. 'I would dismiss any maid of honour in my service who behaved in such a disgraceful manner.'

Before Henry could respond they were stopped by the priest, who was equally appalled by the ladies' light behaviour.

'Sire, will you never cease to come to the house of God without being followed by these women, whose levity within these sacred precincts is a scandalous sacrilege? Silence and reverence are due, even by Your Majesty, in the court of the King of kings.'

Henry could find no fitting response to this, but appeared to take the chastisement in good part, and the royal couple went on their way. Marie secretly smiled with quiet satisfaction.

'I hear that the she-cat is demanding a *lettre de cachet* to send the Jesuit Priest to the Bastille, but His Majesty has refused,' Donna Leonora told Marie with some glee the next day.

'Could she be losing her influence?'

'Too many *faux pas* of this nature and she may find herself banished from court, mayhap for good this time.'

Marie laughed out loud. 'Then let us hope her bad behaviour continues.'

A few days later the King and Queen again attended the church at Saint Gervais, and as they entered saw the priest leaving the sacristy, about to ascend his pulpit. Henry stopped and spoke to him, offering apologies for what had occurred on the previous occasion.

'Nonetheless, *mon père*, I request you in future to administer such paternal corrections in private, if you please.'

Quietly listening to this exchange, Marie thought it sounded a warning to any who dared to criticize not only the King, but his mistress too.

Part Six

THE PROMISE OF MARRIAGE

Henriette ran through the corridors of the Louvre Palace, heart racing almost as fast as her flying feet. On reaching her father's apartments without even pausing to politely scratch on the door, or wait for permission to enter, she breathlessly burst upon him with the news. 'The King has received a letter from James I of England saying that a copy of the *promesse de matrimonio* has been seized.'

Balzac went white to the lips. 'By the grace of God, tell me he has named no names.'

Struggling to catch her breath Henriette continued, 'The English King must have mentioned Morgan, for Henry has had him arrested. Was he not the secret agent my brother used to communicate with the Court of Spain? And the King has summoned *me* to his closet as compromising letters were also found upon his person, some written by yourself. What am I to do, Father? What should I say?' she cried, sinking to her knees before him.

There was an unaccustomed tremor in Balzac's voice as he answered his daughter. 'Say as little as possible. Deny everything. You know nothing, do you understand? Nothing! The letters were merely to introduce Morgan to your cousin, the Duke of Lennox.'

'There must be more to them than that,' was the King's cold response when she gave this answer to him. 'Why would your name even be mentioned?'

Henriette widened her lovely green eyes, carefully adopting her most innocent expression. 'Why would it not? What does it signify if the Duke possessed a copy of the promise of marriage Your Majesty made to me? He is family. Lennox is my aunt's son, my father's nephew. Since I have right on my side why should I not seek my cousin's support in the matter? Is that so wrong?'

'No, no, of course not.' Henry frowned, badly wanting to

believe in her innocence. 'But it depends what Lennox intended to do with it.'

'Nothing. At least, *I* know of nothing being done with it. In any case, it is only a copy. We still hold the original.'

She held out her pretty hands in a helpless gesture, a childlike innocence in her soft smile so that his lust for her brought a fresh ache to his loins. She looked so lovely in her rose and silver satin gown that he longed to set his hands to that tiny waist, pull her to him and sate his hunger. How could she possibly be guilty? Henry struggled to focus his mind. 'It may be that your father is engaged in some intrigue with Morgan. If so, then it would be advisable if you were to tell me what it is.'

'I've already told you, Sire, I know nothing. How could you think otherwise?' She was pouting now, deeply offended by his apparent distrust, and Henry felt again that dread of losing her.

Balzac was summoned. The King walked in the Tuileries Gardens with the father of his mistress, and challenged him on the matter. The Marquis denied everything.

'All I can say is that it was evident Henriette was in some danger should Your Majesty unhappily depart from this world. I therefore sought to protect my daughter by finding her a safe retreat. I sounded out the Prince of Orange, the Duke of Lennox, and the Spanish ambassador on the subject. Surely there is no harm in that? Your Majesty was aware of Henriette's concern over this issue.'

'That is true,' Henry admitted, grasping at anything which would prove her innocence. He could not believe that she would turn against him, let alone to the extent of engaging in treason. 'You know that I have caused one Thomas Morgan to be sent to the Bastille. I believe he may have been intriguing with your son, and that Lennox was a party to the conspiracy.'

Balzac swallowed his fear, striving to sound normal and unconcerned. 'I assure Your Majesty that Auvergne is innocent.' Afterwards, he wished he'd left it at that and said no more. Instead, in his desperation he recklessly continued to press his case. 'Knowing that Your Majesty had formerly given my daughter a promise of marriage, the Spanish envoy did offer to pay two hundred thousand *livres* in exchange for it. My stepson communicated my most firm refusal to the proffered bribe.'

Henry considered this, suspicion a bitter gall in his chest. 'If your son is implicated, he would do well to confess it. You should tell him so.'

Balzac wasted no time in dispatching a message to his son, then promptly shut himself up in his stronghold at Marcoussis.

When Henry sent for Henriette a second time she flew straight into his arms, weeping with relief. 'You believe in me, I can see it in your eyes. Oh, thank God.'

She pressed herself to him, scattering kisses over his mouth and bearded chin, rubbing her soft body against his rather as a cat might, and to his shame Henry felt an instant arousal. She was so utterly irresistible he could never have enough of her. Summoning every ounce of self-discipline he set her from him and gazed at her with sadness in his eyes. 'It seems that your father has been negotiating with Spain on your behalf. Perhaps because you did not trust in my promise to protect you and our children.'

Shocked by this revelation, Henriette's thoughts raced. Had her father confessed? Surely not. More likely he had blundered while trying to salvage the situation. And what of her much adored, but weak, half-brother? Auvergne was as reliable as the wind, incompetent, ineffectual and light-minded, his conceit and ambition a danger for them all. Why her father had agreed to go along with his crazy schemes she would never understand. Yet hadn't she too been led astray by his scheming, motivated by her own disappointed ambition?

No doubt Auvergne was now hiding in his château in a state of desperate inactivity, dithering over whether to run, or trust the King to pardon him a second time. Whatever he decided, Henriette realized there was no one she could turn to now for protection, but instead must rely upon her own wit. She pouted seductively as she swiftly manufactured a few tears.

'If I did not easily rely on your protection, Sire, perhaps it was because I'd seen little evidence of Your Majesty keeping *his* word.'

'Are you confessing that you knew of this plot?'

Henriette felt something like cold terror unfurl inside. 'Have I not already answered this question? I am innocent, I swear it.' Sliding her arms about his neck she kissed him full on the mouth, letting her tongue dance with his, almost smiling with triumph as she felt his desire harden against her. 'How can you be so cruel as to accuse me of such mischief? You know how much I love and need you.'

And because he wanted to believe in her so badly, Henry made no protest as she led him to a shadowy corner away from busy-body courtiers, lifted her skirts and, hooking one leg about his waist, swiftly guided him deep inside her. Powerless to resist, within seconds he was thrusting hard, her little gasps and cries exciting him to greater urgency. But then one of the things he loved most about Henriette was her complete lack of inhibition, or need for foreplay.

No more was said on the subject of intrigue, at least for today.

Henriette was relieved when the King continued to treat her with his usual consideration and friendliness, even inviting her to accompany him to St Germain, where her children were being reared with those of Gabrielle d'Estrées and the Medici woman. But then one day when she approached the little dauphin to kiss his hand, as required by etiquette, Henry stepped in and prevented her from doing so. In that moment she realized that however much he might protest, the King no longer trusted her. The very next day she returned home to Verneuil, taking her son with her. Thereafter, she refused to see him. Whatever blame he was laying at her door, Henry would soon desist if he didn't see her for a while. It was ever so.

There were risks attached to such a ploy, since the King's fondness for pretty maids of honour was well known. But Henriette believed that the only way to make him realize how much he loved her was to stay away from court until Henry's need for her made him edgy and miserable. He'd come looking for her fast enough then.

So it was that Henriette was still residing at Verneuil when her younger sister arrived in a state of great distress. 'What is it, what has happened?' Heart pounding in alarm, Henriette stood awkwardly by, observing Marie-Charlotte's tears but not quite able to offer comfort when she was so filled with fear for herself.

'Our father has made an attempt upon the life of the King.'

Henriette stared at her in horror. 'What are you saying?'

'It was all my fault. I chanced to mention that the King had flirted with me and . . .'

'You flirted with the *King*, with *my* Henry?' Henriette inter-rupted, enraged, and slapped her sharply across the face. 'Can I not even trust my own sister in my absence?'

Marie-Charlotte sobbed all the more, holding a hand to her hot, stinging cheek. '*I* did nothing, you know that I love Bassompierre and hope to marry him. It was the *King* who made the moves, because he was missing *you*. I'm sure it was only harmless fun but Father took the matter seriously, or as an excuse for revenge. He accused Henry of propositioning me, then sent a party of fifteen men who hid in the forest, and when the King rode out hunting they attempted to take his life. By a miracle they did not succeed.'

'It would take more than fifteen men to beat Henry,' Henriette scoffed. 'His mount is good and he rides well, but what on earth possessed Father to be so foolish? Do we not have enough trouble?'

'I cannot imagine.' Marie-Charlotte was wringing her hands in agony. 'Father tried to force me to make an assignation with the King and lure him out alone. Fortunately, I managed to find a way to avoid that happening, partly by leaving Saint Germain and coming here to you. I refuse to become embroiled in the family's plots and mischief.'

'You did well to come.' Henriette addressed her sister as a queen might speak to a minion, haughtily summoning every scrap of her dignity. 'I myself have persistently denied all knowledge of this intrigue, laying the blame entirely on our brother. I have even written to Rosny, fervently declaring my innocence in the matter and explaining that I sought only to leave the realm to secure my own safety from the furies of La Florentine.'

'But did you know that on hearing how you betrayed him, our brother delivered up to Rosny all the letters which you addressed to him during this last year?'

Henriette's knees suddenly gave way and she sank on to the garden bench beside her frightened sister. 'Oh no, what did I say in them? Can you remember? Did I compromise myself? Was I discreet?'

'You are ever discreet, in letters anyway,' Marie-Charlotte assured her with a wry smile. 'Auvergne has also accused you of indulging in an affair with Bellegarde.'

'*What?* But that is a lie! At least, it wasn't what I would call an *affaire* exactly. Are we falling out among ourselves now? Surely the King won't believe a word of such nonsense?'

'I do not know what His Majesty believes. But how can you defend yourself, sister, if you refuse to see him, even though the King has begged for an interview here at Verneuil, or Malesherbes, whichever is convenient.'

Henriette put her hands to her cheeks and found them to be ice cold. Had she played the game wrongly? Should she have gone to Henry and wept in his arms? Instead she had stuck to her old trick of playing hard to get in order to make him want her all the more.

'The King forgets that *I* am the one who has been wronged. I must stand up for my rights. Oh, but I'm so glad that you followed me here. I need you beside me. We mustn't quarrel as you are the only one I can trust.'

Marie-Charlotte warmly hugged her elder sister, but was able to offer little by way of comfort. 'The King's guards still search for the promise of marriage.'

'They won't find it,' Henriette hissed through gritted teeth.

'But if Father does not relinquish it, the King could have him arrested and sent to the block. Particularly if he ever discovers it was Father behind this latest attempt on his life. We should return to Paris immediately, sister, and beg for his life. Our mother will not do so. It is up to you to speak to the King.'

Now it was Henry's turn to absolutely refuse to see Henriette. She sent numerous requests for an interview, but no such permission was granted. After only a few days he ordered her to return to Verneuil.

Henriette was filled with terror. If the King no longer needed her, then she had nothing left.

Worse, the moment she arrived back, Henriette saw that in her absence a search had been made at her château, which had resulted in the discovery of some letters from her father. Would they implicate him further in the intrigue, or even herself? In her panic, she couldn't quite decide.

'I do not believe they will compromise me, or Father, in any way, although there may be letters among them which mention my fondness for Bellegarde. But that does not prove I was intimate with him, does it? Oh, what are we to do? It is all unravelling. We are undone! I dread to think what might happen next.'

'Write to the King.'

'I shall do so at once.'

'Your brother is in hiding. The King has requested his presence but although he keeps promising he will set out for court, he never does so. He fears he will be arrested the moment he sets foot in the Louvre.' The Countess d'Auvergne had arrived and was explaining the situation as best she could to her sister-in-law. 'He is in a fever of anxiety, his guilty conscience troubling him most dreadfully. He spends his days pacing the rooms of his ancient château, starting at every sound, constantly gazing out over the mountains as if expecting to see the King's archers arrive at any moment. His men report any strangers in the vicinity, although he rarely goes abroad. Should he ever step outside, even for a moment, he keeps two fierce hounds by his side at all times. He lives in peril of his life.'

Henriette listened in dawning horror, the true folly of the risks she had run by connecting herself with this conspiracy only just beginning to penetrate. 'Does he know then of Morgan's arrest?'

'I wrote myself to inform him before taking refuge with my father at Chantilly. You too must take care, Henriette; the privy council is seeking to arrest all members of the Balzac family.'

'They will not come for me, the King would not allow it,' she confidently predicted, hoping that was true. 'Besides, I did nothing.'

'Nor did you do anything to stop it either. To some that will be enough. Rosny is watching the entire family with his customary vigilance.'

'And I am left to stew alone, without protection, while my coward brother hides?' Henriette snapped.

The Countess stiffened. 'You forget how he has already tasted the tribulations of the Bastille, the first time he was arrested with Biron. He has no wish to repeat the experience.'

'I have little appetite for it myself.'

'But Morgan is singing like a canary, naming other nobles involved. It will not be long before they have the evidence they seek, or else contrive it. I pray you write to your brother and beg him to confess. He will not listen to me, his own wife. If he falls upon the King's mercy he may yet keep his head. Henry has offered a pardon if he will agree to three years' exile for his crime.'

'Dear God, is it as bad as that?' Henriette felt her throat constrict with dreadful apprehension. 'This was not how it was meant to be. I refuse to believe that any treacherous evidence will be found against us. Yet in protecting my brother, do I run the risk of damning myself?'

The Queen had taken herself into seclusion, deciding she preferred to keep well away from these political troubles. She had with her Prince Louis, who was almost three years old now; a quiet, rather serious child, whom she adored. Princess Elizabeth was more delicate, both in her features and in health, but a darling all the same. The three children of Gabrielle also lived in the royal nurseries, although Marie largely ignored them, save for César who was still her favourite. They were all cared for and properly disciplined by Madame de Montglât.

But Marie longed for the opportunity to make this into a brilliant court of art and culture. She was tired of the restrictions, the quarrels and moods of her rival, the neglect she was forced to endure. She ached for the company of her husband, to have him in her bed again, yet whenever Henry asked to speak with her in private, she insisted that Donna Leonora or Concini be present. The King would often be obliged to stand at the door of her cabinet pleading for admittance.

'What must I do to regain your favour?'

'You know what needs to be done, husband. I am weary of La Marquise ruling our lives for want of a piece of paper.'

At times Donna Leonora was obliged to call on Rosny to act as mediator between the royal pair as she could not cope with their endless squabbles, or their conflicting orders. But it was she who brought the news that not only had the trial of Morgan commenced, her rival's father had also been arrested.

'The King's archers found Balzac in his bed, and, despite his attempt to buy his freedom with the bribe of a casket containing fifty thousand *livres*' worth of jewels, they wasted no time in bearing him off to the Conciergerie in Paris. The entire court is humming with the tale, Madame.'

Marie was scarcely able to disguise her delight. Could she hope that the she-cat herself would be implicated in this intrigue? She was quite certain in her own mind that must be the case.

'And have they found the promise of marriage?'

Her *dame d'atours* shook her head. 'More arrests are even now taking place, the plotters being rounded up like recalcitrant sheep. The King instructed his archers to keep searching for the document until it was found. As a consequence, letters from Auvergne were discovered, and one signed by the King of Spain himself. This stated that on the death of Henry, France would be invaded by Spanish troops, and the Duke of Lennox would take Province. Not only that, Philip III would recognize the son of the La Marquise, and not our own beloved dauphin, as heir to the French throne.'

Marie went pale. 'Thanks be to the God that this iniquitous plot was discovered in time. But will the King ever discover that pestilential promise?'

'I am doing all I can in the matter,' Henry testily informed her when she asked him this question directly. Marie wasn't satisfied, the need for it to be in her own hand burned like a brand in her brain.

'How? In what way are you doing all you can?'

Henry grunted his displeasure. The Grand Duke had been right to ask how it was that a hero who had conquered France inch by inch could not manage two unruly women. 'The High Court has examined the documents submitted by Morgan but have declared the one claiming to be the promise of marriage as invalid.'

'Invalid? What does that mean?'

'That it is but a copy, a fraudulent document. I have ordered my archers to return to Malesherbes and search for the genuine article. Balzac is claiming that I have no servant more faithful than he. I believe the fellow lies. But if he is so keen to save his own skin then I have offered to suspend investigations into his part in the plot. I will even pardon his son, whom I believe to be the one truly culpable, if Balzac will only surrender the document to me.'

Marie thought about this for a moment. Did she want Balzac's head? Or Auvergne's? No. She simply wanted an end to this illegal challenge to her son's right to the crown. She wanted to feel secure in her marriage at last. 'That seems fair,' she agreed at last. 'Will he accept, think you?'

'He'd be a fool not to,' was Henry's tart response.

'And what of La Marquise? Is your strumpet also involved?' Marie regretted the question the moment she noted the instant puckering of the King's brow. Had she pushed him too far?

Henry paused as he considered recent correspondence he'd received from Queen Margot. Despite being many miles away, secure in her fastness at Usson, she was nevertheless a remarkably accurate source of news with regard to events in his own court. No doubt because she had so many gossipy friends here who relayed it to her. His former queen had warned him many weeks ago of a possible intrigue by the Balzac family, and he had ignored it. More, perhaps, because he had no wish to hear the truth, rather than any lack of trust in Margot. She had frequently been a source of intelligence on state matters for him, as well as having saved his neck more than once in the past. But did he even now wish to believe in his mistress's guilt?

'Henriette has been avoiding me of late, so at this juncture I cannot say further than that she declares her innocence in the matter.'

'Perhaps some independent person should speak to La Marquise on the subject, in order to confirm her lack of guilt,' Marie drily remarked.

Marie-Charlotte slipped her arm about Henriette's slender shoulders so that she could whisper in her ear, terrified of being overheard. They were again in the gardens, where they were obliged to take their private conversations. Even so, they were fearful someone might be lurking behind a nearby bush, ears wagging. 'There is more news, I'm afraid.'

Henriette's face was pale and pinched as she regarded her sister. 'Not good, by the look of it.' And when she hesitated, Henriette snapped impatiently, 'Well, what is it?'

Marie-Charlotte took a breath before answering. 'A messenger arrived this morning from Marcoussis to say that being in fear for his life, Father has finally handed over the *promesse de matri-monio* without further protest. It is the genuine article this time.'

Something inside of her died in that moment. 'Then it is over.'

'I'm afraid so. Did you know that he kept it rolled up in a bottle, stoppered with a cotton rag and secreted in one of the castle walls?'

Henriette made no response to this question, merely stared, unseeing, at a wilted rose. 'Henry finally has what he always wanted.'

'Indeed! And our father has perhaps saved his life by relinquishing it,' came the gentle reminder.

'So where does that leave me?'

With great trepidation Marie-Charlotte handed her a letter. 'This is from the King.'

Henriette unrolled the parchment, the colour rising in her cheeks as she quickly scanned its contents. 'How dare he! *How dare he!* He threatens to take my son. *My son!*' Ripping the paper to shreds she began to pace back and forth in a lather of fury. She stormed for hours, alternately raging and sobbing, till her head throbbed and she felt sick. Marie-Charlotte strove to calm her.

'Pray compose yourself or you'll be ill. I know that as a mother you would miss little Henri, were he to return to St Germain. But the King loves him and would take good care of him.'

Henriette looked at her sister askance. 'What are you talking about? I do not worry about *missing* Henri. He is only a child, I barely see him. His daily care is in his nurse's hands, not mine, you stupid girl. But *my son* is to be the next King of France, not a mere plaything in a royal nursery. I need him here with me because he is the only card I hold to protect myself.'

Marie-Charlotte was accustomed to her sister's audacity, yet she was shocked and appalled by this evidence of her selfishness. That she should care more for herself than her own child was quite outrageous. 'You speak of your son as if he were a weapon, or a political pawn in some game or other.'

'What else would he be? What other purpose could he have? He is a king's son, and should be dauphin of this realm. I will not have him seen as a mere bastard.'

Later, Marie-Charlotte persuaded her sister to take some soothing poppy syrup, and put her to bed, then quietly went to her own, pondering on this complicated woman who was her own sister.

★　　★　　★

Henriette was woken at dawn by the sound of a horn, and within minutes, or so it seemed, her bedchamber was invaded by a party of men.

'Get out, you have no authority here!'

'We have the King's authority, Madame. His Majesty recommends you depart at once for the château at Caen, since you seek a safe haven from the Queen's wrath. Your son, however, is to be conveyed to Saint Germain.'

'Do not dare to touch him!'

But neither her tears nor her disdain had the slightest effect. The King's guards picked up Henri out of his cot, and bore him away. In a torrent of rage his mother screamed abuse at them as they rode off, but made no attempt to give chase. Before they were even out of sight she was calling for her sister.

'Start packing, Marie-Charlotte, we at last have the safe haven I have striven so hard to achieve. But I must first speak to the King.' Henriette stormed through the hall and up the stairs, picking up vases and figurines to fling them in temper against whatever wall she happened to be passing. 'He will not get away with this. I will *not* be pacified. I shall demand he return my son, *and* grant me sovereign rights over the city of Caen.'

Marie-Charlotte scurried behind, desperately trying to curb the damage, picking up the gowns and petticoats Henriette ripped from their coffers. Thinking of her own beloved and fatherless child, she wondered whether this was truly the action of a broken-hearted mother, or a scorned woman who had failed in her ambitions?

There was joy in the court, the Queen emerging with a smile from her self-inflicted confinement. Marie felt a surge of new hope, a promise of a better future at last. She ordered magnificent feasts to be held, entertainment to delight the King whose good humour was also restored. Even the children raced about laughing with glee. Husband and wife were reunited, friends again as if there had never been any friction between them.

The she-cat still had to be dealt with, of course, and would be if Marie had her way. But in his mistress's absence Henry had not taken long to find a replacement to warm his bed. She was the young and pretty Jacqueline de Beuil, who happened to be Bellegarde's niece. The King was wooing her furiously, showering her with gifts and compliments, and Marie did all she could to encourage this latest vanity on the part of her elderly husband. There was almost a desperation in him, which she found rather sad, but the Queen was hopeful the girl would help Henry to forget his former mistress. And at least she was respectful towards herself, unlike the waspish wickedness of her predecessor. La Marquise was still at Verneuil, her mother in attendance, having failed to persuade the King to return her son, which might serve to hold her rapacious ambitions in check.

Quite by chance, Marie was with Henry when the Countess d'Auvergne arrived to fling herself at the King's feet. 'Your Majesty, they have arrested my husband and taken him to the Bastille.'

'Indeed, I am sorry to hear it, Madame,' Henry mildly replied. 'What is it you would have me do?'

'I beg you, Sire, to spare him. He has done nothing wrong. He is no traitor.'

'Mayhap you think too highly of him, as did I. I pardoned his folly once before, even trusting in him sufficiently to allow him to continue his communication with Spain. And all because I swore to his father, Charles IX, on that blighted king's deathbed, that I would show indulgence to the Count.'

Queen Marie brought the weeping Countess gently to her feet. 'The King can do nothing, you must let the courts decide, Madame. Remember, that promise of marriage has hung over my husband's head like a sword of Damocles for years. It was long past time for him to secure possession of it.'

Henry acknowledged this truth with a slight inclination of his head. 'I felt tolerably certain it might be found at your husband's château, Madame, or else that of your father-in-law. A search was implemented, and it has indeed been discovered at Marcoussis.'

'I know not if my husband has unwisely become involved in some intrigue. It may have been out of ignorance of the implications, or else for the safety of his sister, with whom he is close.'

Henry thought of a recent letter he'd received from Margot in which she had offered more serious warnings, giving several names, which, added to the information that Rosny had unearthed, he now took more seriously. 'These are grave charges, Madame.'

'I humbly beg Your Majesty to pardon him, as you did out of love for him once before.'

Marie marvelled at the woman's humility, in stark contrast to the unswerving arrogance of her sister-in-law, La Marquise. She could see that the Countess's earnest efforts to save her husband had touched the King's soft heart. Marie too wept along with the woman cradled in her arms. Her own heart swelled with pity for her, thinking how she too would beg for a beloved husband.

'May I second the Countess's petition for mercy, Your Majesty, on the grounds you have yourself outlined. At least spare his life.'

But Henry feared for his own life now, and frowned upon the woman. 'Deeply, Madame, do I pity you, and sympathize in your suffering, but were I to grant what you ask, I must necessarily admit my wife to be impure, my son a bastard, and my kingdom the prey of my enemies.'

The Countess succeeded only in gaining the King's permission to visit her husband. Such was the gentle countess's devotion to her lord that being presented with a pass, she braved the rigours of the prison and asked Auvergne what he desired of her. His reply was that she might send him a good stock of cheese and mustard, but that she need not trouble herself further.

'His arrogance will be the death of him,' Henriette mourned.

Growing tired of the country, as she generally did, Henriette returned to Paris. For all the promise of a supposed safe haven she dare not accept the offer without her son by her side. Little Henri was still her one hope of salvation. If something were to happen to the Queen, perhaps in childbirth, the King would surely turn to her for comfort, and the boy could take up his true inheritance as he so deserved. But if she retired to some distant castle, Henry would soon forget her. She'd already heard rumours that he'd taken a new mistress, that he'd found the girl a rich husband and even presented her with the beautiful little house in the forest at Fontainebleau which he'd once bestowed upon herself. All of this troubled Henriette immensely.

But he would come for her soon, she told herself. Some chit of a girl could not keep him entertained for long.

It was a cold day in early December, and she was alone at her mansion on the Rue de Tournon Faubourg Saint Germain when there came a hammering on her door. The next instant the house was filled with the King's archers.

'Madame, we have a warrant for your arrest.'

The words fell upon her ears like a death knell.

Henry had sent Brulart de Sillery, but as this trusted envoy handed her the document she barely glanced at it, the words dancing before her dazed eyes, making no sense. Henriette listened in stunned disbelief as he coldly instructed her to make a full confession.

'The King is disposed to grant you a pardon, and also to pardon those whom you might wish to nominate for this favour. Think carefully, Madame, before you decline this offer. Your unfortunate father is enjoying a miserable time in prison. He is allowed no visitors, not even family, and it was several hours before he was even granted the indulgence of light in his cell, or a fire to warm him. Food too is in short supply. All you need do to secure his release is to declare your guilt.'

'I am guilty of nothing!' She was on her feet now, facing her accuser with open contempt.

'Madame, you are charged with high treason against the King. It is claimed you borrowed the keys of the Sainte Chapelle from His Majesty in order to take part in a secret interview with the Spanish ambassador.'

Henriette was outraged. 'These charges are false. I sought only to provide myself with a place of safety because of the threats by the Queen to have me put into perpetual imprisonment, should anything untoward happen to the King. Such an establishment was eventually granted to me, but at the cost of losing my son I refused to accept it. I would be obliged, sir, if you would take your men, quit my house, and leave me in peace.'

'I am instructed to carry out the King's orders.'

Hot fury roared through her veins. 'I do not fear to die. On the contrary, I desire release from my earthly tribulations. Nevertheless, it would be always said that the King had put his wife to death – for I was the true and lawful queen before La Florentine.'

Turning to the archers, Sillery issued the necessary commands, which were instantly carried out. Her servants were dismissed save for one elderly old crone left to attend her, the keys to all the doors collected up, and the Captain of the Watch put on guard.

'You will remain under house arrest until you confess, or the King decides otherwise. No man may have access or speak with you except in the presence of the Chevalier du Guet, or his deputy, who will guard you.'

And so they left her. Henriette was utterly distraught, barely able to sleep or eat as she railed against her fate. She was quite unable to believe that Henry would treat her with such cruel disregard. Had he lost all love for her? What was she to do? How could she save herself if she was locked up here, and her father and brother in the Bastille?

The next day was even worse as Parliament ordered she be brought to the Conciergerie to answer charges.

'Dear God, would they put me too in the Bastille?' She sank to her knees in floods of tears, but not for long as she again fell into a raging tantrum, as was her nature.

Later in the day Sillery brought her the glad tidings that the order had been rescinded on the instructions of the King. She was to remain under house arrest, as first agreed. 'His Majesty bids me remind you that he asks only for a confession to your wrongs and you will be pardoned. Your mother, the former Marie de Touchet, appears to have left her home and cannot be found.'

'My mother was ever wiser than me,' Henriette drily replied.

Yet she took heart from Henry's defence of her. Had she not known that he would never see her imprisoned? He wanted only to humble her, to prick her pride and frighten her into apologizing for her arrogance in daring to claim her rights and thereby raise the status of their son. Lifting her chin she met Sillery's studiously blank gaze with soft tears in her eyes.

'I swear I knew nothing of this intrigue. I disown my half-brother, and all knowledge of his scheming. I deplore the calamitous fate he has brought upon my father, whose sole crime was that he loved me too faithfully.'

'Madame, letters in your own hand written to Auvergne have been discovered which refer to correspondence with Spain. These are now held by Rosny as proof against you. Confess all, and the King will pardon you. Not only yourself but all for whom you may intercede.'

'Perfidy is written in the soul of Auvergne. For my part I have no confession to make. I demand nothing but pardon for my father, a rope for Auvergne, and justice for myself.'

The questioning continued for some hours, Henriette being formidably interrogated not only by Sillery, but also Achille de Harlay, the President of Paris. She held fast to her argument, and even managed to gird her temper.

During the course of the interview Sillery revealed that papers had been found at Marcoussis bearing the cypher of the King of Spain, and its key. 'These were used in communications between the Spanish ambassador and your brother.'

'But not by me.'

'There were several letters, one from Philip III, in French, addressed to yourself, as well as others directed to your father and brother. The Spanish king stated that should your son, Henri de Bourbon, be delivered to his guardianship and custody, he would recognize him as the true dauphin of France, and heir to the crown. Depending on the success of this policy he would also assign to him five fortresses and a pension of fifty thousand gold *écus*, and yourself twenty thousand ducats and a residence within his dominions. There is more. Need I go on, Madame?'

But Henriette was immune to his bullying, her bearing and tone as arrogant as ever. 'I am not responsible for what the King of Spain promised as a result of my brother's wicked machinations. Where is the evidence of treason you hold against *me*?'

They could find none. Henriette's personal correspondence to her relatives in France and in England was indiscreet, to say the least; her language regarding the Queen deeply offensive. Yet Henry was most hurt by love letters found addressed to her from the Prince de Joinville, among others, which he read with avid interest and a bitter heart. Several courtiers had apparently fallen under her spell; even the Queen's own cousin, the Duke de Bracciano, had successfully beguiled her with his gallantry. It was evident she had not been as faithful as she had claimed, which was heart-rending to learn. Could he ever trust her again?

He had at first refused the pleas of her supporters to see Henriette. 'Her offence is not against my person, but the State,' he had told them. Now he was having second thoughts, as despite all the advice he still received from Queen Margot and from Rosny, no truly damning evidence had been found against her.

In recent weeks he'd enjoyed a mild affair with Jacqueline de Bueil, who had started life as a penniless orphan until she'd been adopted by the Dowager Princess de Condé. She was young, blonde and beautiful, with a dazzling complexion, large luminous eyes and exquisite porcelain shoulders. But he had grown weary of her already. Her want of intellect bored him, and Henry constantly found himself comparing her with the dazzling wit of La Marquise. Despite the dangers she presented, he wanted Henriette back.

As always when in difficulty, the King turned to Rosny.

'Go and see her. Force her to confess so that I may pardon her without risk of criticism.'

Much against his will the minister presented himself at the residence of Madame de Verneuil, but he saw at once the fruitlessness of his mission. Her self-possession and her confidence appeared undimmed. Far from offering up a humble confession, she instead demanded concessions from *him*, complaining loudly about her living conditions, her lack of servants, her daily discomforts and loss of freedom.

'The King has defiled my honour with these calumnious accusations. *He* should apologize to *me*, rather than the reverse.'

Rosny blinked at her impudence. 'A king does not apologize to a mere subject. And you have done nothing to save yourself from this dangerous situation.'

'Have I not more than once attempted to leave court to save my mortal soul, and yet the King himself always insisted on my return.'

'May I remind you, Madame, that you are a prisoner under suspicion of treason, one who might consider herself fortunate to be permitted to expiate your crime by self-exile to any country you choose, save for Spain. But first you must confess and be pardoned.'

'And may I take my son and daughter with me?'

'Indeed not.'

'Then I refuse, although I would gladly accept exile if my children, my parents, sister, and my brother, could come with me. But do not imagine, Monsieur, that I have any intention of leaving the kingdom and taking up an abode with strangers to risk dying by hunger. I am by no means inclined to afford such gratification to the Queen, who would doubtless rejoice to learn that this had been the close of my career. I must have an income of a hundred thousand *livres*, fully and satisfactorily secured to me in land, before I leave, and this is a mere trifle compared with what I have a legal right to demand from the King.'

Rosny's expression was grim. 'I shall submit your proposition to His Majesty, Madame, and acquaint you with the result. Though I offer little hope of the King agreeing to such a request.'

He accused her of disrespect towards the Queen, of insulting Marie de Medici by calling her 'the fat banker's daughter', of indecency, impertinence and absurd affectation. 'You are not royal, Madame, yet you preen and disport yourself as if you were, as if your bastard children were on a par with our royal offspring. You would be wise to throw yourself at the feet of the Queen and entreat her pardon for the wrongs you have done Her Majesty.'

Henriette listened quietly to every word of this lecture, which continued for some time, detailing every facet of her licentious life, some details of which she had quite forgotten herself and was amused to be reminded. Yet she felt a certain sadness that Henry had discovered evidence of her lack of constancy in their union. She had bluffed him so well until now, particularly over Joinville. Throughout the diatribe Henriette displayed exemplary patience, and then stifling an ostentatious yawn, wearily thanked the minister for his unasked for advice. 'I need to reflect further upon all you have said, before I can decide upon what measures to take.'

'If you do not confess and beg forgiveness, there can be no guarantee that a trial would not end badly.'

Henriette answered with a placid smile. 'I doubt the King would agree to such a damning indictment.'

The festivities of Christmas and the New Year were over, and on 2 February 1605, the Parliament convicted Balzac, Auvergne and Morgan of *lèse-majesté*, the crime of violence against the King. Throughout the trial Auvergne had sat miserably upon a low wooden *sellette*, answering every question at length, in the desperate hope of saving himself. To no avail. The nobles were deprived of all their honours and privileges, and committed to be decapitated at the Place de Grève. A few days later on 11 February, the court further ordered that Madame de Verneuil's head be shaved and that she be confined to the nunnery of Beaumont les Tours, for life. The Queen herself had stood as witness against her, at last able to air her indignation and contempt for her husband's favourite.

The King made no protest to his wife venting her anger, perhaps relieved it was no longer directed against himself. Already he was secretly hoping to find a way to pardon Henriette, once she'd been suitably humbled. This punishment, however, was somewhat extreme.

Marie Touchet, Duchesse d'Entragues, and her younger daughter, Marie-Charlotte, cast themselves at his feet, imploring his clemency. As always Henry was deeply moved by the women's tears, particularly the mother and sister of the woman he still loved. He raised them up with tears in his own eyes.

'You shall see that I am indulgent. I will convene a council this very day. Go, Mesdames, and pray to God to inspire me with the right resolutions, while I proceed in my turn to Mass with the same intention.'

'Do not grant them any favours,' Queen Marie sternly warned. She felt outraged by the very idea, held a great desire to wreak vengeance upon this trollop and her reprobate family who had inflicted such pain upon her marriage. She wouldn't now be against seeing heads roll. 'You should be done with offering pardons. What safety is there for myself and our children if the heads of these persons guilty of so foul a treason do not fall?'

The privy-council agreed with her, insisting that by granting pardon to crimes of so serious a nature the safety of the kingdom would be put at jeopardy, and bring contempt upon the judicial authority. 'If this decree be not executed, the sentences of the High Court will be seen to be debased instead of, as of old, a power to control the evil-doer and to avenge crime.'

The majority of the populous likewise supported the council. Henry IV was a much-loved king, and the people of Paris would not tolerate any interference with the peace and prosperity he had brought to the realm.

But Henry did not possess the bloodlust necessary to destroy relatives. 'Can I doom to the scaffold the son of Charles IX, and the uncle of my children? Can I decapitate the grandfather of my children?' He sought advice from England, and the Duke of Lennox brought letters from King James and Queen Anne requesting him to defer the sentence.

Finally, following further discussions with the council, a compromise was agreed. The King ordered that the death sentence be commuted to perpetual imprisonment, and that Henriette should remain under arrest at her mansion on the Rue de Tournon.

When she heard she'd been spared a humiliating and horrific fate, Henriette sank to her knees shaking with relief. The commune of sixty Benedictine nuns had a reputation for austerity and strict rule, and despite her many declarations of piety in the past the prospect of spending the remainder of her days in such an establishment was chilling. Not that perpetual house arrest greatly appealed to her either, although infinitely preferable to a convent.

Henriette had been determined throughout the interrogations and subsequent trials not to beg or show any sign of humility which might indicate guilt. She was, however, greatly distressed by the fate of her father and brother. To be incarcerated for life in the Bastille was no sinecure, and she wrote to Rosny begging for him to intercede on their behalf.

'As for myself, let the King consummate my perdition. Where there is no crime it is ignominy to solicit pardon.'

She expected no mercy from the King now. It was a bitter blow to be exiled from the court life she loved, to be a prisoner confined within the boundaries of her own estate; the Medici woman no doubt rejoicing in her disgrace. Nevertheless, a great deal could happen in the months ahead, she told herself, swiftly shrugging off her momentary display of weakness. Henry would soon come knocking at her door, once he felt he'd punished her enough. She must simply hold fast to her courage.

Meanwhile, her anger spent, Marie wept with despair, sunk into melancholy as she feared Henry meant to forgive La Marquise. It was but a matter of time before the she-cat would be back in her husband's bed.

Part Seven
QUEEN MARGOT

1605–1606

Queen Marguerite de Valois sat at her window, looking over red-tiled roofs which reminded her of Nérac, watching the sun rise over the mountains of the Auvergne. How many dawns had she witnessed during the nineteen years she had spent incarcerated in this grim fortress in the foothills of the Pyrenees? It must be thousands. She had been a young woman in her early thirties when first brought here by her husband's guards. Now she had turned fifty. The summer of her life was long gone, with only autumn and the winter of her days left to enjoy. A deep sadness enveloped her at the thought. Was she to spend her final seasons on this isolated rocky outcrop where the damp gave her rheumatic pains, and her only solace the correspondence of old friends?

How she had depended upon those. Were it not for the generosity of Mesdames de Nevers and Retz, not forgetting her beloved sister-in-law, Elizabeth of Austria, now sadly demised, Margot thought she might well have starved in this ancient Cathar stronghold.

She had been married against her will, incarcerated twice, first in the Louvre following the Massacre of Saint Bartholomew, which had taken place within days of her wedding, and later here, in Usson. She had begun her life as a prisoner, but once she'd taken the castle with the help of men sent by her lover, Guise, it had become instead her safe haven. Margot had gathered about her a band of loyal supporters, and made a life of sorts for herself. She'd done what she could to assist the vine growers, and help them repair their cottages. She'd become a part of this small community.

But despite the magnificent panoply of mountains over Puy de Sancy, with nothing more exciting to divert her than the chickens pecking in the courtyard below, Margot knew she'd be glad to leave this dour castle in Les Gorges d l'Aude, situated as it was in the middle of nowhere.

'I sometimes think of those early dark days, when I was obliged to run for my life,' she told her *dame d'honneur*, speaking her thoughts out loud. 'I fled amidst wild accusations of attempting to poison my husband, of plotting against my brother King Henri III with my younger brother Alençon, and arousing his jealous temper; even of secretly giving birth to two bastard babies. I do not count myself innocent of all charges levelled against me, but most certainly of all those.'

The dry old lips of Madame de Noailles curved into a placid smile as she warmed a cup of morning chocolate over a burner for her mistress. 'Your Majesty was famously adventurous in her youth.'

Margot laughed out loud. 'Some of the rumours of my scandalous behaviour are undoubtedly true, I do not deny it. I did so love to intrigue and to live as freely as my husband. What is good for the goose . . .'

'You were, I believe, the fashion icon of the French Court. Where the young Princess led, the other ladies would surely follow.' The older woman set the dish of chocolate on the table, Margot's favourite *croustarde de pomme*, baked by the castle *boulangerie*, beside it.

'I was indeed.' Margot sighed. Noailles had not been with her in those far off days, her first woman of the bedchamber then being her beloved Madame de Curtin, who had been like a mother to her. But it was true that in her prime she had been quite captivating, with sparkling brown eyes and dark luxurious hair often worn loose, although on more formal occasions it was tucked beneath a tightly curled, fashionably blonde peruke. She liked to think that her skin was still flawless, and pale as silk. Her bosom remained reasonably firm if not quite as pert as it once was, and she had admittedly grown somewhat plumper than in her younger days.

Margot felt a keen nostalgia for the days of her youth, sighing softly for the glorious balls and ballets in which she had loved to take part, the music and games, challenging Guise at archery, stepping out in the pavane with him, aching to have him kiss and make love to her. Which he frequently did with consummate skill. She smiled now at the memory even as tears sprang to her eyes at the thought of Henri de Guise, the love of her life, tragically slaughtered at the hand of her own brother, King Henri III.

She remembered reckless La Molle, the beautiful Champvallon who was her *coup de foudre*, and poor sad Aubiac who paid the ultimate sacrifice for his love. Men had doted on her, and willingly died for her.

'But had I done half what I was accused of, or slept with a quarter of the men named as my alleged lovers, I would have been a busy woman indeed. I simply believed in enjoying the same freedom as my husband in the political union that passes for marriage in royal circles. Where is the wrong in that?'

'None, Your Majesty. Without doubt you were a much maligned and misunderstood young woman. A woman, perhaps, born before her time, as men will never agree to such equality.'

'You speak true. I've been interrogated, besmirched, dishonoured, ignominiously searched by Henri Trois' men, and had my life threatened on more than one occasion. I have no wish now for intrigue and adventure. Oh, but how I ache for some diversions and entertainments to enliven my last years. I am filled with a yearning to go home.'

'And why should you not?' Noailles settled in a chair beside her mistress, the two women often sharing breakfast for the pleasure of each other's company.

'Henry will not allow it, but before I die I would so love to walk again in the beautiful Tuileries Gardens created by my mother, to see the sun rise over the Seine instead of these bleak cold mountains. I ache to again be part of a court where poets and artists gather to speak of their art, to discuss and argue over the mysteries of life.'

'The King might allow it now.'

Margot cast her a sceptical look. 'Many times over the years I have sought my ex-husband's permission to return, but he has always denied me that right. We were friends of a sort once, even lovers, although not *in* love, if you can understand the difference.'

The old lady smiled. 'I think I can still remember how it feels to be in love.'

'But then we fell to quarrelling, over *his* women, *my* lovers, my settlement and property, and the fact I refused to grant him the divorce he needed to marry Gabrielle d'Estrées.'

'But that young lady is no longer a threat,' Madame de Noailles gently reminded her. 'You not only gladly signed the papers but the King has married his Florentine princess. Since that glad day Your Majesty has frequently written to Queen Marie with respect and congratulations at the joyous news of a birth, and you have been most helpful to the King during the recent travails.'

'That is certainly true. Did I not frequently come into possession of many interesting nuggets of information regarding Balzac and Auvergne, sent to me in the gossipy correspondence from my many friends at court?'

'Which you did not hesitate to pass on to the King. His Majesty's gratitude is such at this moment that he may finally grant the permission you seek.'

There was a small silence in which Margot set down her dish of chocolate untouched. 'You are right, Noailles.' Hope soared in her, a giddy sensation akin to flying. 'That rascal Auvergne was the recipient of a substantial inheritance from my mother, Catherine de Medici, which should rightly have been mine. Perhaps this is the moment to petition parliament and make another attempt to retrieve it.'

Madame de Noailles brought paper and ink and set it beside Margot's breakfast plate. 'Since the Count has been sent into perpetual imprisonment he will have little use for such a fortune now. This may also be a good time to write again to the King, for permission to leave Usson?'

'It may indeed, but we will not wait for his reply, Noailles. I shall simply inform him that I am coming home.'

Margot's journey across country from Usson was a good deal more comfortable than her last travels when she'd fled for her life from Agen. On that occasion she'd abandoned side-saddle in order to make greater speed bareback, and suffered blistered thighs as a result. When she'd grown too weary to stay upright, she'd ridden pillion behind Aubiac. Her loyal band of supporters had crossed precipitous mountains, forded raging rivers, and frequently got lost in thick forests, obliged to avoid all roads in case she was being pursued by her enemies.

Now she rode on a cushioned seat in a coach of relative comfort, passing through some of France's most beautiful countryside. She stopped to rest at Toury, and again for a time at Villres-Cotterêts, which formed part of her heritage from her father, Henri II. Her brother Charles IX had loved to escape to this hunting lodge deep in the forest of Compiègne when suffering from one of his black moods.

She had received no response to her letter, as yet, from the King, but several from friends. 'They are warning me not to enter the capital without Henry's permission. I am growing ever more nervous, the nearer we get to Paris. What will I do if he denies me entry? I cannot bear the thought of being forced to return to Usson.'

'I'm certain it will not come to that,' her *dame d'honneur* assured her.

The party were in the small village of Cercote, her gentlemen tending to the horses while Margot rested in her chamber, when, all of a sudden, there came the sounds of a disturbance in the courtyard. There was the clatter of hooves, shouts of the grooms; clearly a large party arriving.

Margot groaned. 'Someone has come; find out who it is Noailles, but pray do not allow them to disturb me. I must needs sleep.'

Sleep was forgotten, however, when moments later her attendant rushed in with news. 'It is Baron de Rosny himself come to meet you, Madame, and he's brought his good wife with him.'

Dishabille as she was, dressed only in her *robe de chambre*, Margot welcomed him warmly. 'My old friend, how good it is to see you again after all these years. And how well and prosperous you look.'

'And I see Your Majesty's beauty is undimmed by the years.' Rosny grinned, making his delight in seeing her again all too evident.

She laughed out loud. 'Ever the flatterer, but I cannot tell you how pleased I am to see you here.' Only seven or eight years younger than herself, Margot knew him to be a loyal servant of the King since Henry's days as the Prince of Navarre, although, unlike his master, he had refused to convert to the Catholic faith. 'When first I met you, you were but a boy, a student, I seem to remember, studying at the College of Bourgogne at the time of the Saint Bartholomew's Day Massacre.'

'From which I fortunately escaped unscathed by wisely contriving to be seen carrying a Book of Hours under my arm.'

They both laughed, as if it were a joke and not a matter of life and death. 'Would that it had been so easy for Henry and myself. How is the King?'

'His Majesty is well. I have business in Châtellerault, but he bade me come to meet you on your journey. He wishes me to sound out your intentions and thank you for your assistance in dealing with the malcontents. My wife also eagerly awaits the opportunity to be the first court lady to compliment Your Majesty on her return to the world.'

They talked for some time, as the old friends they were, discussing the troubles in Limousin, the intrigues of Biron and then Auvergne. Margot explained how she had already petitioned parliament for the return of her inheritance, and Rosny offered his full support.

'But what of the King and Queen, how do you think they will react to my presence?'

'I believe the King is secretly looking forward to seeing you again. I assure you, Madame, you will be well received by both the King and Queen.'

'Would that I could believe you.' Margot felt deeply vulnerable. As the last Valois her position and alleged wealth was coveted by many, yet her years away from court had changed her. She was no longer that beautiful, adventurous young princess, but a stranger now in the court that had once been captivated by her charms. 'I am nothing more than a divorced wife, a barren queen with nothing to offer.'

'You can offer your friendship, your loyalty, which have never been in doubt.'

Again she laughed, gurgling with pleasure at the repartee. 'You grow ever more diplomatic, but do not twist the facts, old friend. My friendship and loyalty to the King were most sorely tested, and doubted, on numerous occasions. Scandalous rumours about me were rife, one would not be exaggerating to say they were at times the life blood of the court.' Then just as abruptly, she grew serious. 'I beg you to give me your word that no further harm or dishonour will befall me. I want nothing more than to enjoy my last years without censure or apprehension.'

'I pledge, on my honour, that you will be safe.'

Later they dined together, and Margot spent a happy day with the Baron and his lady, before Rosny went on his way and the Queen's party continued on to Paris.

Margot arrived at the Château of Madrid on the outskirts of Paris on 19 July 1605. She could find no fault with her reception as the palace had been magnificently prepared for its long-absent mistress. She was greatly encouraged by the trouble taken, and by the fact she was met by César, the young Duke of Vendôme, who had been sent by the King, together with his tutor, to welcome her.

'The excitement among the people is high,' he told her, most seriously. 'They are eager to welcome back their beautiful Queen, the last of the Valois who was so outrageously and disgracefully evicted from court.'

Margot was enchanted by the boy, a precocious child if ever there was one, and allowed him to kiss her hand then take her on a tour of the palace, as if he were the one responsible for making her feel at home. Afterwards, she penned a note to the King, waxing lyrical about the nine-year-old's charms.

'I believe, Monseigneur, that God has given him to Your Majesty for special service . . . He is a royal prodigy truly worthy of Your Majesty.' She added a postscript. 'I took extreme precaution that the journey taken by this delicate little angel of yours should do him no harm, and I exhorted him very zealously not to pass through Paris. Your Majesty will pardon me if I presume to say that you are not careful enough about his health.'

Queen Marie, when she read this letter, was deeply offended. César was a favourite of hers too, yet she took exception to Margot's comments. 'How dare she criticize the arrangements we made for him? He was perfectly well escorted on his journey, and properly guarded.'

Henry gave a wry smile as he fastened on his cloak, attempting to pacify his queen who had become increasingly insecure of late, the cause for which could no doubt be laid at his own door. 'Marguerite is somewhat extravagant in her praise but she means no harm by it. She is a woman of great character and passions, full of *joie de vivre*, and possesses great tenacity and courage. She is articulate and well educated, a lover of poetry and art, politics and religion, skilled in languages, and indeed fond of young children. It is a tragedy that she had none of her own. I am sure that when you meet her, you will find that you have a great deal in common.'

A chill wind flickered down Marie's spine as she listened to her husband sing the praises of his former queen. Had she not enough trouble with mistresses without an ex-wife to contend with as well? 'Meet her! Are you intending to receive her at court?'

'Of course I will receive her. How could you imagine otherwise?'

'But I'm not sure that *I* can. I should feel most awkward. She was your *wife*, after all.'

He pulled on his leather gloves, one by one. 'That is all in the past. Will you ride with me now to greet her?'

Marie stiffened, a tremor of nervousness in the pit of her stomach, yet she held fast to her resolve to keep her distance from this new threat. 'I would prefer not to.'

'Very well, then I shall ride out alone,' Henry agreed in his equable way. 'You can make the necessary preparations for receiving her later.'

Marie watched him go with a heavy heart. Should she have accompanied him? Had she again made the wrong decision?

The meeting between King and Queen, one-time husband and wife, was surprisingly warm considering the fierceness of their quarrels over the years. Henry arrived at about seven and they sat and talked all evening, much of it concerning the details Margot had learned concerning the intrigues of Madame de Verneuil, and more serious worries involving the assignment of Marseilles, Toulon, and other cities to the Spaniards. Henry thanked her for generously agreeing to a divorce so that France now had the heir she needed, and for the deference Margot had shown to his new queen. But most of all they enjoyed reminiscing about the past.

'I give you due warning not to expect too much. The courts of your brothers, both Henri Trois and Charles IX, were far more luxurious and brilliant than my own.'

'You were ever parsimonious,' Margot teased. 'Particularly when it came to soap, I seem to remember. I do hope you have learned better hygiene and do not trouble your present queen by attempting to visit *her* bed with dirty feet, as you did mine.'

Henry grinned. 'I doubt she would wash them for me, as you did.'

'I was ever a woman of high standards. You know that I like my perfume, my diamonds, and my splendid gowns.'

'And your dancing and cavorting, your ballets and banquets. I am only too aware of your ability to spend money,' Henry gently admonished. 'While I, as the King, must think first of the treasury before my own pleasures.'

'Which is why you are so loved by your people. You have done a great deal to improve their lives: building roads and bridges, repairing the destruction left behind by my brother, as well as lowering taxes. Henri Trois bled them dry, you succour them.'

'I believe if every Frenchman can afford to have a chicken in his pot on a Sunday, he will be a contented citizen.'

'I do not seek to make problems for you, Henry,' Margot added, suddenly anxious. 'I trust we are going to be friends.'

'You will be my very dear sister.'

She smiled at him, resolutely putting behind her all their former differences. 'I would like that very much.'

'There are only two things which I must request Your Majesty to concede. The first is that for the sake of your health you will refrain from turning night into day, and day into night. The second concerns those pecuniary affairs of which we speak. I beg you to be less liberal in your expenditure.'

Margot laughed out loud. 'Sire, I will strive to please you in all things. But your first request will be difficult to comply with, for such has been the habit of my life from childhood. As to my liberality, I fear to make such a promise. I am a Valois and a Medici, profligacy and heedless munificence have ever been the failings of our family houses.'

The King sighed. 'I can but hope for the best.'

The court was buzzing with anticipation. At last the two queens were to meet. Marie was trembling with nerves, not quite sure what to expect. 'That woman has spent her entire life making mischief for you,' she reminded Henry. 'Why should she want to come here and bother you now?'

'I believe I have made as much trouble for her, and it is time to leave the past behind us. She is lonely. Be kind to her, Marie. It is a humiliation to lose a crown, and a sadness to her in old age to find herself without children. We are the only family she has left, we can afford to be generous.'

'We do not all have your heart of gold,' Marie tartly responded. 'It is humiliating for me, as all of Paris will see this beautiful queen they have lost and may prefer her to me.'

He tenderly kissed her forehead. 'Now why should they do that? Are you not handsome too, and didn't you give France a dauphin? Now here she comes; smile and offer your deepest curtsey.'

Marie looked sharply up at him, not quite able to believe this last instruction. 'You wish me to offer obeisance to my predecessor?'

'I wish you to treat a fellow queen with proper respect. She is the daughter of a King, three of her brothers were Kings of France. She was herself Queen of France and Navarre. I will have her treated accordingly.'

Marie was inwardly alarmed but outwardly contrite. 'Of course, Your Majesty. I wasn't thinking.'

But as Margot approached in stately fashion, she felt overwhelmed, as if she were a humble subject being presented to a monarch who was regal in every line of her beautiful body. For this was no sad old crone. This woman may have grown older, and plumper, but was every inch a queen, and still a beauty. She sparkled with gems, ablaze with diamonds, from those in the shape of stars that she wore in her ears, to the precious stones studded all over her satin gown, which was in her favourite orange. The style brought forth a few whispered comments as it was hooped in the fashion of those worn in the time of Queen Catherine de Medici. Queen Marie favoured a more draped, flowing style, but, judging from the ladies' reaction, she accurately surmised that in a frighteningly short space of time hoops would again become *de rigueur*.

As Margot walked towards the royal dais with perfect grace, none could deny her loveliness. She glanced to her right and left, smiling and nodding to the nobles and their ladies who crowded the salon, eager to see this woman who was a living legend; treating them with the kind of ease that Marie, a foreigner in this land still, could only envy.

Henry presented his former queen to his new one with delicate precision. Marie graciously dipped a curtsey, as instructed, and rather clumsily embraced her predecessor.

'You should have stepped forward to meet her,' Henry grumbled in her ear. 'It was churlish of you to make her walk those few extra steps. Did I not remind you that she is more royal than either of us?'

Marie blushed to the roots of her carefully coiffed hair, feeling suitably chastened and woefully inadequate; a frump with her limp gown and over-powdered hair. Queen Margot wore her own hair lightly powdered, as did La Marquise. It was vexing to always be slightly out of step with fashion.

A few desultory words were exchanged between the two queens, Marie making polite enquiries about her journey and her health. Queen Margot then asked after the children.

'They are in the nursery, with their governess,' Marie coolly responded.

'I would love to see them. I cannot wait to meet the little dauphin. I have heard he is a fine, healthy boy who excels at his studies.'

The mother in Marie melted at this compliment to her son. 'He is strong, yes, and his tutors are pleased with him.'

Margot was insistent that she must be taken to see him forthwith, proclaiming herself enchanted when he came towards her and politely bowed. 'Ah, but they did not lie. How beautiful he is. What a handsome boy!'

Marie's maternal pride swelled, and her attitude towards her husband's former wife softened just a little. But in her heart she knew that she had not conducted herself well. In this first exchange, Queen Margot had won the day.

Throughout August, as the guest of the royal family at Saint Germain, Margot revelled in her stay at court. She couldn't remember when she'd enjoyed herself more. She joked and teased Henry as they had used to do in their youth, Margot reminding him of how she had been the one to instruct him in the courtly steps of dancing, and how she could always outride him, so long as he didn't cheat. 'Although I never persuaded you to stop eating garlic.'

'Or from drinking good Gascon red wine,' Henry agreed.

'I may be an optimist but never expect the impossible. And do you still hunt boar with reckless abandon, and climb in bare feet?'

Laughing, he shook his head. 'The former on occasions, but not the latter. I have grown a little older, if no wiser.'

'Oh, I think we both know you were never quite the fool you pretended to be, although my mother was frequently taken in by your innocent-seeming charm, I do recall. Save for where your particular weaknesses are concerned, of which we will make no mention.'

Marie always felt rather left out during these witty exchanges, as they referred to a time in which she played no part. They spoke of a shared youth, of many failed attempts to escape the Louvre and Catherine de Medici's menace, of adventures she could only guess at.

Margot enjoyed renewing other old acquaintances too, particularly with regard to her favourites: Bellegarde and Roquelaure, even Jacques de Harlay, Marquis of Champvallon, which she thought rather generous of Henry to allow him to attend. He had been her Narcissus, and she perhaps a touch indiscreet about their passionate relationship. All water under the bridge now, of course, but it was good to see him again and discover they could remain friends.

'Are you still writing poetry to your lovers?'

Champvallon smiled. 'None ever stirred my heart as did Your Majesty, so the skill has rusted, I fear.'

Margot chuckled with delight. 'As quick-witted as ever, I see.'

But as well as enjoying the court festivities she visited monasteries and convents, happily chatting with the nuns, and sitting with them to help with their embroidery or repairing the lace adornments for the altars, at which she was an expert.

'There was little else to do in the long days of winter at Usson,' she told them with her usual frank candour, and not a trace of self-pity.

Marie watched all of this with increasing unease and envy. You could not fault Margot in any way. She always gave precedence to herself, the queen, and treated her with the utmost respect and even warmth. Yet how was it that this woman, who had been accused of such scandals that she'd been banished to live far from civilization for years, could so easily slip back into the court routine? The court ladies who remained cool and condescending towards Marie, were almost grovelling to be a part of Marguerite's circle. It was galling in the extreme that she, the true queen, who had tried so hard to fit in, was still looked upon as a stranger.

And in addition to a divorced wife, she still had her husband's mistresses to contend with.

It was not until September 1605 that letters of remission were granted to Balzac and he was at last allowed to return to Malesherbes. At first he was under surveillance, although his guards were soon dismissed and his wife allowed to join him in their home. Henry claimed the reason was because he wished to show regard for the ambassador of his good brother and ally, the King of England, as the Duke of Lennox was his envoy and a close relative of the Balzac family. Marie knew it was for love of La Marquise.

Auvergne was left to moulder in the Bastille.

Letters of abolition were also issued which pronounced Henriette innocent, and forbade further investigations into her case. As expected, she had been pardoned.

The people of Paris were furious that the decree of a respected tribunal was so easily overturned. It proved to them how very much the King still desired her. Henriette shared that view and wrote a passionate letter to Henry expressing her sincere gratitude. She received a reply written in his usual loving style, one that caused her dampened spirit to soar with fresh hope.

> *My dear heart, I have received three letters from you, to which I will make but one reply. I consent to your seeing your father, whose guards I have had removed. But remain with him only one day, for the contagion from him is dangerous. I deem it good that you should go to Saint Germain to see our children . . . Love me, my little one, for*

I swear to thee that all the rest of the world is nothing to me in comparison with thee, whom I kiss and kiss again a million times.

She wrote again, and Henry responded within days. Their correspondence continued, every word simmering with repressed passion, and of course kept a secret from the Queen. Henriette realized with a sense of joyful triumph that her affair with the King was by no means over.

'Have you seen how they flock to her salon?' Henriette asked of her sister. 'Margot has settled in the Hôtel de Sens, holding court as if *she* were queen, and not the fat banker. She counts the Duchess of Retz, the Princess Dowager de Condé and the Duchess of Guise among her guests. All leaders of fashion. Not to mention several of the finest poets and artists in the land.'

'And you wish to be included?' teased Marie-Charlotte.

'I wish to meet with the King again, and I am told Henry is a regular visitor.'

'You were ever audacious, sister, but I think you expect too much, too soon.'

Henriette flounced over to her desk, a wry smile on her face. 'Perhaps I have reason to believe I would be welcomed. I shall write and request an audience.'

The reply came swiftly and was not quite as she'd hoped. Queen Margot thanked Madame de Verneuil for her kind words of welcome, noted her request for an audience, but stated that regretfully she must ascertain the King's pleasure before offering an invitation.

'Which will take no time at all,' Henriette haughtily assured Marie-Charlotte. 'The King has forgiven me, and still writes to me of his love. He wants *me*. Only *I* can make him truly happy.'

But weeks went by and no such invitation arrived.

'They are saying that the King is still enamoured of his little Jacqueline, now risen to the title of Madame de Moret,' Marie-Charlotte quietly informed her sister.

Henriette ground her teeth with fury. 'But *she* cannot entertain him as *I* can. The chit has no wit, no sparkle, and has a pale insipid beauty. What is it about her that he likes?'

'She is young and biddable.'

'And available, whereas I still do not have permission to return to court; neither Queen Marie's, nor Queen Margot's. It is most frustrating. Letters from Henry are all very well, but I want more. I need to see him, and how can I find out where he is, or what is going on if I cannot gain entry?'

'I think I may know of a way. I will ask Bassompierre if he will help, and in return, once you are back with the King, you can ask His Majesty to grant us permission to marry.'

Unexpectedly, Henriette kissed her sister. 'I knew you would find a way to help me.'

The chamberlain's assistance was not needed in the end as the King himself came calling upon Henriette a few days later. She could barely contain her excitement and was thankful that she'd always made a point of wearing one of her finest gowns every day, just in case. Today she was in sky blue and turquoise, which set off her green eyes to perfection, the décolletage suitably revealing. She swiftly ordered Henry's favourite repast of sausage and cold meats, slapped a goggle-eyed maid who fell into some kind of trance at sight of the King, and with rapidly beating heart sank into a deep curtsey before him.

Henry raised her up and gave her the usual three kisses by way of greeting, but on her cheeks, not the lips. She cast him a smouldering glance from beneath her lashes, suggesting he could take more if he wished. He made no move to do so.

'I'm glad you came, Sire. I have so longed for this day.'

'I too, dear heart, although my visit must be short. I'm preparing to leave on campaign as there is trouble in Sedan, but I wished to see you before I departed, to assure you of my very deep affection.'

Henriette poured him a goblet of wine, leaning close so that her gown fell forward slightly, revealing a silky shoulder and the soft curve of her breasts. 'I have ordered your favourite dinner. The best of everything. Whatever hunger you have, I can quench it.'

Henry snatched up the goblet and took a long swallow of wine, taking time to collect himself. He had not meant to tangle with her today, had vowed to resist, yet the mere sight of her set his senses swimming. Setting down the cup with a sigh, he gave her a stern look. 'You should not have avoided me. Had you been more open with me from the beginning, we might not have had all of this trouble.'

Henriette pouted provocatively and, sinking into the seat beside him, slid a hand fondly over his knee which she then began to knead with her long, slender fingers. 'I was afraid. I thought I had lost you. Oh, but I missed you so.' Her hands instinctively slipped about his neck, stroking his beard, taking off his plumed cap and tossing it aside so that she could run her fingers through his hair. 'Did you miss me?'

'Of course, my love.' His breathing was growing more rapid as his pulses raced, his resolve melting at her touch.

But Henriette wanted more. She needed to be sure of him, to enslave him again. She began to unlace the bodice of her gown, slipping it slowly from her shoulders, baring herself to him. 'Perhaps you have forgotten what it is exactly that you are missing?' Freed of their restriction her breasts tumbled full and warm into her own hands. She laughed, a low, gurgling sound deep in her throat as she rubbed a thumb over nipples taut and dark, teasing him, knowing he wanted to take their place with his own.

'I–I have . . .' He stopped, cleared his throat, started again. 'The Queen is not happy, and I have no wish to upset her further.' The fever in his eyes was sheer delight, a balm to her wounded pride. Henriette pulled away slightly, took a slow sip from the King's own goblet, arching her throat as she drank, aware of his burning eyes upon her nakedness. She set the cup down, brushing a hand lightly over wine-darkened lips. 'We must take great care not to upset Her Majesty.'

She kissed him then, full on the mouth, nipping, touching, her tongue darting and sparring against his. She was opening his shirt, slipping her hands inside to slake her claws down his back. He could not resist her, no more now than ever. In no time at all his mouth was where her own hands had teased, then he was seeking his pleasure beneath her petticoats, slaking his lust fast and hard as he'd done many times in the past.

Afterwards he lay back on the couch, replete. Yet for Henriette there was a slight sense of disappointment. The coupling had not been quite as it should be, taking less time than she would have liked. She'd never troubled much with foreplay, but somehow after their lovemaking today she felt dissatisfied, as if Henry had held something of himself back. And he seemed more tense than usual. Then he told her.

'I am informed by Rosny that your father has made an attempt to help Auvergne escape from the Bastille.'

'Escape?' Henriette sat up, horrified. This was the last thing she needed, just when she was about to win Henry back. 'I swear I knew nothing of this.'

He regarded her with a steady gaze. 'I'm sure you did not, dear heart. Apparently ropes and pulleys were found concealed in a loft at Malesherbes, ready to be used to affect a rescue. Balzac has been interrogated, your mother too, but no further evidence has been elicited.'

Henriette's heart almost stopped beating at this news. She knew only too well what such interrogations could involve. 'I'm sure Father must have had some other reason for the presence of these implements in his house.'

'Such was his claim. His answers were certainly prudent, if not entirely satisfactory,' Henry shrewdly answered, giving nothing away. Rising from the couch he quickly began to adjust his clothing, little of which he'd troubled to remove. 'The matter is now closed, but a watch will continue to be kept on your relatives. Your brother Auvergne will henceforth be deprived of visits from his friends, and his wife permitted to see him only once a week. I trust we shall have no more affairs of this nature.'

She was beside him in a second, pressing her naked body against his with a fluid, feline grace, her claws now sheathed. But as he smilingly set her aside and took his leave, for the first time Henriette experienced a shadow of doubt in the power of her charms.

Queen Marie accompanied the King on his latest campaign but did not stay long as she was again *enceinte*, and soon returned to Paris to rest. Henry wrote to her every day, showing very real concern for his wife's health, and in early November Marie met him at Fontainebleau to warmly welcome her husband home. They enjoyed a happy time together: walking in the gardens, Henry riding out into the forest, hunting and fishing, savouring the country pursuits he'd always enjoyed since boyhood. Marie loved to have him to herself, and when he was so content and relaxed he was a different man, her own beloved husband. He took her into his confidence on many state matters; sharing with her the mysteries of government, even listening to her opinion should she have one to offer.

'You are my Madame *la Regente* when I am away on campaign, so must understand the demands made upon a monarch. And should disaster befall me, you will be well prepared.'

Marie was horrified. 'Do not speak of such things. I have no ambitions in that regard. I am content to be your wife.' And your only love, she might have added, but refrained from doing so.

The King looked sad for a moment, as if he wanted more from her, but then softly agreed. 'You are right not to wish to survive me, for the close of my life will be the commencement of your own troubles.'

It was with some regret that they returned to Paris in December, in time for the Christmas festivities. But in the New Year Marie's tranquillity was shattered when Donna Leonora came to her with news of the reconciliation. 'I have it on good authority that His Majesty is again seeing La Marquise.' The *dame d'atours* softly dropped this whispered poison into her mistress's ear. 'They have been meeting regularly for some weeks now.'

The Queen looked so devastated the Italian thought she might be about to faint.

'I trust I have done no harm in telling you this, Madame. Concini said I should not trouble you with it, but I insisted that you would wish to be told.'

Marie felt the old hot rage bubble up inside her as she coldly responded. 'You did right to tell me. Oh, but how could he do this to me after all we have been through? And when I am again carrying his child! I swear I shall not receive her, nor any lady, however august her rank, who has visited or even spoken in public to La Marquise. Do you understand?'

'Yes, Your Majesty. I will let your wishes be known. Pray calm yourself. Think of the babe. Let me help you into bed. You must rest.'

But Marie refused to rest. She was in a rage, storming back and forth in her bedchamber, proclaiming what she would do should the she-cat dare to appear, even on the streets of the capital. 'I shall have her bodily ejected by the Swiss Guards.'

Donna Leonora now deeply regretted not having listened more closely to her husband's wise advice, and rushed to bring a soothing syrup. But on further interrogation by the Queen she was obliged to also inform her that La Marquise was again installed in her château on the Rue de Tournon. 'And the King has allowed her to spend two days at Saint Germain in order to see her children. Concini saw the letter he wrote to Madame de Montglât informing the governess to prepare for her arrival.'

'Dear God, does she again lead the old fool by the nose?'

Donna Leonora was stunned into silence for a moment, shocked to hear the King so addressed. 'There were rules; apparently she may lodge in the castle for one night to see her own children, and those of Gabriel d'Estrées, but may not see the Dauphin.'

Marie turned to her uncle, Don Giovanni, for support, but received only lectures.

'You must moderate your temper, as the Grand Duke has already advised, and learn to tolerate the presence of Madame la Marquise. Do not give yourself the vexation of enquiring about her activities.'

Marie raged all the more as a result of this advice. She'd been pleased when he'd first moved to France to act as ambassador, as he was family. Now she fervently wished her uncle would go home as he was always so very disapproving, both of the Concinis, and of herself, which only served to make her feel ever more isolated.

For a time she sulked, refusing to converse with Henry, turning her back on him whenever he spoke to her. And she withdrew all intimacy, although she was near to her time so that hardly signified. She was endlessly restless and unhappy, claiming herself quite unable to sleep.

Henry, deeply concerned for his wife and the child she was carrying, urged her to rest more during the day. 'It is essential that you remain calm and happy. Think of the babe.'

'How can I rest when I know not where you are or what company you keep? It is impossible for me to feel either calm or happy while you prefer the society of persons who are obnoxious to me. My very dreams are haunted by this knowledge, and doubly so when I know they are false to you, and, moreover, detest you in their hearts. I pray, I *beseech* Your Majesty to abstain from the company of these personages, at least until after the birth of my child.'

Mindful of her condition Henry said no more, save that she might speak to Rosny should she be in need of him and know not where he was, then he kissed her tenderly and left her in the capable hands of her loyal attendant.

Rosny recommended a mediator who might help the royal couple through their domestic turmoil. Nothing came of this suggestion as the King, although perfectly willing to oblige, believed it to be entirely unnecessary. Marie feared blame would be cast for her distress on the Concinis, and that they would be sent back to Florence, so she declined.

'If it is any consolation to you, Madame,' Donna Leonora said one morning during the Queen's *levée*, 'the King is also betraying the she-cat. He is still visiting his little Madame de Moret, and has taken a new mistress: Madame d'Essarts.'

'Isn't it ever the case when I am in this condition? I shall save my pity for myself,' came the sharp reply.

On 10 February 1606, Marie gave birth to a daughter, Christine. It was an easy labour, and the Queen made her usual speedy recovery. Celebrations were called for, and this time Henry went further. He awarded Rosny the title of Duke, an honour the minister had previously declined, claiming his wealth could not maintain so exalted a position. Now the King insisted he accept, letting him decide on his own estate to finance the honour. Rosny chose to be the Duke of Sully.

'It is fitting recompense for your loyalty and devotion to the crown,' Henry told him, slapping him on the shoulders in that robust and friendly way he had. 'Does he not deserve it?' he asked his queen, seeking her approbation.

'Indeed, the minister's advice is ever sound. Perhaps we should both learn more often to take it,' Marie drily remarked.

Margot was revelling in her new freedom. She held music or dancing, poetry readings or dramatic recitals most evenings, the revels often going on into the early hours. Her banquets were munificent in their splendour. But then she was a Medici, in name and nature. The talented, the rich, and the brave flocked to her salon. The finest musicians and poets could be found there. Madame la Marquise became a frequent guest, and if Queen Marie heard of it she made no further protest, perhaps on the grounds that if the she-cat must be present in a court, let it be that of the *other* queen, and not her own.

'I am done with the quiet life,' Margot told her friends. 'Now that I am back in the world, I mean to enjoy it.'

There was no more talk from Henry about Margot's profligate spending habits, as he too was often present at these soirées, enjoying this relaxation away from the more staid royal court. Margot, however, was only too aware that her funds were limited, and was pursuing her petition to parliament to retrieve her inheritance. She had great hopes of success, particularly now that Auvergne had again fallen into disfavour. In the meantime she was determined to lead an impeccable life, no further scandal, no mischief or intrigue. An unblemished existence.

She even resolved to take no more lovers. 'I am done with men,' she would cry, even as she teased and flirted with some handsome *chevalier* or other.

The Queen still had her favourites, of course, including several footmen who, as well as handsome, must always be blonde so they could provide her with the hair she needed for her perukes. These young men would vie with each other for her favours, each trying to outdo the other with some love poem or recital to please her.

Content with her new life, she installed her household in the Rue de Seine, Faubourg Saint-Germain, near the Pré aux Clercs, a much finer mansion.

Learning that she now had two rivals, Henriette was not only furious but filled with a new fear. Her banishment from court and the intrigue of the last months with her father and brother had left her isolated, and she'd lost some of her hold over the King. She was itching to know how often Henry saw these other two women, who were little more than whores in her opinion. Did he grant them any particular favours? Did he love them as he claimed to love her? Any information she could discover might help her devise a way to extinguish these rivals from the court.

Usually, when the King's messenger, Bassompierre, arrived with letters from Henry, she would tell him to leave them on the table while he hurried off to see her sister. The pair had been lovers for some years and Marie-Charlotte was anxious to marry him, not least because she had borne him an illegitimate child, although Henriette was less convinced of the chamberlain's honourable intentions. The son of a noble family who were supporters of Guise and the League during the wars of religion, Francis de Bassompierre was one of the most handsome and sought after men at court. Charming, amiable and gallant, he could take his pick of the nobles' lovely daughters. Henriette very much doubted he would choose Marie de Balzac. Nevertheless, he was a useful contact, so she encouraged him. Today, when he came, instead of idly dispatching the fellow, she engaged him in conversation.

'Do you carry other letters for the King?' she mildly enquired, indicating his pouch.

'But of course. His Majesty relies upon me completely. I have a second letter to deliver today.'

'May I see the address?'

'Madame, I'm not sure I can allow it.'

'Nonsense, I allow you to see my sister, do I not? I ask only to see the address, where is the harm in that? I promise not to open it.'

Reluctantly he handed over the letter, and, ignoring her earlier promise, Henriette immediately broke the royal seal, and read it.

Bassompierre cried out, appalled. 'Madame, what have you done? The King will never forgive me.'

The contents of the letter having yielded nothing of any value, Henriette tossed it back at him. 'You can easily get it resealed, then engrave it with the royal cipher. Henry will never know.'

A day or two later Marie-Charlotte flounced in to confront her sister. 'Do you know what you have done now? Because of your stupid curiosity you have endangered my beloved Bassompierre.'

Henriette gazed impassively upon her sister, her face the very picture of innocence. 'I have not the first idea what you are talking about.'

'Oh, yes you have,' snapped Marie-Charlotte, for once standing up for herself. 'Your breaking of the King's seal meant that Bassompierre had no choice but to follow your suggestion and get a new one. He sent his valet to an engraver with the letter, so that an impression of the broken seal might be taken and a duplicate made. Unfortunately, this ploy was discovered by the court jeweller who cut the original seal for the King. Bassompierre was alerted to this by his valet, and was obliged to accept the blame by saying that he'd broken the seal himself, by accident, thinking the letter was addressed to him. What other reason could he give?'

Henriette shrugged. 'What of it? It is but a love letter; the matter is hardly likely to be set before the Privy Council.'

'This is a violation of the King's privacy!' cried Marie-Charlotte, in despair. 'And by a circuitous route the King himself heard of this alleged accident, and called Bassompierre to account. Will you never learn discretion, sister?'

'And did the King send your lover instantly to the Bastille for having so violated his privacy?' Henriette scornfully remarked.

Marie-Charlotte gave a little shake of her head, nervously clasping and unclasping her hands. 'Thankfully, no. As always with the King, he took it in good part and laughed at Bassompierre's distress. He told him to find a new mistress with a name and address less similar than Madame de Moret's.'

'Well, there you are then, no harm done.'

'Exceeding harm has been done. The King may not trust Bassompierre so well in future. And the Queen was less easily fooled. After the interview, Her Majesty spoke to Bassompierre, astutely placing the blame where it was properly due. You do yourself no favours by this sort of foolishness, Henriette. The King will lose patience with your tricks in the end.'

'You can mind your own affairs and keep your advice to yourself, madam!' And giving her sister a stinging slap, Henriette stormed from the room.

On the thirtieth of May the law courts declared the ex-Queen Marguerite to be the lawful heir to the counties of Auvergne and Clermont, the barony of La Tour, and other estates which had appertained to the late Queen Catherine de Medici. These estates had hitherto been in the possession of Charles de Valois, who had wrongfully taken the title of Comte d'Auvergne. Parliament directed that the said territories should forthwith be transferred to Queen Marguerite, to whom they rightfully belonged.

When she heard of this decision, Margot celebrated a special mass in the church of St Saviour, causing a Te Deum to be chanted in gratitude. She then donated the recovered estates to the Dauphin, keeping only the income for life, so that Louis should inherit all on her death.

Margot loved the little boy as if he were her own son, and would often visit him and the other children in the royal nurseries where he was being taught to ride and tilt, even to dance, as he was doing today. He too had grown fond of her and would always run to her in delight, calling her *maman-fille*, which thrilled her.

'The King seems to be a good father, is that not so?' she asked of Madame de Montglât.

'Oh, indeed he is,' the governess vehemently agreed. 'Our little dauphin is somewhat headstrong and if he stubbornly refuses to do as he is told, I am instructed to whip him. Queen Marie, who is much softer with the boy, disapproves strongly, but the King insists that he must not be mollycoddled. He says that at his age he was often soundly whipped, therefore he commands me to take the same firm line.'

'I am sure His Majesty knows best.'

'He also showers all the children with great love and affection, personally regulates their routine, their welfare and education, demanding daily bulletins of every childish ailment. He is a devoted father, and visits them daily whenever he is resident at Saint Germain.'

As if on cue, Henry arrived at that very moment. 'Ah, are you too a slave to the charms of my children?' he teased.

'I am. I adore your sons, little Louis and César, and Henri of course. The princesses too are delightful, such pretty little girls, and clearly very attached to you.' She laughed as, squealing with delight, they ran to their father to be swung up into a loving embrace.

Henry planted exorbitant kisses on cheeks and curly hair, on snub noses and tiny fingers, then set his daughters down on the floor where they instantly demanded a pony ride. 'They have me entirely in their thrall,' the King groaned, obediently going down on all fours to allow them to climb all over him and whip him on, as if he were a real pony. 'This is my sweet Elizabeth who will one day be affianced to a grand king or prince. And here we have the naughty and lovely Gabrielle, the daughter of Madame de Verneuil, and as much a coquette as her mother,' he teased, gathering up the giggling child to tickle her.

'I trust you will grant them some say when it comes to choosing husbands,' Margot mildly remarked, and Henry raised dark eyebrows in surprise as he cast her an amused glance.

'Are you saying that had you been given a choice in the matter you would have declined to marry me?'

'You know full well that I would. You and I were sworn enemies from the start.'

'I seem to recall you not battling with me greatly on our wedding night.'

Margot flushed bright crimson, a rare occurrence for her, but it was true. She had feared and dreaded that night, wanting only to lie with her beloved Guise, but Henry had surprised her, skilfully fulfilling his role of husband and lover. 'Have a care. Do not speak of such things before the children,' she sternly chided him. 'I accept our marriage did not turn out as badly as I had feared, and might have fared better in different circumstances.'

'Aye, there is some truth in that. At least my girls do not have Catherine de Medici for a mother.'

'Indeed, that is an advantage,' Margot drily remarked. 'I ask only that you choose wisely for them.'

His eyes were soft as he watched his two pretty daughters gallop away on their pretend horses. 'You can be sure that I will take the utmost care.' Then directing the warmth of his gaze back to her, he continued, 'I thank you for bequeathing your personal fortune to the Dauphin. It was most generous of you. And your gifts to the clergy and the poor of Paris are becoming almost legendary. I hear you have donated money for a new monastery for monks of the reformed Augustine order.'

'That is something I promised to do while still a captive at Usson. Do I not need to recompense for all my sins?' she said, chuckling with good humour. 'Every morning I do penance in bare feet.'

'And by evening you are clothed in carnation silk, reposing upon velvet cushions while a musician strums you a love song.'

Margot laughed out loud, for there was much truth in the jest. 'But I never fail to give a tithe of all that I possess to the monks, even though I confess my favourites cost me far more.'

And if she took some of them as lovers she was ever discreet. More than enough men had died for her.

Marie was quickly falling into a melancholy. She had at first rejoiced to discover that Henry had taken not simply one, but two other mistresses. There is safety in numbers, Donna Leonora had assured her, and surely it would put the she-cat's nose out of joint. But Marie was beginning to have doubts. It meant only that she must suffer the pangs of jealousy three times over. She had rather hoped, nay, expected the affair with La Marquise to be over long before now, but it was evident that her husband's visits to the château on Rue de Tournon were as regular as ever.

Yet the entire court knew that La Marquise was no more constant to the King than he was to her. It was rumoured that the young Duke of Guise was also paying her excessive attention. And as if that were not enough, the Duke of Longueville, ever reckless in affairs of the heart, was now paying court to Jacqueline. What a blind fool Henry could be in these matters.

All of these unseemly capers added to Marie's own humiliation, and forced her to withdraw more into herself, hiding in her apartments with her Italian companions for hours at a time. She was deeply angry, couldn't help but feel bitter at the circumstances of her marriage, and again refusing to speak to Henry. Marie felt she had been as unfortunate as her mother, her life blighted by an unfaithful and neglectful husband.

Henry too was in despair. 'How am I to deal with her?' he asked his favourite advisor.

'You could always renounce your mistress, Sire, and offer complete loyalty to your Queen,' came the predictable reply.

Henry scowled. 'Or my wife could moderate her temper. Speak to her, I beg you. I am weary of these other women, of Mesdames de Moret and des Essarts, who have no wit and simple minds. I almost prefer a stormy interview with the Queen since she at least has some fire in her, which I greatly admire.'

'You wish me to tell Her Majesty this?'

'I do. And tell her that I am not responsible for Madame de Verneuil's wicked tongue.'

As always Rosny, or Sully, as he should rightfully now be called, tactfully intervened and yet again a shaky peace was forged between husband and wife. Which was just as well, as the official baptism of the royal children was about to take place and arrangements needed to be made. Each child had been given a private one at birth but now a grand, state occasion was planned. Once these arrangements had been set in motion the royal couple were sufficiently reconciled to go together to Saint Germain to spend some time with the children, which was always a joy to Marie. They stayed until the first week in June when they set out to return to the capital.

They were being driven in a coach drawn by eight horses, the day wet and miserable, the roads muddy due to a steady downpour of rain. With them were the Princess de Condé and the Dukes of Vendôme and Montpensier, attended by several gentlemen on horseback. It was still pouring with rain when the cumbersome vehicle reached the river at Neuilly, which they found to be running at such a flood that the horses struggled to draw the coach on to the ferry. One suddenly took fright and lunged forwards. The others followed and minutes later Marie was screaming.

'It is going over! We are sinking.'

Henry managed to quickly extricate himself, and seeing that his son was in danger of drowning, managed to grab him by the cloak and drag him to the shore.

Madame de Condé had fortunately landed in shallow water and was able to save herself with a little assistance from the Duke of Montpensier, although she fainted on reaching the bank.

But the Queen was still trapped inside the coach, which was sinking fast.

Seeing this tragedy unfolding before his very eyes, Henry plunged back into the swirling waters to save her. He was beaten to it by La Châteneraye, who, catching the Queen by the hair, ignominiously dragged her to the surface and helped her to the shore.

Marie lay pale as death in the mud, her rescuer and the King doing their utmost to revive her. At length she opened her eyes, and her first thought was for her husband. 'Where is the King, is he safe?'

'I am here, my love, and by the grace of God, so are you. I think the immersion has done me good,' he joked. 'Before that

I was suffering from a furious toothache, which now seems to be cured. And if any of us dined too heartily on salted meats, we have the satisfaction of having been able to drink freely.'

'How can you jest about such matters? We almost drowned. Where is César?' Marie looked about her in a panic.

'The little fellow is safe too, my love. We did not drown, and will hold a service of thanksgiving to celebrate our survival.'

Châteneraye was granted a private audience and presented with a jewelled star worth 4,000 *livres*, plus an ample pension and post as captain of Her Majesty's bodyguard, the Queen forever trusting him to keep her safe.

Paris was agog with the tale, giving their own prayers of thanksgiving for the rescue of their Queen consort. But within hours of returning to the capital Henry called upon La Marquise. She listened to the tale with glee, eyes round with amusement.

'Goodness, had I been there, once I had seen that *you* were safe, I should have exclaimed *la Reine boit!*'

Perhaps caught unawares by her wit, as so often in the past, Henry laughed. He was ashamed of this later but, unfortunately, the exchange was overheard by Concini, and when the King's reaction was relayed to the Queen, Marie was livid.

'Am I ever to be humiliated and vilified by that woman? And now by the King too who shares in her wicked wit? Am I to be nothing more than a source of ridicule to them both?' She felt deeply hurt and offended, her dignity as queen compromised to such a degree that she refused to receive her husband. The truce was over. 'I am done with him,' she cried. And although her anger gradually faded, and this, like all their other spats, eventually passed after an estrangement of three or four weeks, a part of her love for him did die as a result. Stung to the heart, it was one humiliation too many for the sensitive Marie.

Part Eight

THE END OF AN AFFAIR

The baptism had to be postponed as plague stalked the streets of Paris during August, and it was therefore decided that the ceremony should be transferred to Fontainebleau instead of the Church of Notre Dame. Queen Margot's household suffered the loss of three of her servants, and she hastily removed herself to a picturesque house at Issy, returning in early September for this grand state occasion. Marie, in a high state of nervous tension, and anxious not to be outshone by the former queen, chose to wear a lavish gown of cloth of gold set with thousands of precious stones. Now she stood before her Venetian glass in tears, knowing it was a complete failure.

'I cannot possibly wear this. It is far too heavy.' The weight of the gems were such that she could hardly move. It was not a good omen for the day.

'Your Majesty will be equally beautiful in something less oppressive,' Donna Leonora assured her, sending the maids of honour scurrying for a replacement gown.

'And Fontainebleau is far too small,' the Queen sobbed. 'Have you seen the numbers of guests arriving, and what of the spectators who will come to view the pageant later? How shall we manage?'

'All will be well, Madame, I promise you, and if it is not then Sully will be the one held responsible, not Your Majesty. Now breathe slowly, let us prepare you, then you can visit the children before the ceremony commences.'

'Oh, Leonora, what would I do without you?' Marie cried, allowing her *dame d'atours* to dry her tears.

Little Louis was five, old enough to understand, or so the King believed, the meaning of the rites to be administered. Princess Elizabeth was a pretty child of four. And then there was baby Christine. There had been some initial difficulty over who was to be godfather, since James I of England thought he should have been asked before the Pope, and the latter refused to share the role with a heretic, that is Anne of Denmark, the Protestant queen of James, who had been invited to stand for Madame Christine. Eventually matters had been resolved as diplomatically as possible, and Donna Leonora was proved right – all did go remarkably smoothly despite this fracas and disappointment over the venue.

'All praise to Sully for the extensive planning involved,' the Queen said as, at the end of a long and tiring day, Donna Leonora helped her to remove the substitute gown. And if it had not possessed quite the splendour of the first, or that of Queen Margot's extravagant creation in silver tissue draped with pearls, it had certainly been more comfortable to wear. 'It has been a remarkable and wonderful occasion. How splendid the crimson draperies, the canopy of silver over the font, the glorious processions, and how good the children were. Did you see how little Elizabeth looked about her in wonder? She missed nothing. What an intelligent child she is. Everything was perfect.'

But after the smallest of pauses, the Queen continued more quietly, 'Save for the King making unwelcome advances upon Madame de Nevers. In her innocence the dear lady at first accepted his compliments as being simply admiring of the calm serenity of her person. But once she realized that Henry was proposing to replace La Marquise with herself, she has fled to her estate at Nevers. Why will he not behave?' Marie sighed heavily, in near despair.

'Did Your Majesty note the number of great ladies now wearing enormous hoops in the style of Queen Margot?' Donna Leonora gently enquired in an attempt to change the subject.

'I did indeed.' The thought brought no greater satisfaction. It seemed at times that every one of Henry's women were able to influence him, and the court, save for herself.

There was one other woman who had caught the King's eye at the baptism, or rather a girl. Her eyes were huge, a soft brown set in the sweetest face that had no need of powder or paint. Her figure was slender but shapely for one so young. Her hair, which hung in shimmering waves down her back, was the fairest and silkiest the King had ever seen. Henry knew, the moment he set eyes on her, that he wanted her.

'Who is that girl?' he asked Sully.

'She is Charlotte Marguerite de Montmorency, the youngest daughter of the constable.' The minister glanced anxiously at his master, noting how the dark eyes glittered with interest, a look he knew well. 'And barely thirteen years old, Sire.'

'Is this her first time at court?'

'Mademoiselle de Montmorency has led a quiet, sheltered life at Vincennes, educated by her aunt who loves her dearly, her mother being dead. I believe she is somewhat neglected by her father, who only shows interest in the girl when he receives yet another offer for her hand. It is said that she had a half-dozen before she was twelve years old.'

'She is a rare beauty,' agreed Henry, almost salivating as he watched her gracefully walk in the procession beside his infant daughter. 'There is a beguiling innocence about her.'

But in the weeks and months ahead Henry had little time to think of this luscious young beauty as fresh domestic turmoil broke out between his queen and his mistress. Henriette was growing increasingly demanding, and Marie was again refusing to admit her to court. Henriette could be difficult, he conceded, and even cold towards himself if she was in one of her moods, of which Henry was growing somewhat weary. On one recent visit she had actually ordered him to leave.

'You have never brought me anything but misfortune,' she screamed at him.

Henry had felt deeply offended. 'Reflect a little, Madame; I do not deserve this treatment.'

Yet she continued to engage in these outbursts, and he continued to endure them, although perhaps with less grace. At other times she could, of course, be most loving, as exciting and daring as ever. But that would be when she wanted something, such as the time she wished to secure the bishopric of Metz for little Henri. She was also growing increasingly possessive. Henriette, like the Queen, seemed to demand exclusive rights over him, something Henry was quite unable to give.

Why were they both so quarrelsome? Did neither of them care to simply give him the love and peace he craved?

Henriette was in despair. Her power seemed to be slipping from her grasp with frightening speed, and her hope of igniting the

King's love through jealousy, by dallying with the Duke of Guise, did not seem to be working. Weary of seclusion and yet another banishment from court she wrote to Henry repeating her request to retire to London, or Madrid. 'I wish to devote myself to religion, and preserve my honour and dignity at least.'

This time it was not entirely a ploy. She was desperate to get away, anywhere there was some life and fun to be had. She was dying from frustration and boredom cooped up in the country with no companions but her servants and her sister. Henriette had never loved the King, only the role she'd played as a royal mistress. If that was lost to her, or no longer what it should be, then far better to gain her freedom and look elsewhere. But she still needed protection in the form of favours for her children, and a pension for herself. The Queen could not have things all her own way.

Henriette sent her son a Spanish missal, suggesting it might help him to learn the language, but received a furious letter back from the King when he discovered it one morning at prayers.

'How dare Henry interfere with what a mother chooses to give her son,' she railed at her sister, ever the butt of her fury.

Marie-Charlotte sighed. 'Because he is the King, and the boy's father.'

'Read this letter, read what he says. No, I shall read it to you. "This morning at matins I took a book of prayer in Spanish from your son. He told me the book was your gift. It is my will that my said son shall not even know that there exists a Spain." What think you of that?'

'I think you should take care, sister, or your rivals will warm his bed more often than you would care for.'

Never one to give up easily, and remembering how the Queen's *dame d'atours*, Donna Leonora, had helped her once before, Henriette decided to make use of the woman again, and quickly dashed off a letter to her. Perhaps the Italian could gain her admittance to court circles again, where the King had failed.

A reply came within days, although it did not please her. 'Damnation, the woman refuses to help. This letter comes from her husband, Concini, in which he expresses regret that duty to the Queen prevents both himself and his wife from espousing the interests of a woman whose tongue daily inflicts outrage on her royal mistress. How dare he speak to me in such tones!'

'Barring the insult to your good self, sister, I am sure there is some truth in what he says. Donna Leonora is an insipid, humble creature, entirely devoted to the Queen and in thrall to her ambitious husband. Concini's one weakness is that he hates to be ill-thought of by the nobles of the court. He wishes to be considered their equal.'

'He will never be accepted, not when even the King dislikes him.' Her eyes brightened on a new thought. 'In fact, I would be doing Henry a favour were I to rid the court of the Italian's obnoxious presence. Bring paper and pen. Hurry, I have other letters to write this day. I shall teach the arrogant rogue a lesson for trying to best me.'

'Matters are getting entirely out of hand,' Marie complained to the King in some agitation, having great difficulty in controlling her fury. 'My uncle the Grand Duke informs me that he has discovered a plot to have Concini killed. And the source of this latest intrigue is none other than your harlot!'

Henry frowned. 'Guard your language, wife.'

'Why? That is exactly what she is. It seems La Marquise begged for my equerry's help, and that of Donna Leonora. They were apparently expected to persuade me to have her received back at court, and when they refused, she decided upon revenge. It is an outrage! The woman is a threat to the safety of my household, if not the entire nation.'

'I think you greatly exaggerate her influence.'

'I do not!' Marie snapped. 'And why would she imagine that such a plot could ever succeed unless she were sure of *your* blessing in ridding the court of my favourite.'

Henry almost spluttered with anger. 'If there were any truth in this—'

'Oh, there is indeed proof. La Marquise hired assassins and may well have succeeded with her nasty little scheme had not one of her brigands found himself arrested for some trifling theft in Florence. Papers were found on him outlining the plot. Praise God, the Grand Duke informed me in good time, and although my other uncle, Don Giovanni, is treating the matter as unimportant, it is very far from that. I will not have the lives of people I most trust and rely upon, put into danger by Your Majesty's strumpet.'

Henry's face now turned purple, his rage matching hers. '*If* there is indeed proof,' he repeated, 'the fellow has only himself to blame. He is far too arrogant and full of himself. He had the insolence to enter the lists at a grand tilting at the ring the other day at the Rue St Antoine. He did this in *my* presence and without asking my permission.'

'You are only annoyed because he won the prize you coveted for yourself,' Marie scoffed.

'The scoundrel is presumptuous.'

'He is skilled. Accept defeat gracefully, Sire. Even a King must lose sometimes.'

Henry growled his disapproval. Since he could not control his wife, either of his women in fact, winning at his favourite activities was even more important to him. He devoted much of his days to hunting and field sports, and his nights to gaming. It served as some sort of solace against the waning passion he felt for La Marquise, and his boredom with her so-called replacements. But Marie wasn't done with him yet.

'I hear you are now lusting after a mere child.'

'Then you hear wrong, Madame. It is but gossip. I have not touched the girl.' Too late he realized he'd fallen into her trap, for she hadn't even mentioned a name. And indeed he would touch her, if he had the chance. Sadly, the delectable Charlotte had withdrawn to the country again, with her aunt, and he could find no way to lure her back to court, as yet.

'Forgive me if I find that hard to believe,' Marie scornfully remarked, her lip curling with disgust. 'Am I to be forever humiliated by your women, and used by you so that you can procure them? You'll no doubt grant her a title and order me to accept her too within my circle so that she is conveniently available. Then you'll take her to your bed, despite the forty year difference in your ages. While I will be expected to bear the shame of it, even if you do not.' Never had she spoken to the King so brutally before, nor with such deep loathing in her tone. Marie could feel the anger churning in her stomach, scalding her like hot acid.

Henry, hating emotional scenes with a cowardice he had never shown on the battlefield, turned his back on her and strode from the room.

'Do not walk away from me!' Marie screamed, stamping her foot in rage.

The only answer was the slamming of the door.

Harsh letters were exchanged between them, even the Queen's competence as regent brought into question. Neither would back down, the King determined to exercise his right as monarch, and the Queen feeling her anger to be highly justified. Sully again attempted to intercede, but the royal estrangement lasted even longer this time; an aloofness between the royal pair as painful and absolute as a divorce. Marie might alternately weep and rage, and Henry suffer from an almost equal confusion of kisses and reproaches from Henriette, but this time there was no sign of a rapprochement.

The dispute ended, ironically, when Concini himself informed the King of another plot, this time against His Majesty. 'The only way to frustrate it is to restore marital harmony between yourself, Sire, and the Queen. The plotters will then have no reason to proceed with the plan.'

'And where is the source of this alleged plot?' Henry wanted to know, hoping against hope it could not be traced back to Henriette.

But he had underestimated the Italian's cleverness. 'I believe much of it springs from Don Giovanni, the Queen's uncle.' A man Concini had long hated.

The King and Queen were duly reconciled and Don Giovanni ordered to return to Florence, much to the delight of both Marie and her favourites.

'Let him be sacrificed,' the Queen agreed. 'We are well rid of him.'

So it was that by 25 April 1608, when Marie gave birth to a son, Gaston, the royal couple were on reasonably affable terms. The King was so pleased with his wife that he granted her the sum of twelve thousand *livres* towards decorating her château at Monceaux. And to Marie's particular delight, this time there was no corresponding *accouchement* from the she-cat.

Henriette was placated somewhat when, by the end of the year, she was at last permitted to return to Paris. Even the Queen made an attempt to be civil to her, and once asked after the health of her son when Monsieur de Metz was suffering from some childish complaint. Henriette begged to have her children come and stay with her, as strict rules were set upon her access to them. They remained firmly under the care of Madame de Montglât, who had orders from the King not to allow Madame de Verneuil anywhere near the children without his written permission. He did, however, agree for them to take a short holiday at the country home of Roquelaure, where Henriette might enjoy their company for a few days.

The same restrictions were placed upon her visits to see her father at Malesherbes. Her brother Auvergne remained a prisoner in the Bastille, only his wife being permitted to visit him once a week.

'My brother is ill,' she sobbed to the King. 'You must free him from that dank, dreadful place. He is innocent of this charge of treason. He should not even be there.' Henriette flung herself into his arms, kissing him with all the skill that had once excited passion in him. Now he set her from him with a sad shake of the head.

'I will grant no indulgences to Monsieur d'Auvergne.'

Henry's soft heart did allow the Count to be transferred from his dark and dank prison chamber to one in the tower of the Arsenal, which boasted a barred window through which he could look out on to the fortress garden and watch Sully tending his beloved vegetables. A mixed blessing so far as Auvergne was concerned.

Convinced she was losing her hold over the King, Henriette sought solace in affairs. She readily took the dashing young Duke of Guise to her bed. Not only was he a passionate and exciting lover, but a rich husband of prominence was exactly what she needed. There was no greater house than that of the Princes of Lorraine. Henriette used all her wiles and skilful tricks to make him happy, and smiled to herself when the *chevalier* soon began to profess his love for her.

'But we must keep this from the King,' he warned her, thinking of his own safety as much as hers.

'Of course, my love,' Henriette agreed, even as she secretly hoped otherwise. In the past such dalliances had always provoked jealousy in Henry, and brought him to heel. Let him see how little I need him, she told herself. Let him writhe in agony to hear of me giving pleasure to another. She hoped and prayed the ploy would work again. Even if Henry tired of the empty-headed Jacqueline, there would surely be others eager to replace her. One way or another she had to secure her own future.

'Are you spreading the whispers?' she asked of her sister, ever reliable in such matters.

'Exactly as you instructed.'

'Then why is the King not pounding on my door? Try harder, you stupid girl,' Henriette snapped, peevishly pinching Marie-Charlotte's arm. 'And make sure you feed the gossip into the right ears.'

But still the King did not come, was in fact said to be chasing Madame de Nevers again. Henriette was therefore overjoyed when Guise asked for her hand in marriage, which she gladly accepted. Marriage into the House of Lorraine would be a most satisfying revenge upon the King for his rejection of her.

There were other, surer ways of settling the score, such as those instigated by her own father, which at times still occupied the recesses of her mind. Her father and brother had risked all and lost. How much was she prepared to gamble to see her son upon the throne? Would not such a triumph mean that she could then grant them their freedom herself, as regent? A heady prospect.

The King, of course, was still alive and well, and for now Henriette hoped he might come to realize how much he missed and needed her. She longed for Henry to be tormented by jealousy, as in the old days of their passion. Failing that he could at least give the permission she sought to create a new future for herself.

Time enough to contemplate other measures if he failed to oblige.

Using false names to disguise their intentions, Guise put up the banns. But when Henry finally got wind of the scheme, as nothing could ever remain secret for long in this court, he put a stop to the plan at once. He had no more wish now for La Marquise to come too close to the throne than he had the first time she had considered marriage with Joinville, or any of the other *chevaliers* who had fancied her charms and recklessly offered for her. Were that to happen, say by her marrying into the House of Lorraine, she would become an even greater threat to the Queen. He absolutely refused to grant his permission, coolly reminding the reckless young duke of the number of times he'd needed forgiveness in the past for his indiscretions and offences.

'I forbid you to pursue a purpose so distasteful to all those who have your honour at heart.'

The King's refusal brought fresh hope to Henriette. 'There you are, you see, he does still love me,' she cried in exultation to her ever-patient sister. 'Henry will be here to see me within the week.'

But he wasn't. The King did not come running to her side as he might have done in days gone by. He was weary of her tricks and schemes, and no longer felt the same desire for her. Clever she may be, but perhaps, on this occasion, too cunning for her own good. Even Henriette could see that in desperately attempting to win back what she had lost, she had succeeded only in extinguishing the dying embers of his spent passion. Henry was done with her. He had quite a different quarry in his sights now.

Oh, but how her heart beat with the need for revenge.

Charlotte was beside herself with excitement. Everything was going right for her at last and she couldn't be more happy. She was even about to dance in a royal ballet organized by the Queen herself. Her life thus far had been spent quietly at Chantilly with her Aunt Diane, Duchesse d'Angoulême, who until now had resisted all efforts to allow her to come to court.

'The French Court is a wicked place,' the old lady would say to her niece. 'I should know, as I was raised there, largely by Diane de Poitiers, mistress to King Henri II. Not at all a place for innocent young girls.' But being now somewhat old and infirm, and Charlotte only months from her fifteenth birthday, she had finally relented.

The event which had persuaded the old lady to change her mind was that Charlotte had become engaged to be married.

Weary of the endless offers for her hand her father, Henri de Montmorency, one of a long line in the family to be Constable of France, had invited the young Ducs de Roquelaure, d'Epernon, Zamet and Bassompierre to his house in order to choose one as a husband for her. Charlotte had hoped it would be the latter, as she was already most attached to him. Bassompierre was so handsome, and a perfect dancer.

'When Father has chosen, will I then be able to go to court?' she'd asked her aunt.

The Duchess smiled, and kissed her cheek. 'Charlotte, dearest, you are young, with all your life before you. I know you are eager to taste whatever excitements the court can offer, but proper arrangements need to be made. I will agree so long as you are first betrothed to be married. You will then be permitted to accompany your affianced to court, accompanied by myself as chaperone of course. But you must guard your chattering tongue, child, and mark well my warnings. Keep yourself chaste and pure until you are safely wed.'

'Oh, I will, Aunt.' Excitement had bubbled up in her, and her hopes were high. Her father had always favoured Bassompierre, thinking him more worthy than most of the nobles who'd come panting at his door for love of her. But would he agree? 'What if Bassompierre should say no?' she'd asked, her lovely elfin face suddenly pale with concern. The *chevalier* was so deliciously handsome that Charlotte could hardly bear the thought.

'Why would he do such a foolish thing when you come with a substantial dowry of one hundred thousand *livres*?' her aunt had replied, giving one of her barking laughs.

Charlotte hadn't wanted to think too deeply about such practical concerns. She thought only of love and the gallant charms of her chosen *chevalier*. Seeing her niece's quick frown, the old lady softened a little to give her an affectionate hug, stroking back the fair curls that sprang with a life of their own above the high forehead.

'How could he resist your fragile beauty, my sweet one? He will feel as if he has been granted possession of the crown jewels.'

The Duchess was proved to be entirely correct. At the end of the banquet, her father had brought the eager new suitor to meet her. 'I have always loved you as a son,' he told Bassompierre. 'Now I give my daughter to you in the full assurance that the marriage will be a happy one. *Mon fils*, behold the wife I have in store for you – embrace her.'

Bassompierre looked as if he was quite unable to believe his good fortune in securing such a prize, and far better than continuing to tangle himself with Marie-Charlotte. The deal, it seemed, was agreed.

'Accept him, my dear, and you will make me the happiest of fathers.'

Charlotte was more than happy to do so. Blushing with delight she dipped a curtsey and readily gave him her hand to kiss. In truth she had no real choice in the matter, yet as well as being anxious to please her stern father, she was half in love with him already.

Instructions were immediately given to draw up the marriage contract without delay, but then Roquelaure and the other nobles advised caution. 'If, Monsieur Constable, you have affianced your daughter without previously informing the King, it would be deemed an act of contempt which His Majesty never would pardon.'

Montmorency was obliged to accept the justification of this. He already had one son-in-law in the Bastille, Auvergne being the husband of his elder daughter. He certainly had no wish for another. 'I see the sense in what you say. Unfortunately, His Majesty and I are not on the best of terms at the present time. We recently disagreed over a proposed alliance between my son and his daughter, the little Mademoiselle de Vendôme.' Clapping Bassompierre on the shoulder in a friendly manner, he continued, 'Why do not you inform the King yourself, and seek his blessing?'

The young man looked stricken. 'His Majesty will say that I have nothing to offer, and it is true. I am neither of princely birth, nor have a fortune to bestow on my intended bride.'

Charlotte listened to all of this with deepening fear and trepidation. Nothing must be allowed to go wrong. She desperately wanted to go to court, and to marry her *chevalier*.

'You have honesty and good taste, sir. Charm and breeding, and I have long been fond of you. I see no reason why the King would not grant it.'

Roquelaure stepped quickly forward. 'Perhaps we might be of assistance in this delicate matter by informing His Majesty of your intentions, perhaps tomorrow night at the *coucher*.'

Montmorency sighed with relief. 'Thank you, good sir, that would serve well. Let it be known to His Majesty that I am ever mindful of my daughter's honour. I want only the best for her.'

So here she now was at the Louvre, dressed in a faintly ridiculous costume of green and yellow gauze, about to appear in the royal ballet as one of seven nymphs to Queen Marie's Diana.

'It is all so thrilling,' she giggled to one of her fellow performers. A harp was playing and the girls were practising their steps and pirouettes with much laughter and teasing.

'Look,' her companion whispered in sudden urgency. 'See that man by the door watching us. It is the King himself.'

Charlotte laughed. 'Are you sure? He looks so old.'

'He *is* old, past fifty. You can see that by his grey hair and beard. But it is His Majesty, I am certain of it.'

'Then let him see us dance.'

On impulse, Charlotte tossed back her blonde tresses and pirouetted gracefully across the room, then lifting her bow aimed the arrow at the King's breast. Laughing, he put up his hands in mock surrender, and with a teasing glance she sank into a swift curtsey before running giggling back to her comrades.

Henry remained where he was for some moments, watching the girl dance, admiring her lithesome figure, recalling her angelic little face, an innocent coquette smiling up at him. He had been informed by Roquelaure of the coming nuptials between this lovely creature and Bassompierre. Now, having remembered the first time he saw her at his children's baptism, he decided to investigate the matter more closely before granting his permission.

Following the ballet, Henry paid several more visits to the Queen's apartments, and on occasions spoke privately to the girl. He would flatter and tease her, could see that she was warming to him, no doubt thinking him a rather nice old man. He offered her gifts, not too many, as he had no wish to overwhelm her. She was such a gentle creature, a dear little angel who reminded him so much of his beloved Gabrielle. Henry tried to tell himself that not for a moment did he expect to become her lover, while he knew all along that was exactly what he longed for. He merely demonstrated kindness and affection, as a father might, although she appeared not to mind the difference in their years. And if at fifteen she was old enough to marry, she was surely of an age to know her own mind on how, and to whom, she granted her favours. He asked for her views on her coming marriage.

'As my father has commanded me so to do, I am well content to accept the suit of Monsieur de Bassompierre.' Charlotte smiled, thinking the King sweet and caring. But Henry saw that she was head-over-heels in love with the scamp already, which was troubling.

The courtiers were up in arms over the alliance, which they thought entirely inappropriate. Other family members of the Montmorency House considered Bassompierre quite beneath them. Henriette had also heard the rumours and was furiously demanding that the King refuse to give his permission.

'The scoundrel has been dallying with my sister for years. She even had a child by him. He has injured her greatly, has betrayed her under a promise of marriage, and should not be rewarded with so fair a prize.'

But the more Henry learned about the girl, the more time he spent in her company, the more Henry wanted her for himself. He did not see any problem with their age difference. He had never failed to win a woman; still thought of himself as reasonably good looking and a vigorous lover. And he was the King after all. The very idea of seeing her with Bassompierre was keeping him awake at nights, tormented with jealousy.

'Mayhap the new husband and I could come to an agreement,' the King mused.

Roquelaure issued a warning, which Henry knew in his heart to be true. 'Sire, if you marry her to Bassompierre he would quickly gain her affection, and she is so fond of him that she would likely remain a faithful wife. Your Majesty needs to consign her a husband who would be less demanding, and more agreeable to Your Majesty's terms.'

Henry leaned forward in his chair, taut with interest. 'I am listening. Who do you suggest?'

'The young Prince de Condé. As he is a Bourbon, a member of your own family, he is regularly at court, so you would daily meet her on intimate terms.'

'Ah, that is true.' Henry was thoughtful. 'But why would he agree? He is a Prince of the Blood and could marry whom he pleases.'

Roquelaure shrugged. 'I'm not so sure that he could. Suspicion still lingers over his mother's possible involvement in the poisoning of his own father, your beloved cousin and comrade-in-arms, Henri, Prince de Condé.'

A shadow crossed the King's face. 'That is true. He was not an easy man, being austere and filled with fervour for the reformed religion, but he was my very dear friend and cousin. His wife may well have been innocent, but it could never be proved.'

'Furthermore,' Roquelaure continued, 'his son is more interested in the chase, and in military matters, than feminine charms. I dare say he would be willing to allow Your Majesty precedence, so long as it was made worth his while.'

Henry beamed his pleasure. 'I will speak to Bassompierre forthwith.'

Unfortunately, Charlotte's father, the Constable, was laid low with gout for a while, as was the King. But when Henry was sufficiently recovered to sit up in bed and receive visitors, he sent for Bassompierre. Unsuspecting, the young man knelt before his sovereign, and Henry could see in his young handsome face that he came eager to hear that permission had at last been granted.

'My dear fellow,' Henry began, propping himself comfortably up on his pillows, 'I must tell you that I have hardly slept this night as I have been thinking of you. I wish you to marry and be happy.'

'Then Your Majesty's wish will soon be granted,' Bassompierre brightly assured the King. 'It would have been already were it not for the Constable suffering from the same complaint, but new arrangements have been put in place and—'

'No, no,' Henry hastily interrupted. 'I was thinking of offering you the hand of Mademoiselle d'Aumale, and of restoring in your favour the confiscated title and honours of that house.'

Bassompierre looked stunned by this news. 'B–but Your Majesty, I cannot marry two wives!'

Henry leaned forward, soft tears of pity in his eyes. 'Bassompierre, I am going to speak to you as a friend, and not as your king. I am desperately enamoured of Mademoiselle de Montmorency. If you marry her and she loves you, I shall hate you. If she loved me, then *you* would hate me. Let us not, therefore, risk the destruction of our friendship, for *mon ami* I care for you and your interests greatly.'

'What are you saying, Sire?' Bemused, the young gallant gazed into the King's face, an ache of fear starting up somewhere around his heart.

'I have resolved to give Mademoiselle de Montmorency to my nephew, the Prince de Condé, and so bring her into my own family. She will become the consolation and solace of the old age now before me. I will give my nephew an income of one hundred thousand *livres*. He prefers hunting to the society of ladies, so she will be no loss to him. And I desire nothing more from Mademoiselle de Montmorency than her regard. I neither pretend nor covet more.'

This last was a lie, and they both knew it. Not for a second did Bassompierre believe the denial. He knew only too well that Henry coveted much more than mere friendship from her.

Too stunned to speak for some long seconds, at last he gathered his thoughts sufficiently to realize there was little he could do but agree. This was the King, after all, and if he foolishly and ungraciously refused to accept the inevitable, then Bassompierre knew he would run the risk of losing His Majesty's favour entirely, and not just a beautiful wife.

Inclining his head, he strived to keep the tremor from his voice as he answered with as good a grace as he could manage. 'I ask only to serve Your Majesty, to evince my gratitude and complete devotion. I will do as you ask and relinquish my claim on the lady. Great though my sorrow and disappointment is to lose her, I pray that this new attachment may bring Your Majesty felicity and content.'

Henry put out his arms and embraced him, clapping Bassompierre on the back with great affection. 'I shall further your fortunes as though you were one of my own natural children. Know that I love you dearly, and be well assured that your frankness and friendship will be richly rewarded.'

And as his defeated rival took his leave, backing out of the royal chamber as etiquette demanded, the King privately congratulated himself at concluding this delicate affair so well. Dealing with Condé would be even simpler by comparison.

The Constable attempted to protest, stating that his daughter already possessed a fiancé and had no need of another, and, as great-uncle to Monsieur le Prince, neither had he any wish for a closer relationship with him. But it made not the slightest difference. As always, the will of the King prevailed. Condé himself was entirely agreeable, and even the young Charlotte, when informed by Henry of this change of plan, philosophically accepted the inevitable. As she left the royal apartments and passed her rejected suitor, she resignedly shrugged her slender shoulders, smiling kindly at him.

Suddenly overcome by what he had lost, Bassompierre turned on his heel and strode from the Louvre, quite certain that his would-be bride had no notion of the King's true plans for her.

'I shall be a princess now,' she happily told her aunt. Charlotte knew very little about her new fiancé, nothing of his temperament or his interests, but felt sure her increased status would be some consolation for the loss of the gallant Bassompierre.

The Duchess was less certain. 'Better a wife than a mistress, certainly,' she sharply retorted. 'And so long as the Prince is permitted to fulfil the role of husband.'

Charlotte stared at her aunt blankly. 'Why would he not be?'

'My dear child, what an innocent you are. Take my advice and do not allow yourself to be alone with the King.'

'But he is so sweet to me, and so generous. Yesterday he gave me a bracelet of garnets which he said matched my ruby lips.' Charlotte giggled. She was deeply flattered by the interest the King was showing in her personal affairs, and loved all the attention he showered upon her. 'He is an old man. Where is the harm in it?'

The Duchesse d'Angoulême frowned, worrying over how much she should say to warn her niece. Was it treason to block a King's pleasure? 'I ask only that you keep yourself pure for your husband, whoever he may be.'

Some part of her aunt's message must have penetrated Charlotte's childlike mind for a new thought struck her. Would she, by marrying Condé, gain a prince but lose a King?

No time was wasted in bringing the couple together and the betrothal took place within weeks in the great gallery of the Louvre. If Charlotte noticed the King keeping one arm clamped about her former fiancé's shoulder so that he could not escape, she paid it no heed. She was overwhelmed by the majesty of the occasion. Henry had presented her with the most beautiful wedding robes which must have cost over 10,000 *livres*, and the

Queen gave her jewels valued at twice that sum. The wedding itself was solemnized at Fontainebleau on 17 May 1609 and Charlotte revelled in the attention being paid to her, dancing with happy delight at the ball that Queen Marguerite gave to celebrate the occasion.

A few months later in July, fifteen-year-old César was also married, to Françoise de Lorraine, a wealthy heiress to the duchies of Mercœur and Penthièvre. Henry was in such high spirits, and determined to show off his youthful vigour and prowess to Charlotte, the new Princess de Condé, that he took part in all manner of jousts and tilting of the ring in a bid to impress her. In the evenings when there was music and dancing he wore perfumed collars and dressed in his finest robes, decked out in the kind of rich colours you would expect to see on a much younger man.

'Yet again he is making a fool of himself,' the Queen mourned, feeling helpless even as she wished to protect the girl of whom she was quite fond.

Donna Leonora listened with every sympathy, but knew, as did the Queen, that if the King had set his mind on the empty-headed little chit, there was nothing anyone could do to prevent the inevitable. Nevertheless, she wanted to ease her mistress's concern. 'I hear the young couple are not getting on too well. He, poor boy, has fallen head-over-heels in love with her, but his love is not reciprocated. Perhaps Your Majesty could speak with the girl and encourage her to be more generous.'

'Does she still pine for Bassompierre?'

'Possibly, but she also sees a great deal of the King.'

The two women looked at each other, almost reading each other's mind. 'Does the child not appreciate how she plays with fire by pandering to the royal infatuation? Someone should warn her new husband.'

'I suspect Condé is well aware of the danger. The girl's father has suggested they take a short sojourn at one of the summer palaces.'

'An excellent notion. Keep me informed, Madame.' The wedding festivities had already become a trial to her, and Marie was desperate to have done with them and leave.

Donna Leonora bowed. 'I will, Your Majesty.'

★   ★   ★

At that precise moment Charlotte was cavorting on her balcony in a diaphanous *robe de chambre*. The King, who was urging her to call him by his given name, had earlier begged her to step out and show herself to him. 'I cannot sleep for thinking of you, dearest angel. Pray be generous to an old man,' he had begged her.

Of course she'd agreed without demur, and protested at this description of himself, as was expected. 'You do not appear old to me, Sire, but as handsome and gallant as any courtier. I saw you in the lists taking on men half your age, and winning.' Not that any *chevalier* would dare to defeat a king, but Charlotte had the wit not to suggest they would willingly allow Henry to win.

'You are my angel,' he told her. 'The light of my old age. You fill my heart with joy.'

She blushed prettily, enchanted by the attention he lavished upon her and eager to show her gratitude. 'Do not say such things, Your Majesty; I am a married woman now.'

'Perhaps you could bestow a kiss on your royal admirer?' And giggling delightedly, Charlotte blew him one.

Now she was positioning herself before the bright blaze of light coming from the torches on the wall behind her, aware that by doing so the King would be able to see every curve in the outline of her naked body beneath the translucent, Grecian-styled robe she wore. Oh, but this was the King of France whom she held enthralled in her hand. What delicious power there was in that. But then seeing how he waved to her from the garden below, how he gesticulated and begged her for more, even Charlotte quailed before his implied demands, and, scarlet-cheeked, hurried back inside.

'Goodness, it is hot this evening,' she told her maids, who hid their smiles behind their hands.

Her husband was less amused by such scandalous behaviour, and particularly incensed when he learned that she had secretly sat for her portrait at the wishes of the King, for all it was a simple pastel. Charlotte was proving to be a compliant wife, in every way, save for this childish desire to allow herself to be so foolishly flattered. And Condé could guess only too well where that was leading.

The wedding festivities of the young Duke of Vendôme were

drawing to a close, not least because the Queen's uncle, the Grand Duke Ferdinand, had recently died and Queen Marie had gone into mourning. Condé took his wife home to Chantilly and ordered her to remain there.

'Also, you must accept no more gifts from the King,' he sternly instructed her, and was obliged to direct his gaze away as her beautiful face crumpled with disappointment.

'Why should I not when His Majesty is so generous and so persistent?'

'You are my wife; it is unseemly for you to receive presents from other men, even from a king.' He might have added, particularly this king. 'There will be no more royal ballets, no more private meetings, no portraits painted without my express permission. You must know that I love you, that it hurts me to see you fawning for attention from that old lecher, Henry Quatre.' His expression was both bleak and pleading.

Charlotte returned his gaze unmoved. Did he not understand how very important it was to obey a king? 'What can I do,' she asked, 'when he makes his desire for my company so plain?'

'It is not simply your company he craves.' Should he tell her that he had already got wind of a plot to have their marriage dissolved? Would that make her more or less intransigent? All Condé wanted was to make his wife love him, but he couldn't quite work out how to achieve this seemingly impossible task when she was so besotted by the King's dubious courtship.

Henry wrote ordering him to return to court, but Condé stubbornly refused. Instead, he sent a messenger to the Low Countries, seeking assistance and protection from the Archduke and Archduchess.

The King spoke to Sully, as always needing the help of his favourite advisor. '*Mon ami*, Monsieur le Prince has been playing the devil. You would be in a fine passion, as well as ashamed of all the evil things which he says of me. My patience at length will tire out, and I shall speak my mind.' The King went on to instruct Sully to refrain from paying Condé's next quarter's pension.

'But Your Majesty promised this to the Prince as part of the deal, Sire?'

'Now I have changed my mind,' Henry roared. 'If this does not restrain him, I must adopt other means.'

Prince Condé's response was to bravely confront the King and ask to leave the court. 'I wish us to reside at my mansion at Saint Valery.'

'Absolutely not!' Henry retorted. 'You will stay here, where you belong and are needed.'

But the Prince was beyond cajolery or bribery now. 'Your Majesty desires to seduce my wife, and by that intent you annul all the benefits that your royal generosity conferred upon me. By the grace of God, I will not submit to such tyranny, nor will I be made the object of the contemptuous pity of your court.'

Henry was inflamed with fury at such defiance. 'Never in the course of my life have I acted as a tyrant, save that I have compelled everyone to acknowledge you for what you are *not!*'

Condé went pale. Was the King implying that he was not his father's son, that his mother was indeed guilty of the senior Condé's death? This was all becoming far more serious than he had bargained for.

Meanwhile, annoyed by the strict rules imposed upon her freedom by her new husband, Charlotte did what all dissatisfied brides do, she ran home, in this case to her aunt and father. 'I will not tolerate such control,' she cried, pouting pettishly.

'You will certainly please the King by coming to Vincennes,' her aunt mildly conceded. 'His Majesty may at this very moment be on his way here to see you. But by running away you deeply offend your husband, and does the poor fellow deserve to be so treated? He loves you, dearest. Why can you not appreciate what you have, instead of crying for the moon?'

'But the King loves me too, and I cannot bear to remain in that dull château a moment longer. I wish to return to the gaiety of the court.'

The Duchess considered her niece with sadness in her heart. 'There is more to life than merrymaking and feasting. And far better to be a wife, than a mistress, even to a king.'

Henry arrived the very next day, exactly as she had predicted, ostensibly to offer comfort to the poor abused bride. 'You have only to ask, dear angel, and I will do all in my power to help you free yourself from this vagabond.'

'Oh, but . . .' Charlotte began, realizing she had perhaps implied things about her new husband which were not strictly true. The Prince had certainly been nothing but entirely kind and agreeable to her. But if that were true, why did she wish to leave him?

Queen Marie quickly stepped in to assure the confused young woman that her exile from court need only be temporary. 'Your wifely duty demands that you leave with the Prince your husband, but I promise that when my *accouchement* is imminent, I will send for you, and summon you back to my side.' Marie had doubts on the wisdom of doing even this, but she could not bear to see the pretty child so miserable. 'I am sure Henri de Condé will make you a good husband, given the chance.'

In the end it was the Constable who settled the matter, insisting that his daughter obey her husband, as she had vowed to do in the wedding service, and accept a sojourn at the summer palace, as he had earlier suggested.

Condé made every effort to please his bride, being most attentive and considerate. Although, to her intense disappointment the young couple were accompanied on their wedding journey by the Dowager Princess, Condé's mother. Even worse, the old lady seemed determined to keep a very close eye on her daughter-in-law indeed.

Back at court Henry raged back and forth, far from pleased to hear that the young *chevalier* had disobeyed him. Even Sully agreed that the young prince was audacious to have taken his bride even further away. 'He is wracked with love for her, Sire, and jealous enough to spirit his new wife out of the country.'

'I will not allow it,' Henry stormed, and ordered the young couple to return to court forthwith.

Condé dare not refuse the summons entirely, but he came alone to face his monarch, without the company of his wife who remained under the close guard of his mother. Henry was so incensed by this obstinate refusal to comply with his demands that he next turned to his old ruse of disguise. Donning a long false beard and rough clothing he set out to attend the hunt at Muret, pretending to be a servant in a bid to secretly meet with his heart's desire, as he had once done when courting Gabrielle.

The plan failed. Condé's chancellor, Rochefort, brought his master warning of the ploy, possibly by devious means from the

Queen herself. The Prince made sure he was present at the hunt, and that his wife was nowhere to be seen. Furthermore, he warned his mother not to let Charlotte out of her sight, in case the King should present himself at the château.

'He will not best me,' Henry cried, and invited all the ladies to a feast. Charlotte came, looking as beautiful and desirable as ever, but her mother-in-law came with her, and was in close attendance throughout. Henry found no opportunity to speak to the girl in private. 'It was vastly frustrating,' he told Sully, who wisely made no comment whatsoever.

When the time came for the Queen's lying-in, Henry ordered her to summon Charlotte to court. Marie considered her husband with cold disdain but did as she was bid. Where was the point in arguing? She would succeed only in upsetting herself and the unborn babe. Fortunately, Condé had the temerity, or the courage, to visit the Queen and refuse.

'Sadly, Your Majesty, I cannot allow my wife to accept your invitation.'

'It was not an invitation but an order of the King. Besides, since the health of your mother the Dowager Princess precludes her from attending me, it is surely only fitting that your wife takes her place?' Even as Marie protested, she secretly admired the stance this young prince was taking.

'I regret, Your Majesty, that will not be possible, for reasons I am sure you will understand.'

The Queen flushed with embarrassment, but did not ask for any further explanation. Nor did she want one. 'Very well, I will inform the King of your decision.'

Condé bowed and took his leave, but spent the next few weeks constantly glancing over his shoulder, expecting at any moment to be arrested for defying the King. 'I must get her away,' he told Rochefort. 'I beg you to help me to protect my wife, and my marriage, from this fierce attachment the King has formed towards her. I intend to visit my sister Eleanor, the Princess of Orange, at Bréda, and beg for her protection.'

'Will the King give you permission, think you?'

'I shall not ask for it. I cannot see how even the King could object to my introducing my new wife to my only sister.'

'Then take care not to alert him to the plan, or he may well attempt to stop you leaving the realm.'

Fearing yet another summons, or worse, Condé visited the Duchesse d'Angoulême, and confessed that he may have offended the Queen. 'May I beg you, Madame, to offer Her Majesty my sincere apologies for my discourtesy in opposing her commands. Please assure her that I will personally escort my wife, the Princess, to the Louvre in but a few days' time.'

The Duchess regarded him with a steady and shrewd gaze, not at all taken in by this sudden change of heart. 'I shall be glad to do so, and wish you well.'

Condé quietly took his leave and recklessly called upon Sully that same afternoon to issue the same message. The minister was at once suspicious.

'Be warned that His Majesty knows full well how to quell rebellion. You would not be the first royal prince to suffer wholesome restraint.'

Condé was privately shocked by this implied threat, yet even more determined to carry through with his plan, and at once set about secretly borrowing the necessary funds from close friends and family to implement it. He openly declared his intention of visiting Muret for a few days, after which he would return to court with his wife in time for the Queen's *accouchement*. The young couple set out at dawn the very next day, but within hours of their arrival news was brought to them that the Queen had been delivered of a girl child, Henrietta Maria. There was no more time to be lost as Her Majesty, no doubt under orders from the King, would be sure to summon them back to court.

'Dearest, I have decided to hold a hunt, and it would please me greatly if this time you were to attend.'

Charlotte considered this request with a puzzled frown. 'I doubt I'd be much good at chasing the boar, husband.'

Condé smiled and kissed her brow, teasing her delightful blonde curls with gentle fingers. 'Sweet one, I should never ask such a thing of you. But there will be feasting afterwards. You would enjoy that, would you not?'

'Oh yes,' Charlotte cried, clapping her hands with childish

delight. 'I should indeed. I shall wear my new green gown, the one with the russet embroidery around the hem.'

Condé smiled indulgently at his bride's excitement, which was good to see. He had been up half the night finalizing his plans with Rochefort, and it was hard to hide his nervousness. Were the King to get wind of his intentions to escape the realm he might well send his guards to apprehend him.

The next morning, thrilled to be included, Charlotte and two of her ladies climbed into a coach drawn by eight horses, having first attended matins in the castle chapel. With them was packed several hampers of food, which they happily picked at as they drove along. Condé rode on horseback alongside, together with Rochefort, Virrey and other gentlemen of his party. The November day was damp and drizzling with rain but spirits were high. The weather didn't trouble Charlotte in the slightest. She was only too delighted to escape the boredom of the castle, the endless embroidery to which she'd been subjected day after day, as well as the company of old women, in particular her mother-in-law. It felt good to be out in the open air, and to have gentlemen around admiring her with their eyes and making flattering remarks.

The jolting of the coach lulled her to sleep for a time, but then she woke with a jerk to stare out of the window where there was no sign of any forest, not even a single tree. A long empty road stretched before them. 'Where are we? It is taking a great many hours to reach our destination. How far distant is the *rendezvous de chasse?*'

'Not much further, dearest,' her husband lied, not slackening his pace.

Less than an hour later it finally dawned on Charlotte that she had been tricked. She began to weep. 'Where are you taking me? Have you abducted me? I can see we are travelling away from the forest in an entirely different direction.'

Seeing her distress, Condé reigned in his horse and came to sit beside her in the coach, holding her hands warmly between his own. 'My love, I am taking you to my sister, where you will be safe and your honour properly protected.'

Charlotte stared at him, round-eyed. 'Your sister?'

He gave her what he hoped was a reassuring smile. 'Our destination is the palace of the Prince of Orange at Bréda.'

'We are to leave France?' She stared at him, wide-eyed with dismay.

'That is my plan, sweet one. You will like Eleanor, who is looking forward to meeting her new sister-in-law. Once you are safely ensconced in the Low Countries far from the unwelcome attentions of the King, we can perhaps begin to properly enjoy our marriage.'

Tears filled the bride's eyes, sliding down her cheeks so that Condé's heart almost broke to see them fall. 'I want to go home,' she sobbed. 'I wish to return to court at once.'

By way of reply her husband kissed her softly on her pouting mouth, then left the coach and spurred his horse, and the party, to an even greater speed.

Charlotte flung herself into the arms of her companion, a Mademoiselle de Certeau, weeping extravagantly for some time. At length, that good lady patted her mistress gently on the shoulder. 'See, dawn is breaking; would you not care for some breakfast, Madame?'

Youthful appetite stirred and Charlotte dried her eyes, looking out of the window in wonder at the sun sliding higher in the sky. She couldn't help noticing what a fine figure of a man her husband looked on his mount, and suddenly laughed out loud. She called to the gentlemen galloping alongside. 'We ladies are hungry; could we not stop and partake of breakfast?'

As the party sat in the early morning sunshine Charlotte meekly submitted to her husband's decision. 'Perhaps you are right to take me from the King,' she told him, letting him slip his arm about her waist, even though close to he smelt of horse and a not altogether unpleasing male sweat. 'It is good of you to care for my reputation, and I assure you, husband, that I will be a good wife to you.'

Condé smiled into her eyes as he kissed her, hoping against hope that she meant what she said.

The King was in his closet playing cards with Soissons, Bassompierre and Cramail when news reached him that Condé had stolen his wife away with the intent of leaving the realm. Henry's response was instant fury. 'The blackguard has lured his wife away, I know not whether with the design to kill her in the forest, or to compel her to quit France. I shall seek to learn the truth of this calumny.' Whereupon, he marched into the Queen's bedchamber, demanding to know if Her Majesty had heard anything more.

Startled from her sleep by this sudden invasion in the early hours of the morning, as well as by the import of the question, Marie blinked at her husband and confessed she knew nothing of the matter. 'But if Monsieur le Condé is seeking to protect his wife, then I would not blame him.'

'Protecting her from whom?' roared the King. 'No, do not answer. I must think on this.'

'Indeed,' Marie said. 'Think hard.'

Sully was summoned from his bed and came reluctantly to the Queen's closet, to also advise caution.

'I do not require your comments on what has occurred,' the King snapped at his minister. 'The remedy, I seek the remedy. The Prince is gone, and has carried off his wife!'

'I doubt you can arrest a man for taking his own wife to visit his sister,' Sully drily remarked, a comment which was not well received.

'I command and direct you to arrest the fugitives, to employ all available force at hand. I shall write and dispatch letters this very day to all government officers, commanding them to keep the Prince a close prisoner in the strongest fortress they possess.'

Marie listened with increasing horror to the plans being made. Much as she detested her husband's obsession with *affaires*, she'd rather liked the girl, and could feel only pity for the silly creature who'd become a victim of her own conceit. No doubt the new little princess had protested pitifully over being taken away from the indulgences of a king and the merry delights of court life. Now she was no doubt being kept hidden in some damp and dark forest in order to evade capture by royal forces. What a foolish child to have unleashed not only the passion and fury of an aged monarch, but endangered the life of her young husband. Marie felt deep sympathy for the Prince, and could only applaud his actions.

At the start of the New Year Donna Leonora came to the Queen with news that La Marquise had grown bored with life alone at Verneuil and moved to Marcoussis to be with her mother. Marie's elation lasted no more than a few moments as her *dame d'atours* continued, 'But word is being bruited abroad that she is planning to take revenge on the King for his rejection of her.'

Marie was shocked. 'What kind of revenge? Is she again conspiring with Spain?'

Donna Leonora leaned closer so as not to be overheard by the other maids of honour busily packing gowns into coffers for the court's move to Fontainebleau. 'She is demanding permission to marry Guise, to be granted a pension and permission to remain in France, otherwise she will seek the backing of Spain and swears that should any catastrophe befall the King, she will challenge the Dauphin's right to wear the crown.'

'Catastrophe? She thinks to blackmail *me*?' White to the lips, Marie could hardly speak for the rage that soared through her veins.

The Italian humbly inclined her head in silent agreement. After a moment, she quietly added, 'She has every faith, apparently, that she will succeed in placing her own son on the throne of France. She also seeks the liberation of her brother.'

'Dear heaven, she expects a great deal. And are you certain of all this? Do we have proof?' Evidence of a conspiracy was all Marie needed to bring the woman down, once and for all, to punish her for the pain she had inflicted upon her marriage.

'We have it in the person of one Madame d'Escoman who wishes to be granted audience with Your Majesty, so that she may tell you the tale herself.'

'Does this woman appear to be a reliable witness?'

'She is an old woman, lame and hunchbacked, but claims to have worked in the kitchens at Verneuil and to be in possession of information regarding a conspiracy against His Majesty.'

'What is it exactly that she wishes to tell me?'

Donna Leonora shook her head. 'That is all I know, save that she also warns of portents of doom against the King, of dreams and visions suffered by simple peasant girls, bells ringing without the aid of a human hand and—'

'Enough!' Marie's interest instantly died. Still not entirely recovered from her recent *accouchement*, which was taking longer this time, her patience was limited. 'Predictions and horoscopes prescribing some disaster or other seem to proliferate daily. She's no more than a mad old crone thinking she can make money out of me. Send her to Sully; let him deal with the woman.'

'She is most persistent, Your Majesty. She claims to have seen treasonable correspondence with Spain.'

The Queen sighed. 'Very well, I will try to see her later in the week, before we leave for Fontainebleau.'

But in her eagerness to leave the Louvre for her favourite place of rest and refuge, Marie forgot all about her visitor. Queen Margot listened with more sympathy when the woman accosted her at church one day, although no more believing of her story. She too dispatched her to Sully, who declined to see her and had the woman arrested for debt. It was but one of many scare stories circulating at that time. Why pay it any heed?

Some weeks later, the runaways still not having returned, Marie was dismayed when the King announced his intention of charging them with treason, and for having left the realm without their sovereign's permission. Marie felt both distressed and depressed by the whole business. Henry was even starting to plan a campaign to bring Charlotte back.

'You would start a war over this girl?' she asked him, dumbfounded.

'War has long been impending.' Throughout his life Henry had suffered from a terrible fear of mighty Spain. Had not the Guises constantly intrigued with Philip II in an effort to oust him from the throne? Even the mighty Catherine de Medici had not been immune, her many intrigues and machinations often aimed to appease, or more likely trick France's rich neighbour into settling for peace. In the end Henry had turned Catholic to call an end to the wars and the turmoil.

It made him deeply uneasy to imagine Condé being assisted now by Spinola, Philip III's ambassador, and be so far removed from his control in the Spanish Netherlands. 'We need to put an end to the ascendancy of the House of Austria, and there is every hope of enlarging France as far as the banks of the Rhine.' It was a dazzling prospect, and Henry was ever a man ready to make love and war at one and the same time, although he far preferred the former. Passion and ambition going hand in hand.

'You go too far,' the Queen protested.

'Who knows what mischief they might conjure up between them,' Henry snapped, attempting to justify his planned action.

'Condé has betrayed me by putting himself and his wife under the auspices of Spain; what else could you call it but treason?'

'It is nothing of the kind. You are reading too much into this. Condé is a fine husband, passionately in love with the girl, and she is young and foolish. Let her go, Henry.'

The King's expression set hard. 'She has agreed to divorce him.'

Marie was only too aware where this conversation was leading. If Henry successfully procured a divorce for Charlotte, he would next seek his own freedom. 'I have heard of your efforts to force her to sign papers against her husband by sending young d'Estrées to seduce her. To use Gabrielle's brother for such trickery speaks poorly of your honour, Henry.'

'I dispatched him to Brussels only to bring her back, but the scheme failed as someone warned Spinola, and the Spanish envoy hindered the plan.'

Marie half turned away, not wishing her husband to see her secret smile as it had been none other than herself, with Concini's help, who had warned the ambassador of the danger. The young princess was even now safely ensconced in the Imperial Palace, her doting husband not blaming her in the least for having signed papers against him. Condé was concerned only with keeping those with evil influence away from his beloved wife, and willing to forgive her foolishness. After a moment, Marie smiled up at Henry, her tone warm and gentle, in sharp contrast to his cold anger. 'Pray do not turn into a fool in your dotage, Henry.'

A flush of crimson crept up the King's throat and over his taut jaw. The implied criticism cut deep, but where was the wrong in wanting to be with someone who cared for him? Henry's despondence over the lack of love in his life was making him feel quite ill, not at all himself. Surely he deserved more affection than either his wife or any of his current mistresses were able to give him. 'Dearest Charlotte needed no forcing. It is my will to have her back, and I shall achieve it. No person can prevent or hinder me. I do this for her father, who is one of my oldest servants.'

Marie raised her brows in disbelief, knowing full well this was an excuse, but she said no more. There was no arguing with the King when he was in this mood. Instead she went to discuss the implications of the proposed campaign with her own advisors.

*   *   *

On this occasion Marie did not require their assistance, as it was Sully himself who advised Henry that, should he insist in going on campaign, it would be necessary to make the Queen regent during his absence. 'With certain restrictions,' the cautious minister added. 'A council could be appointed to oversee what she carries out on Your Majesty's behalf.'

Concini, however, warned her against agreeing to the plan. 'The limitation of your power is untenable. Your Majesty's authority would be ridiculed, and your personal influence under-valued. Cease to be a puppet in the hands of a faithless husband and at least compel this coming war, undertaken more for the recovery of a new mistress than any other reason, to be the means of establishing your own rightful position.'

Marie rather liked the sound of that. It made absolute sense as she must, above all, protect her son. Nor did she much care for the idea of a supervisory council, as it meant that her voice would be but one among many, and with only one vote. She had little hope of standing alone against the cardinals, dukes and lords of the realm if they set their mind to something with which she disagreed. 'I concede that may well be the case, and I must think of the Dauphin. But how can I establish my position?'

'By the solemn rite of a coronation.'

Marie gazed upon her favourite in surprise, a new burst of hope in her heart. In all these long years of marriage there had never been any suggestion that she should be crowned as queen in her own right. Now she saw that was most certainly the answer. The Queen consort had suddenly developed a taste for ambition, perhaps because it pained her to see Henry, who had always been a good and kind husband to her despite his flaws, and a caring King to his people, behave so foolishly. For twenty years he'd brought them nothing but prosperity and peace, and for that reason alone they forgave him his peccadilloes, almost loved him for his passion for women and wine, gaming and hunting, because these manly pursuits were never carried out at their expense.

But Marie knew they did not feel the same affection for her, and if the King were out of the realm on campaign, she would need the protection of a crown to give her the necessary powers.

Henry would not hear of it. 'You have chosen the wrong moment for such a request, since you are aware that I have neither the time nor the funds necessary for the indulgence of so puerile a vanity. We cannot afford such a ceremony on top of all the other expenses incurred by this campaign. I must lead an army into Germany and the Low Countries. I have none to waste on fripperies.'

'Fripperies!' Astonished by his careless dismissal, Marie stood her ground. 'Ever since my arrival in France I have been denied many of the privileges which should enhance the majesty of a queen, which my predecessors traditionally enjoyed. Nevertheless, I have patiently awaited Your Majesty's pleasure upon this particular, a patience which I would continue to have exercised had you not been about to cross the frontier. But under the circumstances, I now consider it would be a weakness in the mother of princes to say nothing. How can I rule in your place without the necessary consecration that should precede homage to your regent?'

She sought support from Sully, from the Princes of the Blood, even from the Jesuits, and at length, either worn down by the argument, or else too eager to be off on campaign to delay further, Henry finally, if grudgingly, consented. Although he had to admit that perhaps his beleaguered wife did deserve some recompense for the trials and tribulations he had heaped upon her. He'd never meant to be intentionally unkind to her, and as always Henry's soft heart was won over, which was another reason his people so loved and revered him.

The coronation took place on Thursday, 13 May 1610, at the abbey church of Saint Denis. Marie wore a robe of pale-grey velvet embroidered with gold *fleur-de-lis* that sparkled with diamonds. Her mantle was of ermine, the seven yard train carried by her favourite ladies the Dowager Princess de Condé, the Duchesses de Montpensier and de Mercoeur. Two of her sons, the eight-year-old Dauphin and three-year-old Henri, Monsieur d'Anjou, walked before her holding the lappets of their mother's robe. Following on behind the Queen came the infant Princess Elizabeth, and after her, Queen Marguerite looking magnificent in a diadem of gold and diamonds, a surcoat of crimson velvet covered all over with brilliant gems, again in the shape of *fleur-de-lis*.

Margot had been privately affronted when told she would follow the princess, a mere child, and not walk directly behind

Queen Marie. The occasion was in any case something of an ordeal for her. To see another granted the crown denied to herself was a painful irony. She might well have feigned illness and cried off attending the ceremony altogether, had it not been for the support of her friends, and their urgent appeal that the King would be greatly displeased if she was not present.

Besides, was she not a Valois and had never yet been one to evade her duty? So she walked and smiled with true regal presence, showing none of the regret for what might have been; for failing to provide the King with an heir. None of her several affairs had brought forth a child, despite gossip to the contrary, and there had certainly been plenty of malicious nonsense whispered about her. But then dealing with court intrigue became a necessary part of her life, even as a young girl. The Queen Mother, Catherine de Medici, had blamed her for everything, and always been disappointed in her. But was the fault hers if as a royal princess she was the pawn of kings, and the butt of political ambition, scandal and intrigue?

Now she was unfailingly cordial to the Queen, paying Her Majesty respectful homage, having found to her surprise that she rather liked this plain-speaking, independent-minded woman.

The day after the coronation Henry rose early at five, as usual, having suffered a restless night. He was feeling increasingly harassed, the programme for the week ahead crowded with activities. His departure on campaign had already been delayed by the coronation of the Queen, and there was still her entry into Paris to achieve on the coming Sunday. Before then there was a grand hunt on Saturday, various private matters to be set in order, and on top of everything the marriage of Gabrielle's daughter, Mademoiselle de Vendôme, with Monsieur d'Elbeuf next Monday, followed by the usual state banquet on the Tuesday.

'But come next Wednesday we will don our boots, grasp our swords, and leave. No more delays allowed,' the King told Villeroy when he came for his usual audience at seven. The courtier laughingly agreed. They talked of state matters for a while, postponing some decisions until the council met later at the Tuileries. At eight, accompanied by his son, Monsieur de Vendôme, and others, Henry proceeded to mass.

The day was as gloomy as the King's own mood, grey and cloudy, threatening rain, so the small party hurried quickly towards the monastery Des Feuillants, paying no heed to the several groups of curious onlookers who hovered in the courtyard hoping for a glimpse of the King. Nor did they see one man in particular, known by the name of Ravaillac, who carefully kept himself hidden amongst the crowd, crouching low behind the benches arrayed in the outer court.

There was a moment as the King moved forward, his hand resting on the shoulder of young César, when Ravaillac leaped up, gesticulating wildly, thereby alerting the attention of the guard who summarily ejected him. Henry continued on his way, completely oblivious to this small disturbance.

On his return to the Louvre, the King dined, spending time with his two eldest daughters, before discussing matters to be brought to Parliament, attending council meetings and dealing with other state affairs, finally visiting the Queen in the late afternoon.

Her Majesty's chamber was awash with courtiers, all seeking instruction and offering advice for her entry into Paris. Since his wife was clearly fully occupied, the King laughed and joked with the Duchess of Guise instead, enjoying her wit and beauty.

'Paris is even more crowded than usual, Your Majesty. Packed with strangers come to see the coronation and the entry of the Queen on Sunday.'

Vitry, Henry's captain of the guard, stepped quickly forward to offer more information on the situation. 'Some of the streets are blocked by platforms and scaffolding erected for the decorations to be put up.'

'Ah yes,' said Henry. 'There is much being done, and still so much to be arranged. Why do you not go to the Palais and inspect and report on the progress of the banquet, ballet and masque, which are being prepared to entertain the good Parisians.'

'Nay, Sire. My services would be better used to escort Your Majesty, in view of the great confusion in the city.'

Henry laughed. 'Go, you only want to stay because you like talking to the women. Do what I say. For fifty years I've managed very well getting about the city without the daily protection of my captain of the guard. I believe I can still manage to find my way today without it.'

Then stepping out on to the balcony overlooking the fountain court, Henry called out to his men. 'Is my coach ready? Good, then I must take my leave. My presence is needed at Tuileries and I wish to visit the Arsenal to speak to Sully.' So saying, he embraced the Queen, giving her the customary three kisses of farewell, and hurried from the apartment, his mind already on the next task in hand.

The streets were indeed crowded; already narrow they were well nigh impassable in places. In addition to the throng, which was even greater than reported, there were a number of booths and stalls selling wares, breads and pastries, sweetmeats and other treats on this special occasion. Heavily laden carts trundled by, frequently blocking the roads, and because of the difficulties in making any headway Henry dismissed most of his attendants, save for a small detachment of guards and two running footmen whose task was to herald the approach of the royal equipage and disperse any blockage. In the coach with Henry was Epernon, Liancour, Roquelaure and one or two others. The royal carriage entered the Rue St Honoré, then turned into Rue de la Ferronière, heading for the Arsenal.

Unfortunately Sully was indisposed, so one of the footmen hurried forward to clear the way for the coach to press on, while the other paused to tie a garter, which had come loose. A figure slipped unseen through the jostling crowd. Enveloped in a cloak, head down, he carried his hat as if to shield whatever was in his hand. The footman didn't notice. He was too busy shouting and gesticulating at the driver of a cart that was blocking the royal progress. Henry was showing the details of a paper to Epernon, his hand on the Duke's shoulder as they read it together, his back turned away from the coach windows, the leather curtains of which had been drawn up to allow him to inspect the preparations for Sunday as the coach had rumbled through the streets.

The blow came out of nowhere, striking the King between the second and third ribs. He cried out, 'I am wounded! No, do not fear, it is nothing.'

Scarcely were these words out of Henry's mouth than his assailant struck again. Ravaillac had sprung up on to the wheel of the carriage and stabbed the King. Now he followed this first with several more blows in quick succession, even ripping the sleeve of the Duke of Montbazon's habit as the courtier bravely thrust out an arm to protect his sovereign.

Mayhem broke out within the coach, the horror of the nobles at what was happening indescribable. Henry made one last effort to speak, then blood gushed from his mouth and he collapsed.

'Dear God, the King is dead!'

The cry went up and there were shrieks of terror and dismay from the demented crowd. One of the King's guards threw himself on to Ravaillac, sword drawn, but the assailant made no attempt to escape, merely stood leaning against a wall. The knife he'd used to slaughter his monarch was still in his hand, the King's blood dripping from it, to add to the pool already running from the carriage.

Epernon leaped quickly down beside his colleague. 'Let no one touch the assassin. The King is not dead, he has but fainted.' It was a lie that few believed, but he knew that within seconds the brigand would have been torn limb from limb, and Epernon had every intention of ensuring that he would not suffer so easy a death.

The curtains of the coach were respectfully closed, the noblemen walking behind as the finest king France had ever known was driven slowly back to the Louvre.

The Queen was still in her *cabinet* engaged in making arrangements for Sunday's procession when she heard the rumpus outside. It was a quarter after four and something about the noise, the murmurs and cries of the people, almost like a wailing, alarmed her. She sensed at once that something was wrong, and ran to the window to look out. Seeing nothing untoward, she hurried down the palace corridors towards the grand staircase where by chance she came upon de Souvré, tutor to the young princes.

'What is it? What is the matter?' she asked, her mother's heart turning over with dread. Had something happened to one of her sons?

Souvré fell to his knees before her, kissing the Queen's hand. 'The King has been wounded, stabbed through the heart. He is being brought to the palace.'

Marie cried out, almost collapsed, and had to be half carried back to her apartment where she waited in agony for more news.

The minutes ticked slowly by, only ten or fifteen perhaps though it felt more like an hour. At last the door opened and Sillery, the chancellor, entered. She rushed to grasp his hand. 'Monsieur, the King! This tumult. Is it true? Is the King dead?'

In a small, halting voice, the chancellor answered. 'Madame, be calm, I entreat you. The King can never die.' And stepping towards the young dauphin, he said, 'Behold the King!'

Louis fell sobbing into his mother's arms. In that moment Marie was too stunned for tears. They would come later. Now she shook with shock, her cries as much from anger as grief. How could anyone kill so fine and noble a king, such a great and gentle man? She had hated much of Henry's foolishness, his flaws, his weaknesses. Oh, but she had loved him with all her heart and soul, despite everything. She bowed her head and let the tears flow, mingling with those of her son who would forever miss this much-loved, affectionate father.

Sillery allowed them only a few moments of private grief before clearing his throat and urging the Queen to gather her courage. 'You have lost a great and glorious husband and king this day. Weep and bewail for him from the bottom of your heart, but never forget that you are also the mother and guardian of an infant king, whose realm must be governed by you.'

Marie met the chancellor's steady gaze and knew that he spoke true. The burden of regency now weighed heavy upon her shoulders, and this holy responsibility would require all her strength and fortitude in the difficult months and years ahead.

January 1611

Henriette was in a state of near terror. How could it have come to this? She, a court beauty who had flown so high, to now fall so low. Charges had been brought against her regarding the death of the King. Having been arrested in her own house earlier today, together with three of her ladies, she was now being interrogated.

Interrogated! Even the word chilled Henriette to the bone.

'When did you meet Madame d'Escoman? Was she introduced to you by your ladies? Or by Guise, or Epernon?'

'You waste your time asking the same questions over and over,' she told her interrogators for the thousandth time that afternoon. 'I never met this Madame d'Escoman. I do not know the woman.'

'She claims she was once in your service.'

Henriette paled, fear escalating through her. How was it they knew so much about her? She was in the Bastille, the place where her brother still resided, lying forgotten in some dank cell. Few people who entered this place walked out alive. Henriette's frightened gaze darted about the stone walls of the chamber in which she was being held, empty but for a wooden table and two chairs, fastening with terror upon anything which looked remotely like a possible implement of torture. What did a thumbscrew actually look like? Was that metal tool hanging on the wall the pincers that were brought to red-hot heat and used to extract toenails, or tongues? She quaked with fear at the thought, struggling to keep the panic from her voice as she answered her accusers. 'I cannot remember every maid who has ever worked in my service.'

'She is lame and hunchbacked. Surely you would remember her. She says you also met Ravaillac at Malesherbes. Do you remember him?'

'No, I do not.' Had not the King's assailant been safely disposed of? Dead men did not talk. But they might try to make *her* talk. Would they put her on the rack? Should she lie to protect herself? 'If this woman accuses me of arranging the murder of our beloved king, then tell her to bring forth proof.'

'She claims that a letter, signed by yourself, was presented to Queen Marie in an attempt to warn Her Majesty.'

Henriette began to shake. 'And what did this supposed letter say?'

'Her Majesty burned it unread.'

Relief flooded through her. 'There you are then. Her Majesty clearly was unimpressed by her. She is a wicked woman who accuses everybody in order to evade her own guilt.'

There had been many questions since the assassination. The main one being was it a public or a private vengeance? Was Spain at the root of it? Or some person closer to the King? Suspicion had fallen upon them all, not least the Queen whom Henry had betrayed yet again and was threatening to divorce so that he could marry the pretty Charlotte. Her Majesty had weathered that small storm easily, but then she was mother of the new King. Suspicion had also fallen upon herself, his discarded mistress. Henriette's young son had even been put under guard in his room on the day of the murder, in case anyone should decide to abduct the boy and declare him the rightful king.

'Madame d'Escoman spoke to Queen Marguerite at the church of Saint Victoire, alleging that because of your despair at falling out of favour, and the peril inflicted upon your family and friends, you allied with Guise and others, to avenge yourself upon the King. What say you to this?'

'I say it is a lie. I am innocent of these charges. You will need to look elsewhere for someone to blame.'

Many believed the crime had been inspired by Condé, a way to put an end to Henry's designs upon his wife. While some even fantasized that Ravaillac, the assassin, might have had a sister whom the King had ravished at some time. No evidence of a sister, or private grievance of any sort, had been found. It was clear that Ravaillac, a man of some thirty to forty years of age, was a religious fanatic, prey to hallucinations and misconceptions. His view was that the King was no true Catholic, that Henry had betrayed the Holy Mother Church, therefore he had resolved to strike him down.

But did he act alone, or was someone else behind the plot? Spain perhaps.

Later in that same month of May he had been duly tortured, burned and dismembered, his death drawn out as long as possible so that he might have time to express remorse for his heinous crime. Yet despite the agonies he'd endured, he gave no other name. No one else had been implicated. But that didn't stop Parliament from seeking one.

'Your accuser claims that you intended your son Henri to be raised to the throne, that you were to marry the Duke of Guise who was to be proclaimed Regent during the new King's minority, and Monsieur d'Epernon was to be appointed Constable of France. That you were acting in connivance with the Spanish King.'

'The woman is a fantasist.'

'She also says that she tried to warn the King's advisers many months ago, but none would listen.'

'I'm not surprised. Sully can recognize a mad woman when he sees one, even if you cannot.'

Her interrogator smiled, as if she had made some jest. 'Take care, Madame, Sully is not as powerful as he once was. We have a new regime now. You know that your friend Epernon has also been arrested, since he too was implicated.'

Henriette thought that at any moment she might actually vomit, her terror was so great. 'Why do you not torture the truth out of Madame d'Escoman, rather than harass me?'

'The Queen regent will not allow it.'

'Why, because she fears she might implicate even more important personages than myself? Neighbouring countries, for instance, which could lead to war?'

'Your tongue may be the death of you one day, Madame.'

How many times Henry had said very much the same thing. Would they whip her, or put her in the pillory, place one of her pretty feet into the boot and crush the bones to pulp? Henriette trembled. But as the clock chimed five they decided to release her. No evidence had been found against her. As yet.

'You will be kept under surveillance, Madame, so do not consider leaving Paris.'

It was not until 10 August 1611, that the Dukes of Guise and Epernon, and Madame de Verneuil, were finally absolved of all charges. Their accuser, Madame d'Escoman, was brought to trial and convicted of false denunciation, sorcery and coining. After some disagreement over her sentence the woman was dispatched to the Convent des Filles Repenties, where she was incarcerated in a small stone cell, specially constructed for the purpose in a corner of the courtyard – 'walled up' was the term used – where she died three years later, still protesting her innocence.

Henri Quatre was deeply mourned throughout Europe, not least by the two queens who had been his wives. They sat together now in the royal nursery, the children gathered about them. King Louis, at ten, and the nine-year-old Princess Elizabeth were busy at their lessons, together with other children of the palace courtiers, and Henriette's two children, born at the same time as their royal half-siblings. Three-year-old Gaston was playing with his soldiers, Princess Christine, at five, being taught her letters, while little Henrietta Maria, the newest addition to the family at just two, was sitting on Margot's knee playing with her pearls and trying on her feathered plume. Henri, the Duke of Orleans, was being cuddled by his mother, even though he was now four. But then he was a sickly child and a great worry to her.

'You are fortunate in your family, Madame,' Margot softly remarked as she stroked the dark curls of little Henrietta Maria, very much a Medici with her brown eyes and olive skin.

'I am indeed,' Marie agreed. 'Henry was an enlightened king, exceedingly tolerant, never more so than where his children were concerned. We also have Madame de Moret's son that she had by him, and the two daughters of Mademoiselle des Essarts.'

Margot laughed out loud. 'I doubt we will ever know the full extent of his offspring. It is generous of you to keep them here in the royal nursery.'

'I fear I quarrelled with Henry too much in life, so feel I must respect his wishes after his death.' A tear slid down the Queen's pale cheek and she quickly wiped it away. Margot gently patted her hand.

'Do not blame yourself for what cannot be changed. Henry was far too easy-going, far too good humoured and tolerant for his own good. It is a tragic irony that, like Henri Trois, he should be struck down by a religious maniac. Above all things, he was most tolerant of religion, worshipping God first as a Protestant, as directed by his mother, and later as a Catholic when obliged to do so to end the wars of religion, and for the sake of a crown. He always believed that it mattered not how you worshipped Him, so long as you had faith.'

'The people loved him for that, and for the fact he cared about the poor, that he brought them peace and prosperity.'

Margot smiled. 'Did he not say that every Frenchman would be content if he had a chicken in his pot every Sunday? Henry loved to play the fool but was more politically astute than his enemies ever gave him credit for. But then he needed to be, as he and I both were subject to the worst calumnies and poisonous libels. Yet he remained true to himself, and stubborn to the core. He would have his way when it really mattered. I fought him for years, refusing to grant him a divorce because I had no wish to see him marry his whore.' She smiled at Marie. 'What a relief it was when he finally wed you. And you loved him, Marie, so how could you not object to his fascination with La Marquise?'

Marie looked at this Valois queen she had once so envied and feared and now recognized as a friend, and tearfully nodded. 'It is true, I loved him with all my heart. Our marriage could have been so different had it not been for the she-cat. I shall forever mourn his loss.'

There were tears standing proud in Margot's eyes too. 'I was saved some of your pain, Marie, as I never did love him, not in that way. I would tease him mercilessly when I was a girl, calling him a country bumpkin and constantly complaining about his garlic-tainted breath, and his dusty feet.' She laughed out loud. 'But despite our squabbles and differences he was always my friend, and I shall miss his company and his wise counsel.'

Margot paused for a moment as she let Mademoiselle Christine slip from her lap to run to play with her brother, then smoothing down her skirts she quietly asked, 'And what of the she-cat, as you call her. Will you let her marry young Guise?'

'I doubt that would be prudent.'

'I agree, it would be most unwise.'

The two queens smiled at each other in perfect accord. 'I shall require her to retire permanently from court, where her presence is most unwelcome, and never allow her to marry,' Marie announced, thinking that would be a just revenge upon the woman who had caused such misery in her own marriage. 'She, and her sister, lived their lives as harlots so can end them in the same way, alone at Verneuil. I will not have my son threatened by that woman ever again.'

'Indeed not!' As one they both looked across to where the boy, ever serious, was studying his Latin verbs. 'As regent, the way ahead will not be easy, but be assured, Marie, that I shall stand beside you. I will do everything I can to help you to protect the Dauphin, and your other children. As strong, independent women, we can do that for Henry, you and I.'

Author's Note

The Queen kept her word and never granted Henriette permission to marry. Nor did she allow her unfortunate sister, Marie-Charlotte d'Entragues, to marry either. When Marie-Charlotte brought proceedings against Bassompierre, who had so greatly wronged her, the Queen ensured that the judges decided against her. La Marquise lived on the riches she had accumulated during her time with the King, indulging herself on luxuries and developing such a passion for food that she grew very fat, far plumper even than Queen Margot, and rarely left the comfort of her couch. She finally died of apoplexy in 1633.

Having safely removed Charlotte to the Imperial Palace, and fearful of arrest or even of assassination, Condé had fled to Milan. Eventually, following the King's death, he returned and was reunited with his wife. Charlotte Princess de Condé settled into married life with her prince, and gave him several children. Unfortunately, she indulged in numerous affairs and was never the faithful wife he had hoped for.

Louis XIII married the Spanish Infanta, Anne of Austria, and the Princess Elizabeth married Philip IV of Spain, thus uniting the two warring kingdoms. Henry's second son, Nicholas Henri, the Duke of Orleans, died in November 1611. All his other children married well, including Henrietta Maria who married Charles I of England and was the mother of Charles II and James II.

Marguerite de Valois lived for a further five years, never giving in to age but always dressing as if she were a young beauty still, and not a plump old woman. She continued to hold her soirées, writing many dramatized pieces herself, and acted as a great friend and support to Queen Marie. Ever a political creature she would often attend the States-General on the Queen's behalf, or write to them with her opinions, particularly when Marie was badly advised by Concini. On every anniversary of Henry's death she caused services to be performed in Nôtre Dame and churches throughout the capital, always mourning his loss. When the young King was crowned in Rheims Cathedral, Margot was, to her delight, invited to act as sponsor, and was also asked by Queen Marie to be godmother to her young son Gaston. She died on 27 March 1615 at her Hôtel du Faubourge Saint Germain, possibly from pneumonia, having caught a chill from which she did not recover. She was sixty-two. After her considerable debts were paid, the pensions and wages of her gentlemen and ladies-in-waiting, and a few personal bequests, the balance of her inheritance she left to King Louis XIII. For some unknown reason, possibly the difficulties of state affairs at the time, her funeral was delayed for twelve months, after which her sealed coffin was taken secretly to Saint-Denis, where the monks at first doubted this could genuinely be a Daughter of France. Later, in 1719, the Valois Chapel in which it was placed was pulled down, and her body mysteriously disappeared. In death, as in life, she was a legend.

Sources

For readers who wish to explore the subject further I can recommend the list below as being the most useful to me. I would like to acknowledge the Project Gutenberg collection for many of the out-of-print titles.

The Favourites of Henry of Navarre by Le Petit Homme Rouge. 1910

The Life of Marie de Medici by Julia Pardoe. 1890

History of the Reign of Henry IV by Martha Walker Freer. 1860

Memoirs of Marguerite, Queen of Navarre.

A Gallant of Lorraine, François, Seigneur de Bassompierre (1579–1646) by H. Noel Williams. 1921.

Illustrious Dames of the Court of the Valois Kings: Marguerite, Queen of Navarre by Pierre de Bourdeille and C.A. Sainte-Beuve. Translated by Katharine Prescott Wormeley. 1912

The French Renaissance Court by Robert J. Knecht. 2008